My Soul
To Take

THE THIRD FREAK HOUSE TRILOGY
#3

C.J. ARCHER

Series by C.J. Archer:

The 1st Freak House Trilogy

The 2nd Freak House Trilogy

The 3rd Freak House Trilogy

The Emily Chambers Spirit Medium Trilogy

Lord Hawkesbury's Players

The Witchblade Chronicles

The Assassins Guild

Stand-alone books by C.J. Archer:

Redemption

Surrender

Courting His Countess

The Mercenary's Price

DEDICATION

To all my wonderful readers who joined me for the voyage through the Freak House books. We've climbed mountains together, crossed valleys and traversed treacherous waters. Now that we've come to the end of the journey, I want to thank you for your company. I hope you will travel with me again.

CHAPTER 1

Hertfordshire, Summer 1889

"Cara, you must not leave! I'm begging you to stay a little longer." Hannah gripped my wrist so tightly that my hand began to throb and turn purple. Her bright blue eyes implored me as fiercely as her words. "Sylvia's hysteria will drive me mad if I don't have your company to keep me sane."

I'd already been at Frakingham House for a week, after sending the escaped spirits back to Hell. It had proven to be long enough. Hannah was right, and Sylvia's current glum mood was infecting everyone. Everyone, that is, except her uncle. I'd decided to leave the following day, but only told Hannah so far. I'd not expected her to provide an obstacle to my departure.

"What about Jack?" I asked. "Surely you newlyweds want to spend some time together on long walks in the sunshine? That will give you some peace."

"Jack's too busy for long walks. His absence during our honeymoon means there's a backlog of estate business waiting for him, and there's no one to assist him, with Tommy gone." She swiveled to face me more fully on the sofa. Her hand moved from my wrist to my elbow, allowing the blood to resume flowing.

I flexed my tingling fingers. At her distressed look, I gave her a sympathetic smile.

Her eyes narrowed and hardened. "I know that look, Cara Moreau."

I tried to make my expression a picture of innocence. "I haven't said anything yet."

"You're about to offer me sympathy then tell me Sylvia will probably only mope for another day or two, which we both know isn't true."

She was right there. It would be some time before Sylvia returned to her normal, bouncy self. Her heart was broken; Tommy had been banished from Freak House by her uncle, August Langley. As someone whose heart would forever bear the scars of a love lost, I knew how she felt. She might never be the same again. I knew I wouldn't be, but it seemed I was better at containing my emotions compared to Sylvia. I saved all my tears for when I was alone at night, and didn't talk about Quin to the others. Much. Certainly not as many times as Sylvia lamented Tommy's absence.

"And then you'll tell me your niece needs you," Hannah went on, "when, in fact, I know you haven't had any correspondence from Emily in four days."

I swallowed my guilt. She'd picked out my lie before I'd even offered it. "It's difficult for me to listen to Sylvia go on and on about Tommy when I'm feeling somewhat bruised by Quin's departure." Bruised was an understatement. My heart felt like it had been ripped from my chest, stomped on, shredded, and shoved back in. At least Sylvia had a chance of seeing her heart's desire again.

"I do sympathize." Hannah's face softened. "But with you gone, and Jack out all day, the only person of any sense that I can speak to is Bollard, and a conversation with him is a one-way street." She shot a glance up at the central rosette on the ceiling where, two levels above us, Bollard would be assisting Langley with his latest experiment. "Besides, he still makes me a little nervous."

2

I sighed. I was out of excuses.

"I also have a suggestion to keep us both occupied and your mind off..." She blinked and looked away.

"Something other than playing intermediary between Sylvia and Langley? It will have to be very good, Hannah. I do miss Emily and the children."

"I know." Her voice was heavy with understanding. "We have some research to conduct. Here, this will explain everything." She pulled out a letter from the pocket of her skirt and handed it to me. "It's from Charity and Samuel. Oh, this letter was delivered today too. It's for you."

It was from Nathaniel Faraday, according to the return address. It was the second one that week, and I had yet to respond to the first. I set it aside and opened the other.

The first part of the letter mentioned that Tommy was helping Charity and the other teachers at the orphans' school. "Thank goodness for that," I muttered. "He's well suited to be a teacher there, although hopefully it's only temporary."

"You think August will calm down and ask him to return?" Hannah looked up at the ceiling again.

"He'll come to his senses when he sees that Sylvia isn't recovering from her heartbreak."

"He has to come out of his laboratory to see her, and he hasn't done that all week. Except to berate her yet again over her 'foolish and disgusting display with a servant,' as he called it."

I'd heard him say those exact words too. He'd followed it up by reiterating that she had until Samuel and Charity's wedding to find herself a suitable husband or he'd find one for her. Poor Sylvia. She'd run from the room sobbing. She knew as well as anyone that August Langley meant every word. While he might have allowed her to marry a man who wasn't wealthy or titled, he certainly wouldn't allow his hard-fought social status to sink by having his niece run off with a fellow who used to be the footman.

I pointed to a line on the letter that said Tommy seemed

content with his role, although he hoped to one day return to his friends at Frakingham House. "Have you informed Sylvia?"

"I have. Read on. There's more."

The next part of the letter contained news of Charity and Samuel's wedding plans; the ceremony was to be held at Samuel's ancestral home in three weeks. They then asked if they could stop at Frakingham House after the wedding, since Langley and Bollard had declined the invitation due to Langley's incapacity.

"Are you going to have them here?" I asked Hannah.

"Of course. Not that I think August deserves special attention. He could have gone to the trouble to attend the wedding, Bollard would be there to assist him."

"I think large groups of people make him anxious."

She sniffed. "We should endeavor to venture into territory that makes us anxious from time to time. It's good for building fortitude."

I said nothing. Hannah had an adventurous spirit and had been confined to an attic most of her life. It was no wonder she didn't understand why some people preferred solitude and confinement.

"That's not why I showed the letter to you," she said. "The final page is most enlightening."

The name Myer jumped out at me. I read quickly, then read it again. "This is interesting." While Charity was busy with teaching and wedding plans, Samuel had decided to fill his time conducting some research into Everett Myer, our acquaintance who was last seen entering the portal at the Frakingham Abbey ruins. He could have been anywhere by now, in any realm. He might have even been dead.

Hannah leaned over my shoulder and pointed to the same line that had intrigued me. It wasn't something Samuel had discovered about Everett Myer, but rather his wife, Edith. Or, more accurately, her family. "They all died very suddenly," she said. "They were poisoned."

"Soon afterward, she married Myer." I lowered the letter

to my lap. "That is suspicious. Do you think he killed them?" A shudder rippled through me, chilling my bones.

"I don't know. For all that I don't like him, he doesn't seem like a cold-blooded murderer."

"Yes, but they were poisoned. It's easier to commit murder when one doesn't have to get blood on one's hands."

Hannah blinked owlishly at me.

"So I suspect."

"I'm not sure that I agree with that sentiment," she said. "Anyway, Samuel says it was ruled suicide. I'm sure the coroner thoroughly investigated before coming to that conclusion."

I agreed. "Particularly because they were a prominent family." Edith Myer's father had been a partner in the banking firm, Hatfield and Harrington. His wealth had been vast and his heiress's hand in marriage highly sought after. Everett Myer had been fortunate to capture her, considering his own background was unspectacular. It was difficult to see what he'd brought to the union.

"What else did Samuel say?" I asked as I read further.

"He hasn't got time to look into it, but suggests we should learn everything we can about the deaths."

I handed the letter back to her. "And how do we do that?"

"There are some old newspapers in the attic from around that time. We could see if they contain anything." Her eyes twinkled, and I knew she had something more adventurous in mind. "And we could pay a visit to the delightful Detective Inspector Weeks."

I pulled a face. Weeks was a sycophant and a generally odious man. The sycophant part could be of help, however. The odious part would have to be endured. "Surely he won't know anything about it. It was a long time ago, and I don't believe he's ever worked in London."

"He could write to the coroner and ask for details of the investigation."

"Won't that seem suspicious after all this time?"

She shrugged one shoulder. "Perhaps, but who will mind? Besides, we'll help him think up a convincing story."

"After we convince *him* first."

She smiled ever-so charmingly. "I've found Inspector Weeks to be quite accommodating toward Sylvia in the past. As the new lady of Freak House, I suspect he'll be as equally accommodating to me."

I grinned. "You're probably right. If nothing else, it'll get us out of the house for an afternoon and take my mind off…"

Her smile faded and she touched my hand. "I'll be up in the attic looking through newspapers. Join me when you've read your letter."

I frowned, and it wasn't until she nodded at the letter I'd discarded on the sofa beside me that I remembered. "Oh yes. Nathaniel."

"He's a good man and he likes you."

A combination that was quite rare, I'd found. While I was deemed pretty enough by most gentlemen of means, I was considered too "exotic" to be marriageable.

She winked as she rose. "Besides, he's terribly handsome and charming."

"He's also available," I muttered as I opened the letter. Not at all like Quin, who was condemned to Purgatory where he performed warrior duties for the administrators.

I swallowed down the lump in my throat. I must not dwell on him and his circumstance. It would only bring tears and more heartache, and I preferred to save those for the evenings when I was alone.

Hannah left me in the sitting room, and I read the letter. It was short and to the point. Nathaniel's last letter had asked me when I would be returning to London, and if he could see me when I did. My response had been that I wasn't sure, as my family had removed themselves to Jacob's estate for the summer. Now he was asking if he could visit me there, or at Frakingham if I remained with the Langleys for any length of time.

I folded the single page and slumped into the depths of the sofa with a sigh. I liked Nathaniel, just not in the way that everyone wanted me to. While he was charming, handsome and kind, as Hannah had pointed out, he was no substitute for Quin. I didn't want to receive his attentions because I couldn't return them with any sincerity. Besides, the last time I'd seen him, he'd been disbelieving of the supernatural. If he found out I was a medium, he might think me mad altogether. Perhaps that would be a way to discourage him.

"Cara? Cara...there you are!" Sylvia plopped down on the sofa with a rustle of silk skirts. Her blonde curls danced artfully around her sweet oval face in a way that made my dark tresses seem lackluster and heavy. If it weren't for her swollen nose and red eyes, she would have looked very pretty.

"Can I help you with something?"

"You can indeed." She nodded at the letter in my hand. "Is that from Charity and Samuel?"

"No." I didn't tell her who it was really from. I didn't need another lecture on how Nathaniel Faraday was perfect for me. Despite her own love for someone as unsuitable as Tommy, she still didn't see how I could love someone like Quin over Nathaniel. "Hannah just showed me the letter from Samuel. The information about the Myers was most enlightening, don't you agree?"

She waved that topic away with her handkerchief. "He's safe and sound at the school, thank goodness. I've been so worried he'd fallen into his old ways again, or just...wandered off." It seemed she wasn't prepared to discuss topics other than Tommy.

She dabbed her handkerchief to the corner of her eye, and I saw that it was indeed watery.

I closed my hand over hers on her lap. "He wouldn't wander off. Of course he'll stay somewhere that he can be found easily. Charity and the others will see that he's kept busy. There's no chance he'll resort to thieving or living on the street again."

"Yes, of course. He wouldn't stoop to such depths when there are other choices available to him." She sniffed again. "So, will you do it?"

"Do what? You haven't yet asked me anything."

"Write to him, of course."

I tilted my head. "On your behalf?"

"No, on your own, silly. As one friend to another, the way you would to Charity or anyone else." She patted my hand and gave me a benevolent smile that would have pleased the most pious nun. "It would be nice if you mentioned a little about me in your letter. Perhaps you could tell him that I think about him. That my heart is true."

"Sylvia, is that wise?"

"Oh yes! It would sound better coming from you."

It wasn't what I meant, but she prattled on and I shut my mouth.

"Perhaps you could mention that I'm showing courage under very trying circumstances." She let go of my hand and smoothed out the non-existent wrinkles in her skirt. "Also that I'm being held against my will."

"But you're not."

"I'm not allowed to go to London. I might as well be kept prisoner in my room if I cannot visit him."

"Or go shopping."

"Precisely. You do understand me, Cara."

I somehow kept my smile from breaking out.

"Tell him not to give up hope." Her chin shuddered. "Tell him Bollard is doing his best to convince Uncle that he should allow Tommy to come home."

He was? While I knew the dour mute cared for Sylvia as if she were his own niece, I didn't think he'd jeopardize his position for her over this. Bollard may be more than a confidant and assistant to Langley, but he was still only a servant in his master's eyes. He was still walking a precarious line by standing up for the couple.

"Tell Tommy that *I* am doing my best," Sylvia went on.

She turned those big watery eyes to me and my heart softened. "I care very much for him. I love him, Cara. You know what it's like. You understand that I'll do anything to be with him. Don't you?"

I kissed her damp cheek. "I do."

"Then please write to him. Assure him that if I cannot convince Uncle…" She shook her head.

"That you'll what? Run away with Tommy? Sylvia, are you certain that's what you want?"

"It's *not* what I want." Her vehemence had me jerking away from her. "I want Tommy to live here, with me, in his home. But I will leave here if I have to. I will, Cara."

"So I see."

"But I don't think it's wise to tell Tommy that. Not yet."

I frowned. "Why not?"

"Because he'll disappear without telling anyone where he's going."

She was right. Tommy was a gentleman, and he adored her. He would do what he thought was best for her, even if he thought walking away was the right thing to do. On the surface, perhaps it was. She would continue to live here in comfort, under Langley's protection. She would have a home for life. But she would be miserable.

I knew it better than most. At night, when I lay in bed and contemplated my future, there was nothing but a yawning expanse of nothing ahead of me. Without Quin to share my life, it was simply an endless stretch of days, minutes and seconds, strung together one after the other.

I drew in a deep breath and pushed my own melancholy aside. I now had two things to focus on that didn't involve Quin. Discovering what happened to the Hatfield family, and helping Sylvia and Tommy be together. After that, I would find something else to do. I could conquer this melancholy. I could live a fruitful, interesting life without him. It would just be lived alone.

"I'll write to him this evening," I told her.

"Why not now?"

"I need time to consider what to say. Besides, I promised Hannah to help her in the attic. There are some old newspapers up there we want to check for news of the Hatfield family deaths."

"Can I come? Please let me join you. I need a distraction."

I grinned. "Of course. But on one condition. You do not mention Tommy."

She considered this then nodded. "As long as you don't mention Quin."

"When have I mentioned Quin?" I thought I'd been very quiet about him, in fact, and kept my feelings to myself.

"Not with words," she said, rising. "With your eyes. They're all sad and filled with hopelessness."

I refrained from telling her that I couldn't *mention* Quin with my eyes, but decided it was best to leave the entire discussion alone and focus on the task ahead. It would be best for both of us.

***

"Here's another one," Hannah said, adding a newspaper to our collection of two others.

Sylvia and I joined her at the small table that we'd cleared of knickknacks and read the article. All three articles had appeared on the front pages, and all were rather sensational in their reporting, describing how the bodies had been found and the reaction of the neighbors and police alike.

Sylvia shuddered. "It reminds me of those horrible Jack the Ripper murders last year."

"It's nothing like those," I said. "They were committed in Whitechapel for starters, not Mayfair, and the victims were horribly mutilated. This appears to be poison or something…less gruesome."

Hannah gasped. "How awful. Did they ever catch the murderer?"

I blinked at her, momentarily forgetting that she'd been living in an attic at the time of the Ripper murders with no outside communication. They'd been the topic on everyone's lips and the focus for the journalists and newspapers for some time. "Unfortunately not, but there's been no murders of that nature since, thank God."

"This is new," Sylvia said, pointing to a paragraph in the middle.

I read it and was about to say something when the light coming through the doorway was blocked. "There you all are," Jack said. "I've been looking for you everywhere." He joined us and kissed his wife. She smiled at him and looped her arm around his waist. "There must be something interesting up here to have all three of you sifting through the dust. Sylvia in particular."

His cousin put her hand on her hip and shot him a glare. She waved a newspaper in front of him.

"We're researching the Hatfield family's deaths," Hannah told him.

"Edith Myer's family?" He peered down at the paper. "What have you discovered?"

"Not terribly much," I said. "The deaths of Mr. and Mrs. Hatfield occurred a mere two months before Edith married Myer. They died from poison, which they drank directly from bottles clearly marked 'poison.'"

"Suicide."

"That's the conclusion everyone drew."

"I don't necessarily agree," Sylvia said.

"Nor do I."

She seemed surprised and pleased that she'd jumped to a reasonable conclusion that the newspapers, and perhaps the police, seemed to have missed.

"Two of the maids died too!" Hannah gasped as she read to the end of the article with Jack. "So…murder *and* suicide?"

Jack glanced over the other two articles. "It's not entirely unreasonable that all four committed suicide. A lovers' pact, perhaps, or…" He waved his hand in the air then shrugged. "No, I can't think of any reason why the maids would kill themselves."

"I'm not sure your lovers' pact holds water either," Hannah said. "I know I've lived a sheltered life, but *four*?"

Sylvia nodded. "I agree with Hannah. Even three seems somewhat…complicated."

Jack's eyes danced with mischief, and I suspect he held back a retort for my sake, the only female in the room that he wasn't related to.

"So we're back to either murder-suicide, or four murders." Hannah chewed on her lip. "Perhaps the maids hated their employers, killed them, then killed themselves because they knew they'd be discovered and it would distress their families too much to think of them as murderesses."

"Or perhaps the *maids* were the lovers and Mr. and Mrs. Hatfield discovered their tryst then dismissed them from their positions." Sylvia nodded emphatically. "I do like that theory."

Jack eyed her cautiously. "Your theory is interesting, if somewhat macabre."

Hannah and I exchanged worried glances. Sylvia's doomed lovers theories were most unlike her. We'd best keep our eye on her over the coming days and weeks.

"There is, of course, the most obvious theory," I said. "That Myer himself somehow killed them all."

"But why kill the maids as well as the parents?" Hannah asked.

"Perhaps they saw him direct the Hatfields to drink the poison."

"Hypnosis." Sylvia pressed her fingers to her lips. "Oh my. Yes, of course. He hypnotized them and forced them to kill themselves. That is diabolical."

"And yet plausible," Jack muttered. "You're probably right about the maids. They realized what he was doing and had to die too."

Sylvia plopped down on a chair covered by a dusty sheet. Her dress would get filthy, but she didn't seem to care, or notice. "What should we do with this information? Go to the police?"

Jack snorted. "They won't believe our theory. Besides, too much time has passed. As far as they're concerned, the matter was laid to rest years ago. They're too busy to reopen old cases."

"But he cannot be allowed to get away with this," Hannah said. "It doesn't seem fair somehow."

"We could tell his wife what we suspect."

We stared at him in silence as we thought through his idea. I was the first to speak. "Surely she has considered it already. She possibly even confronted him over it. She knows he's quite capable of the hypnosis side of things."

Hannah nodded. "Perhaps that's why she hates him now."

"So why not divorce him?" Sylvia asked. "Or just leave him?"

I shrugged. "Fear?"

"But she doesn't seem all that afraid of him," Hannah said.

"True. In fact, it's he who avoids her. Perhaps he has suggested through hypnosis that she must never leave him. Is that even possible?"

"I don't know," Jack said. "We could ask Gladstone."

I leaned my hip against the table and scanned the newspapers again. What we needed to do was speak to Myer. He wouldn't admit to anything, of course, but we might know if he was guilty or innocent from his eyes or his mannerisms. While he was secretive, whenever we confronted him over his secrets, he often divulged more information than we hoped for.

The problem was Myer had disappeared through the portal, according to the ghost who'd seen him enter it. He was free. Perhaps that was his intention all along—escape his crimes by traveling to another realm. Except he hadn't been found guilty on this realm yet; he hadn't even been a suspect until now.

"Cara, you're right." Jack's dark voice had us all looking at him.

"But I haven't said anything."

"I know what you're thinking."

Hannah's jaw dropped and she stared at me. "Cara, is that wise?"

"I haven't spoken!"

Sylvia glanced between us all. "What? Why am I always the last to know?"

"Cara thinks we ought to open the portal and find him," Hannah said, turning a hard glare onto me.

I thought it rather unfair to be condemned for *thinking* something.

"And I agree with her," Jack said.

"What?" Hannah and Sylvia both exploded.

"That is the most foolish thing I've ever heard you say," Hannah told her husband.

"Sweetheart." He reached for her hands but she jerked them away and thrust them on her hips.

"Do not 'sweetheart' me. Promise me you won't open the portal, Jack."

He appealed to me, but I held up my hands. I wasn't going to get involved. What I was going to do was find a quiet place to think things through.

I left the three of them arguing in the attic, both women against Jack. He watched me go with a resigned twist of his mouth.

I headed up to the tower room and sat in the window embrasure. The summer sun bathed the countryside in muted light, softening the green of the grass and the blue of the sky. Usually I avoided these quiet, contemplative moments during the day because my thoughts always headed in the one direction—Quin. But this time I allowed myself to wallow in the peace and let my mind wander.

I could summon him and ask him to find Myer for us. Would the administrators let him do that upon our request? Surely if Myer was a threat in another realm they would have sent Quin to fetch him already. Perhaps. I wasn't entirely sure how the rules worked or the degree of interference the administrators had.

We didn't actually need Quin to open the portal. Myer had the book of spells but we possessed a page with the spell to open the portal. But even if we opened it and climbed through, how could we be certain we'd end up in the same realm Myer traveled to? I sifted through the pros and cons in my head but it really only boiled down to one on each side.

Cons: It was dangerous.

Pros: It would give me something to do—and I might see Quin again.

That settled, I went to find the others. Sylvia was nowhere to be seen, but I found Jack and Hannah still in the attic, their backs to one another. Hannah looked close to tears. I went to her and she gave me an arched look that lasted only a moment before her lip wobbled.

Her sniff had Jack spinning round. "Hannah," he murmured, gathering her in his arms. He tucked her head beneath his chin. "Don't cry."

"It's too dangerous," she said. "I don't want you to do it, but I know you. You'll go anyway because you think you must."

"He won't," I said before he could respond. They both looked at me. "Hannah is right," I told him. "She needs you here. You have a life to build together. Samuel and Charity too," I said when he opened his mouth to speak. "And Tommy is not yet fully recovered from his injuries and may never be. I'll go."

"You will not!" Hannah said, pulling away from Jack.

"Agreed." His face darkened and I could see the steel of the man I would have to convince to stay behind while I went through the portal.

"I want to," I told them. "I'd like to see the other realms, for one thing. And secondly…" I sighed. "Moping about here is not doing me any good. I need…activity."

"Take up croquet," he snapped. "Or horse riding."

Hannah's face softened. "It doesn't mean you'll get to see him, you know. Wherever he is."

"I know. But..." I shrugged. "I want to go regardless."

"No," Jack said. "It's too dangerous for a woman."

Hannah dug her elbow into his ribs. "It's too dangerous for a man, too."

"I'll leave you two to think about it." I turned away. "But you can't stop me."

My exit was blocked by a very stern looking Sylvia. I'd never seen her mouth set in such a determined line, not even when she was haggling over the price of a new gown with the seamstress. "I knew you'd do this," she said, not letting me past.

"I'm glad you overheard," I told her. "It saves me explaining my reasons again. I am going through, Sylvia. Please fetch the parchment with the spell on it."

She didn't move. "You are so stubborn, Cara, and Jack is little better." Her eyes flashed at her cousin beyond my shoulder.

"I've decided Jack isn't coming. The parchment, please, Sylvia."

"And if I don't give it to you?"

"I'll search your room until I find it."

She made a huffing noise. "Well, for once, I am ahead of you."

Damnation! "Have you hidden it elsewhere?"

She gave a defiant tilt of her chin. "Better. I'm going to stop you from entering the portal altogether."

"How?"

"I've summoned a secret weapon." She stepped aside, not to let me to pass, but to allow someone else through the doorway.

"Quin!"

CHAPTER 2

Quin gave a deep bow, hiding his initial reaction at seeing me. Of course, *he* had warning. I had none. I would have given Sylvia my sharpest glare if I hadn't been so intent on Quin. I consumed the sight of him, searching his bare shoulders for any new scars or signs of change. There were none. He was the same.

My heart did a giant flip as my stomach dove. I was glad I hadn't eaten since breakfast, some three hours earlier. It would have been humiliating to throw up on his boots.

He straightened, and I steeled myself for the longing in his eyes, an echo of my own. But there was nothing like that in their blue-green depths. His gaze skimmed over me, brisk and ice-cool, revealing none of his thoughts. It did not settle my stomach, or my heart.

"Good day, Cara." That was it. Those three words were the entirety of his greeting. It was difficult to hide my disappointment, but I didn't have to. He'd already turned to the others.

"Hannah," he said, bowing once more. "Langley."

Jack stretched out his hand. Quin didn't hesitate to grasp it in greeting. They exchanged grim smiles.

Hannah moved past us and kissed Quin's cheek. He looked startled to receive such a sweet gesture, but pleased nonetheless. I envied her ability to approach him. I was rooted to the spot and he did not come any closer to me.

"It's good to see you again," Hannah said. "Sylvia, did you summon him?"

"I did." She waved the rolled up parchment with the spells on it then marched into the attic to the table where the newspapers were spread out. She picked them up and handed them to Quin. "I knew Jack and Cara would insist on going through the portal unless a better option presented itself. I decided to take matters into my own hands and present the better option to them."

Quin finally focused on me. His gaze turned colder, and if I hadn't shared a kiss with him and known that he loved me, I would have stepped back beneath its ferocity. There had to be a reason for him to act so distant toward me. Later, when we were alone, I would discover what it was. If we ever got to be alone.

"That would have been foolish," he said. "And very dangerous."

Jack bristled. "I'm not exactly a weakling when it comes to defending myself."

Quin pinned Jack with his glare, but it softened somewhat. "I know, and I understand your need to learn more of where your mother came from. I was referring to Cara."

I bit back a retort. My plan *had* been foolish and dangerous. That was why I'd been prepared to do it. I didn't think Quin would like that explanation, and I wasn't yet prepared to tell him I'd decided to go through the portal in the hope of meeting him on the other side. Or, at the very least, distracting myself from thoughts of him.

"Come downstairs to the dining room for luncheon," Sylvia said, turning her back to us. "I sent word to the

18

kitchen for food to be sent up before I summoned you. I know how hungry you always are upon arriving here. Oh, and your shirt will be ready by now too. I was much more prepared this time." She sounded pleased with herself as she headed toward the stairs.

My heart sank even further. It was *my* job to see that Quin had everything he needed. He was *my* warrior. My disappointment was completely irrational and yet I couldn't shake it off; not even when Quin hesitated before following the others out of the attic. It was only a brief hesitation but it was long enough to give me hope that he did want to talk to me in private at some point. Just not yet. Hopefully by the time we were alone some of his frostiness would have melted.

And I would have found my tongue. I hadn't spoken a word since announcing his name upon seeing him.

***

If I could cook beyond the simple basics, I would have enjoyed cooking for Quin and watching him eat. Even though Cook hadn't prepared a feast by her standards, she'd sent up cold game and ham by the platter full, warm loaves of bread, mashed potatoes, patés and steamed beans. He piled his plate high and ate with enthusiasm. As such, luncheon was a mostly silent affair.

He'd dressed in a simple white shirt, sadly covering all that brawny muscle. Perhaps it was for the best, since I was wont to ogle and he seemed in a humorless mood. When we all reverted to the sitting room after our meal, I decided I'd had enough of his coolness. Getting him alone to talk, however, proved difficult.

"Now that you've had time to think about what I told you," Sylvia said in this new, schoolmarm manner of hers, "will you find Myer for us and bring him back to face justice?"

"Wait a moment," I said, palms up to slow her down. "Quin's job isn't to fetch people from other realms for our sake. You shouldn't have summoned him, Sylvia."

I felt Quin's gaze on me before I glanced in his direction. It was no longer flinty, but it was still unreadable. "You don't want me here." His tone was flat. He did not pose it as a question.

"That's not what I meant! Of course I—" I cut myself off before making a complete fool of myself in front of everyone. I clenched my hands into fists then after a deep breath, fanned them out across my lap. I hazarded a look in his direction, but he was no longer watching me. His attention was on the fireplace near where he stood.

I drew in a deep breath. "What I meant was, we can't ask Quin to do something that might get him into trouble with the administrators of...of his realm." My friends didn't know that Quin originated from Purgatory. If Sylvia had, perhaps she wouldn't have called him.

"I was given permission to come," he said quietly.

"Oh. I see. So...you asked them and they just...said yes?"

"The administrators are not asked. They simply *know* and grant release."

"Does that mean Myer is causing a problem somewhere and you're expected to bring him back here?" Jack asked.

"I don't know what the administrators know. They do not confide in me."

Jack cleared his throat and frowned at me. *What's wrong with him?* he mouthed.

I shrugged. I twisted my fingers in my lap, warring with myself. Should I ask him? Or should I assume it was related to Purgatory business and I was better off not knowing? In the end, my curiosity won out.

But Sylvia got in first. "No time like the present. Let's go down to the ruins and Quin can go through the portal immediately." She picked up the parchment of spells.

"Agreed." Quin pushed off from them mantel and strode to the doors leading directly out to the garden. He couldn't wait to get away from me.

20

Tears stung my eyes as I watched him open the French doors. I hadn't expected him to recover from his love for me so quickly, or at all. Time had no meaning for him in Purgatory, so perhaps our last meeting had been relegated to a distant memory. Perhaps he no longer felt for me what he'd once felt.

"Is there anything you need before you enter the portal?" Sylvia called after him.

"I have my sword." He strode across the paved terrace and over the lawn. The sun glinted off the hilt of his sword and the white of his shirt dazzled. It made my eyes water. At least that's what I muttered to Hannah when she closed her hand over mine.

"Sylvia," she said. "Stay here."

Sylvia narrowed her eyes at me. "Are you sure that's wise?"

"Yes," Hannah responded without hesitation.

I slipped my hand from hers, gave her a nod of thanks, and took the parchment from Sylvia. I tucked it into my skirt pocket as best as I could, leaving the end poking out of the fabric folds. Quin's strides were long and he was already halfway across the lawn by the time I left the house behind. Dignity be damned. I picked up my skirts and ran after him.

His pace didn't change. "Go back to the house, Cara. I don't need your assistance."

"I'm not here to assist you."

He said nothing, just forged ahead, his focus on the abbey ruins nestled on the edge of the lake like a peaceful folly. Yet they were no folly, nor were they peaceful.

"I want to talk to you before you leave again." I grabbed his arm.

He jerked away and kept walking, like he needed to get away from me. Well. It would seem I needed to slow him down somehow.

I ran to catch up and when I drew alongside him, I promptly tripped over my own feet. His quick reflexes meant

I didn't even land on my hands and knees. It also meant he stopped.

With my elbows firmly in his grip, he helped me regain my balance. His gaze warmed and softened, but only a little. He let me go but did not stride off.

"You do not play fair," he said, crossing his arms.

"If I played fair, there would be no contest. You would win. I can't let you win this time, Quin. It's too important. Don't leave like this. Don't let me think you've forgotten me."

"Forgotten you?"

"Perhaps not forgotten. Overcome your feelings." There, that explained it. I bit the inside of my lip until I tasted blood.

He merely grunted and strode off again. I grasped his arm and this time did not let go when he tried to jerk away. The movement only brought me crashing into his side.

He tried to prize my fingers off, but I clung on. I was the picture of a desperate female and I ought to have been ashamed of myself. I was not.

"Don't, Cara. Please. We cannot touch."

"Why not?"

His nostrils flared. His jaw hardened. I skimmed my fingers over the bunching muscles and, to my surprise, they relaxed. He heaved out a deep breath and closed his eyes.

After a moment, he opened them again, but stared down at the ground, not at me. "Every time I come here, I must leave again. Twice now, I've come and gone from you— from this realm." His gaze flicked to me then darted away, as if checking if I'd noticed his admission. I'd noticed. My heart lifted. "Last time was…more difficult than the first."

I flattened my palm to his cheek and was surprised when he leaned into it. "And you think this time will be worse."

He inclined his head in a small nod.

Oh, Quin. "It will be for me too." I placed my other hand on the other side of his face and forced him to look at me, but he still did not meet my gaze. "Yet I refuse to think of this encounter as a bad thing. It's a reprieve, of sorts. A few stolen minutes are better than nothing."

He gave a small shake of his head. "It's too…hard."

"Pretending we don't have feelings for one another isn't going to make it easier." I stroked my thumbs over his cheeks, tracing the smooth skin stretched over strong bones. "Ignoring me will only make me miserable."

His gaze finally lifted to mine. I knew then that he had been as unhappy as I had since his departure. "I'd rather you were miserable and safe here than have you think you can find me, and happiness…elsewhere."

It was my turn to look away. I lowered my hands, but he caught them. It would seem his determination not to touch me had melted away.

"You were going to enter the portal to come to me, so Sylvia said." He nodded at the part of the ruins where the portal lay dormant and unseen to human eyes. "Why, Cara? Were you putting yourself in danger in the hope I would be sent to retrieve you?"

"No!" Yes. Perhaps.

It was his turn to grasp the sides of my face and gently force me to meet his gaze. "Don't. Don't do that. Never step through that portal. The chance of you ever seeing me on the other side is so small that it's almost nothing. You have more chance of seeing me here than elsewhere. It was a foolish notion. You're wiser than that, Cara."

His admonishment stung, because he was right. He'd deduced the core of my reasoning without me even knowing it was the reason. I *did* feel like a fool, and now I felt worse because he saw me as one too. I closed my eyes, not wanting to see the accusation in his. Hot tears slid from beneath my eyelids and down my cheeks onto his hands. He caressed them away.

Next thing I knew, I was being crushed against his chest, his arms pinning me, one hand on my lower back, the other at my shoulder. His heart thundered erratically against my ear, far louder than usual. It matched my own, smashing itself against my ribs.

The embrace was a welcome relief but it wasn't enough. I tilted my face to peer up at him but I didn't get the chance to see him properly. His mouth met mine with a passionate kiss that did nothing to settle my heart; there was none of the sweetness of our other kisses. It was all primal passion, as if our gnawing hunger couldn't be sated any other way. It set my skin on fire and banished all thoughts from my mind, all cares. I had Quin in my arms again. Nothing else mattered.

He broke the kiss. I groaned in frustration and tried to lean into him, but he held me at arm's length.

"People can see," he said shortly.

"I don't care! My friends won't tell anyone."

"The servants…" He swallowed. "Your reputation is too important." He let me go and strode off toward the ruins.

"My reputation is irrelevant now."

He stopped and swung round. "*This* is why I did not want to kiss you again. I should not have—" He dragged his hand through his hair and growled. "Cara." He settled his hands on my shoulders and peered into my eyes, all earnestness. "Promise me you will not throw away your future."

"I promise."

His gaze held mine for a long moment, then he gave a single nod and let me go. I trailed after him, pleased that I hadn't needed to lie. I *did* plan on having a fulfilling future. I would just spend it unmarried. To a man brought up with medieval ideals, he probably didn't think spinsterhood could be a satisfying state for a woman.

We reached the ruins and wound our way through the scattered stones and the low, broken walls. The occasional blood spatter provided a grim reminder of the violence the abbey had witnessed both during its lifetime and after. The area where the portal lay hidden was a little cooler than elsewhere, but otherwise there were no signs that anything otherworldly was nearby.

"Will you return with Myer?" I asked Quin as we stopped.

"Unlikely. I'll send him back when I find him."

And return to Purgatory. "What about the book of spells?"

"It's an earthly book, not an otherworldly one. I'll leave it with him." He nodded toward the house. "After I go through the portal, you must fetch Jack and have him remove the book from Myer when he emerges. Keep it safe."

"I'll make it my life's work," I assured him.

He gave me a sad smile. "I know you will. Be careful, Cara. Stay safe."

I bit the inside of my lip to stop it wobbling. I could only nod in response.

He focused once more on the air where the portal was located. It was some time before he spoke again. "I don't know how long this will take. The administrators will guide me but time moves differently in all the realms. You may not have long to bring Jack here."

"I'll fetch him directly."

He took a step forward and I grasped his arm.

"Quin, you made me promise that I would lead a fulfilling life, and I will ask something of you in return."

"You want me to cross over," he said flatly. "That isn't my choice to make."

"You can ask the administrators. Tell them it's time." He had never told me why he was in Purgatory or why he'd been chosen for warrior duties. At some point, I'd given up asking. At the time it didn't seem to matter, but it did now. "How can they refuse when you've served them well?"

"We shall see."

"Promise me you will not toss your future away," I said, throwing his words back at him.

His jaw hardened. "It's not the same."

"Quin—"

"It's for the administrators to decide."

Part of me rejoiced in the knowledge that he could forever be accessible to me in his warrior form. I could summon him if I needed to, and we could take snatched moments here and there. Yet it was no easy ride for him in Purgatory. From what I could gather, it was a place filled with punishments and endless tasks that he was required to complete. Quin now deserved to move on to his afterlife and the next phase of his soul's existence. If it weren't for me, he might already have done so.

"Quin—" My words were cut off by his kiss. It was achingly gentle and filled with longing. I wanted it to go on and on.

He broke away and pecked my forehead. "No goodbyes." He let me go. "Open the portal."

I fished the parchment out of my pocket and unrolled it. I blew out a breath, then another.

"Cara." Quin's voice held only quiet sympathy.

I dared not look at him as I began reading the strange, ancient words. I wasn't even half way through the incantation when a strong breeze whipped around me, snapping at my skirts and tugging my hair. What was happening? The portal shouldn't be opening yet. The entire spell needed to be spoken for that to occur. I paused and looked to Quin for an answer.

He backed away from the intense, swirling wind and drew his sword. "Get out, Cara!" he shouted at me over the loud *whoosh* of the wind. "Go to the house and lock the doors."

Oh God. Nothing good ever came through the portal, except for Quin, and he was already here.

"Go!"

I turned and ran. I hadn't even left the ruins when I heard Jack's shout up ahead. "Cara! What is it?"

"The portal…it's opening of its own accord!"

"Go inside." He ran right past me, his otherworldly knife in his hand.

"Be careful!" But he was already too far away to hear me.

I stopped on the lawn and watched the scene unfold down at the ruins. Hannah joined me but not Sylvia. She peered through a pair of opera glasses.

"Please be careful," she whispered.

I clutched her hand and watched too. A figure came through the portal. It stumbled to the ground on hands and knees near Quin. Quin jumped back and raised his sword. "It appears to be a human form," I said.

"My God." Hannah handed me the glasses. "It's Myer."

I peered through the glasses. It was indeed the missing Everett Myer. He picked himself up and smacked dirt off his hands. He wasn't holding the book.

"Come on," Hannah said, sounding relieved. "Let's see what he has to say."

We walked quickly toward the ruins, only to stop again before we reached them. Another human figure was spat out of the portal beside Myer. This one landed on his feet in a fighting stance, a long sword in hand. He was shorter than Quin and Myer, but strongly built. He was naked from the waist up, his long blond hair gathered at the nape of his neck with a black ribbon.

Quin's stance changed upon seeing the newcomer. Even from a distance I noticed his body tense. Although he didn't raise his sword, I knew he was poised to strike if necessary.

I broke into a run. Hannah kept pace beside me and we didn't slow until we reached the ruins. Now that I was closer, I could see the scowl on Quin's face, the angry set of his mouth as he bared his teeth at the stranger.

The stranger had been speaking, but broke off when he spotted us. He edged away from Quin, putting distance between them, and watched our approach with undisguised interest. His lips curled in a slick grin that sent a shiver down my spine.

"Now I understand," he said in an accent similar to Quin's, a little harsher than the French I was used to from my father's speech. It was the accent of the upper classes from the middle ages who spoke both French and English, albeit a more archaic form than our modern languages.

"What do you understand?" Jack asked, moving closer to his wife.

"Don't engage him." Quin's voice was as hard as the steel in his blade, his gaze brutal as it bored into the newcomer.

The stranger chuckled low in his chest. "Which one is yours, St. Clair? Or do they both belong to you?"

Jack stepped forward, but Quin put his arm across his chest and Jack halted. The veins on Quin's neck throbbed. His nostrils flared. I suspected he was restraining himself from thumping the stranger.

I glanced between Quin and the newcomer. "You know this…?" What was he? A man? Demon? Something else?

Quin didn't answer me. He was so intent on the stranger that I wasn't sure he'd even heard me.

"Myer?" I snapped. "Where did you go? Who have you brought with you?"

"I, er…" Myer touched his throat where his collar ought to be. It seemed he'd lost it and his tie and jacket too. His shirt was dirty, with sweat stains beneath the armpits, and his facial hair needed a trim. "I'd rather not say, Miss Moreau. You would not approve, but I can assure you, he means you no harm."

"You stole the book from us," I growled at him. "You hypnotized an innocent man to get it."

Myer snorted. "Lawyers are not innocents."

"Where is the book?"

He swallowed heavily. "I do not have it."

"Where is it?" My voice was not my own. It grated through my clenched jaw, harsh and guttural. Everyone turned to me. Myer flinched.

"It's gone." He held up his hands. "Not my doing! Please, Miss Moreau, this is not like you. You're quite agitated. Such a state isn't good for the delicate female constitution."

I lunged at him, but Quin caught me before I could scratch his eyes out.

The stranger laughed. "You allow a *woman* to speak to you in such a manner?" he said to Myer.

Myer simply shrugged. "She has a sharp tongue and I can't control what she says."

"You could if you hit her."

Hannah gasped and clamped her hands down on her hips. Quin's arm tensed around my waist for a brief moment then he let me go.

Myer touched his throat again, as if adjusting his absent tie. "A gentleman doesn't hit ladies these days."

"Then you are as weak as St. Clair." The stranger laughed.

"Quin, who is he?" I asked. "How do you know him?"

It was the stranger who answered, not Quin. "My name is Edward de Mordaunt. I was a friend to St. Clair once."

De Mordaunt! I searched my memory for everything Quin had told me about the fellow, but it was so little. He had been a friend to Quin's brother. His relative—a grandfather?—had come to England with William the Conqueror, and his distant descendent was Lord Alwyn, the rakehell who'd been prepared to harm members of my family if I didn't hand over the book of spells to him.

"*You* were never my friend," Quin growled. "And you were no friend to Guy."

"Ha! It seems you've set aside your guilt. That is unexpected. I'd thought your crime would dog you for eternity. How *did* you manage to forgive yourself?"

Quin lunged and slashed his sword near de Mordaunt's face. De Mordaunt parried it away, but not before his legs buckled from the force. He recovered and stepped back. A humorless grin stretched his lips wide. "You can't defeat me, St. Clair."

"You should not be here," Quin growled. "Return to the dungeons of your own free will or be sent back."

Dungeons?

De Mordaunt snorted. "You think I would come here without permission? Or without assistance?"

Hannah and I glared at Myer. His eyes bulged and he put up his hands. "Not me! I'm of no assistance in a fight."

De Mordaunt snorted again, this time in agreement. Then he said something under his breath that I couldn't hear.

Quin's fingers flexed around his sword hilt. "Langley, get the women inside! Now!" The words weren't even out of his mouth when he struck at de Mordaunt.

The grind of metal on metal filled the air as De Mordaunt blocked the blow and stepped neatly to the side. He did not stop speaking. Or rather, chanting.

Dread filled me.

"Go!" Quin shouted without taking his focus off de Mordaunt.

Jack gave us both a little shove. "Do as he says. Arm yourselves. Something is about to come through that portal, unless Quin can stop him."

Quin was trying, but every time he drew near, de Mordaunt dodged the strike or parried it. Every bone-jarring blow looked powerful enough to send an ordinary man to his knees, but the two otherworldly men kept their footing. And still de Mordaunt continued his chant. The wind picked up speed, whipping at our faces, sweeping leaves and soil into its funnel. The center of the portal widened. Something would come through at any moment.

I tried to drag Hannah away, but she refused to move.

"Jack!" she screamed over the din of the storm and the clang of metal.

"I have to stay and help," he told her. "If Quin is overset…" His didn't finish. Perhaps he didn't dare contemplate Quin's defeat. I certainly couldn't. "Go now. Please." This last was an appeal that he directed at me.

I pulled hard on Hannah's hand and together we ran, stumbling over stones and our own feet in our haste. "Wait," she said when we reached the edge of the ruins. We turned to look back at the portal and the men, only to see a creature covered in fur tumble through the portal, quickly followed by three more.

Demons.

Myer yelped and ducked behind a crumbling wall before the demons caught his scent. Three of them joined in the fight against Quin and Jack.

The fourth sniffed the air. It turned lidless yellow eyes in our direction and its lips pulled back to reveal blade-like teeth. It crouched, a massive paw fisted on the ground, ready to spring. It emitted a hungry, vicious snarl, and saliva dripped from its mouth. It leapt and sprinted straight for us, lumbering on thickly muscled legs that propelled it at frightening speed. There was nowhere to hide, and we could not outrun it.

CHAPTER 3

"Weapon?" I screamed at Hannah as we ran. An earthly weapon couldn't kill the demon, but it could stun it long enough for Jack or Quin to attack with their blades.

"No. Jack!"

I glanced over my shoulder. Jack had heard his wife, but he and Quin were too far from the demon to reach it before it attacked us. Shock and fear rippled across his face, before it set hard. He raised his knife to throw it, even as another demon bore down on him.

"Duck!" The shout didn't come from him, but from the house, and it sounded like...Sylvia?

Hannah pulled me down with her and I slammed into the ground with a thud, scraping my chin and knocking the breath from my chest. The boom of a shotgun echoed around the estate, sending the birds screeching from the trees. Another shot fired, the sound more like the bang a revolver made. I glanced up to see Bollard striding past, shotgun raised to his shoulder, a demon in his sights. Behind him, Sylvia lowered her revolver. Hannah and I scrambled to our feet.

The demon had scampered back, frightened by the noise and the sting of its wounds, and rejoined what was left of the pack. There were now only two demons and de Mordaunt, and those demons were no longer obeying their master. They were afraid of the guns, being too new to this realm to know that the pain delivered from a gun was temporary and couldn't kill them. In time, however, they would learn.

Myer emerged from his hiding spot and joined us. "Ladies, I apologize for this chaos. It wasn't my intention to——"

Hannah slapped his cheek. I slapped his other one. He rubbed them both and eyed Sylvia with caution.

"If it helps, I hope your husband will not be harmed," he said to Hannah.

"Send them back!" she snapped. "De Mordaunt too. They're far too dangerous to have in this realm."

"I can't, even if I wanted to. He's controlling the portal and demons now. There is a way to override him, but I don't remember the spell. It's in the book."

"Which you don't have," I said on a groan.

He looked down at his feet. "No."

"Did you lose it?"

"Not quite."

Sylvia cocked the revolver and his face went white. "I am not in mind to shoot you, Mr. Myer. Yet."

He gulped and glanced over his shoulder at the fight still being played out amid the ruins. Jack and Quin disposed of another two demons, but De Mordaunt continued to chant, bringing more creatures out.

"Why did you bring him here?" I asked Myer. "What is it you want?"

He didn't answer me, but signaled to de Mordaunt. "Come! We're wasting time."

De Mordaunt growled in response.

"What makes you think we'll *allow* you to leave?" I barked.

"You don't seem to have a choice, Miss Moreau."

"You cannot do this!" Hannah cried. "Those things are too dangerous!"

"De Mordaunt will control them. He knows how." Myer held his hands up to fend off our protests. "Let us go peacefully and no one will be harmed."

"Don't be a fool. You cannot promise no harm will be done with so many demons loose."

But I was beginning to see that we had to do as he said. More and more demons spewed from the portal. The only way to stop them was to stop de Mordaunt, and nobody could do that while they were fighting demons. Sweat slicked Quin and Jack's foreheads. Jack used fireballs conjured with one hand to ward them off and then went in with his blade while they were stunned from the flames. His method seemed to be effective. Bollard fired his shotgun, but some of the creatures had already realized that it was no threat. The bullets dug into their fur but did not hinder them. They advanced on him, and that meant Jack had to draw away from the main group and use his fire and knife on them.

The shortness of his blade hindered his effectiveness, and I soon realized Quin could not continue to battle on his own if more continued to come through the portal. Myer was right. There would be no winning.

"Come, de Mordaunt!" he called. "We had an agreement."

Agreement? What in God's name had he promised de Mordaunt? And what did he want de Mordaunt to do for him?

Myer moved off and we let him go. There was no way we could detain him and hope to spare our lives. Hannah didn't take her eyes off Jack. There were tears in them as he dodged a swipe from a demon's claw.

Four demons swamped Quin and another was on its way. De Mordaunt stopped chanting. His creatures continued with their task without his direction, intent now on their prey. The sight brought a twisted grin to de Mordaunt's lips.

"You need not have come here," he sneered at Quin as he backed away. "You always cared too much for the weak, just like a human. That was your problem then and remains so."

"I *am* human. Not like you. You never were."

De Mordaunt snorted. "Nor are you, anymore." He pointed his sword at Quin's chest. "I will see you again."

He peeled away from the carnage to join Myer. They headed to the stables, leaving the demons to finish their work.

Sylvia raised her revolver and aimed it at Myer.

"No!" I cried. "He's unarmed. No matter what he's done, you cannot kill him."

She lowered it with a sigh. "I'm not sure I would have hit him anyway. My aim isn't very good." It was fortunate then that she hadn't tried to shoot any of the demons tangled up with Quin, Jack and Bollard.

We stood by and watched. Quin swung his sword in an arc and slew another demon then used his momentum to cut through another. Their numbers finally began to dwindle, thank God, and Quin and Jack regained the upper hand. Bollard joined us, breathing heavily, the shotgun cocked and ready.

"I don't like this helplessness," Hannah muttered. "I wish there was something we could do."

I nodded. "When this is over, I'm going to take de Mordaunt's sword and keep it. Then I'm going to learn how to wield it and kill those things."

"They're not all bad," Hannah said. "They're confused when they're summoned like this. Confused, terrified and hungry. Once they've feasted and calmed down they regain their wits and kill only in defense."

She was right, of course. Some demons even blended into society if they were the shape-shifting variety, like Jack's mother had been. It was a sobering reminder of the blood that flowed through his veins, giving him the ability to summon fire at will.

I circled my arm around her waist. "People like Myer and de Mordaunt are cruel to use them like this here."

The two men rode out from the stables on Frakingham horses. The driver, Fray, ran after them, shouting for them to halt. They took no notice and rode at speed along the drive toward the gate, hooves kicking up gravel and dust. De Mordaunt streamed ahead, his tail of blond hair flying behind him. Myer looked ungainly by comparison, his arms and legs all over the place, his body rigid. It was a miracle he didn't fall off.

"What do you think their plan is?" Sylvia asked quietly.

"Nothing good," I said, turning back to see how Quin and Jack fared.

Despite gaining the upper hand they were clearly tiring, and it took several more minutes before they ended the life of the last demon. Hannah raced down to Jack and pulled him into an embrace. He was covered in sweat and blood, but she didn't care. He held her tightly and kissed the top of her head.

I wanted to embrace Quin too, but stayed back. Fury pulsed from him in waves as he glared in the direction Myer and de Mordaunt had ridden. Blood stained his shirt and covered his blade and right hand, but he appeared uninjured. I closed my eyes and blew out a long, measured breath in an attempt to mend my fractured nerves.

The sunlight dimmed and I felt his presence draw nearer, despite not hearing his approach. "Are you all right, Cara?"

I opened my eyes and touched his arm. "Yes. You?"

He inclined his head in a nod, but concern furrowed his brow and his eyes looked haunted as he once more stared in the direction de Mordaunt and Myer had gone.

"Let's get you and Jack cleaned up."

"And then we want answers," Jack said, pinning Quin with a sharp glare. "You must tell us everything you know about de Mordaunt."

"I will," Quin assured him. "Then I will find him and send him back."

We trudged up to the house. Jack and Quin left us and headed round to the stables to clean up and assure Fray that everything would be done to get the horses back. The house itself was eerily silent, the servants nowhere to be seen.

"Uncle?" Sylvia's voice echoed in the vast expanse of the entrance hall.

"Here!" Langley's voice came from up the staircase. Bollard must have left him in the laboratory in his rush. Without the use of his legs, he had no way of traveling between floors.

Bollard removed the bullets from the shotgun and handed the weapon and ammunition to Hannah. Then he traipsed up the stairs to his master to inform him of developments. That left us to go in search of the missing servants and refreshments.

I went with Hannah and Sylvia to the gun room to return the weapons, my thoughts not on the task but the twisted turn events had taken. It was all very odd.

"What do you think Myer is trying to do?" I asked them as we headed down to the kitchen.

"I don't know," Hannah said hotly. "The man is an obsessed fool. We ought to speak to his wife about having him committed to an asylum when all this over. Clearly he cannot be trusted."

"He already has incredible wealth at his disposal, so it's unlikely he's using de Mordaunt to help him gain more riches. What is so important that he would risk his reputation?"

"Not to mention his freedom," Sylvia chimed in. "He stole our horses. Jack will see that he's brought to justice over his earthly crime at least."

"And Quin will see that he's brought to justice over unearthly ones," Hannah added. When I didn't respond, she touched my arm. "Right, Cara?"

"I…I'm not sure Quin has the power to do that," I told her. "Unless the administrators allow it, of course."

Hannah cocked her head to the side. "The administrators from…?"

I sucked air between my teeth, delaying my answer. Being afraid of her response might make me a coward, but it troubled me that she and Sylvia would change their opinion of Quin if they knew he was from Purgatory. Their good opinion may not matter to him but it did to me. It wasn't right that people would think him a bad person. He wasn't.

"You're a coward, Mr. Bradford." The housekeeper's voice came from up ahead and around the corner. We three stopped, to avoid interrupting and to eavesdrop. One could learn much from the servants' conversations, particularly between the two senior members of staff. "Tommy Dawson would have been down there helping the gentlemen fight if he were here."

The butler kept his voice low, but we were close enough for it to carry to us. "That's why he's only got one good arm now. I may be a coward, Mrs. Moore, but I'm at least a whole man."

Sylvia gasped. Then she gathered up her skirts and marched down the corridor. Hannah and I quickly followed. Bradford the butler was about to get a piece of the new, fiercer, Sylvia Langley's mind.

By the time we rounded the corner, however, he was gone. Mrs. Moore the housekeeper jumped at our sudden appearance. The keys jangled at her waist as she took a step back beneath the ferocity of Sylvia's glare. It was directed past her, however, in the direction the butler had taken.

"Is everybody all right, ma'am?"

"Fine, thank you, Mrs. Moore," Hannah said. "And the staff?"

"They are…upset." The matronly woman pressed her lips together and shot a worried glance at Sylvia. Sylvia had been her mistress for years before Hannah came into the position upon marrying Jack, and it was understandable that she would appeal to Sylvia for comfort in uncertain times.

Sylvia took Mrs. Moore's hands in hers, her temper having dissolved as quickly as it flared. "Take a deep breath. Now, tell us what happened here. Where is everyone?"

I shared a small smile with Hannah. It seemed she was as surprised at Sylvia's newfound strength as I was. Not only had she fired a revolver and not fled from danger, but her confidence and maturity had grown. She was no longer the skittish, silly girl I'd first met.

"Some of the servants are threatening to leave, including Mr. Bradford," Mrs. Moore said. "Two of the maids suffered fits of hysteria after…what happened down by the ruins."

"What did they see, precisely?" I asked her. Surely from a distance it was difficult to see everything.

"It's not so much what they saw," she hedged, "but what they heard."

"Gunshots," Hannah said grimly.

"Thieves," I told Mrs. Moore. "They stole the horses."

The housekeeper gasped. "In broad daylight! Are Mr. Fray and the stable boy all right?"

"Mr. Langley is seeing to them now," Hannah assured her. "He, Bollard, and our guest, Mr. St. Clair, tried to stop them, but they were overpowered."

"Hmmm." The housekeeper frowned. "I noticed the gentlemen fighting that pack of dogs. We seem to be plagued by these creatures here at Frakingham."

"I'm sure we'll see the last of them very soon."

Sylvia patted Mrs. Moore's hand. "Hopefully we already have."

"Tell the servants they may take the rest of the afternoon off if they wish," Hannah told the housekeeper. "Mr. Langley and I will address them in the morning when everyone has calmed down. We don't want anyone to leave, but if that's what they wish, they will be given full references."

Mrs. Moore bobbed a curtsy. "Thank you, ma'am."

"You are a very brave soul, Mrs. Moore. Thank you for your loyalty."

The housekeeper blushed. "It's my pleasure to work here. This is my home."

"Of course it is, and we're glad you see it as such. Now please have tea and refreshments sent up to the drawing room."

Mrs. Moore departed down the corridor and we headed back to the main part of the house and the drawing room to wait for the men.

"A generous bonus in their wages ought to convince most of them to stay," Hannah said when we were out of earshot.

Sylvia sighed. "It was as I feared. The new servants have been here long enough now to have heard the rumors about *Freak* House." She flounced onto the sofa with another deep sigh. "It's terribly disheartening. Just as I feel as if we are making progress with our reputation, something like this drags us back."

Hannah sat beside her. "It is only a reputation, Syl. At least nobody lost their life this time."

"Thank God."

Bollard and Mr. Langley joined us, and I was relieved to see that the former was uninjured. Langley's face was grave. Bollard's was as impassive as ever.

"What the bloody hell is Myer up to?" Langley growled.

Sylvia's cheeks flamed at his foul language. "We don't know, Uncle. He didn't confide in us."

"He's a madman. Ought to be flogged for what he did here."

Sylvia's fingers twisted together in her lap, turning the knuckles white. The silence stretched painfully thin until Jack and Quin arrived in fresh clothes, their hair still damp. Quin must have borrowed a shirt and trousers from Jack. Unlike Jack, he did not wear a tie, waistcoat and jacket. Seeing him dressed as a gentleman from this time and realm made my chest ache. It could never come to pass for real.

Mrs. Moore and a nervous maid delivered tea and refreshments. Jack closed the door after they left again. Our conversation required privacy.

"Who was he?" Langley snapped at Quin.

Quin refused the offered teacup and stood by the window where he angled himself so he could see across the lawn. I thought he wouldn't answer at first. He was so secretive about his past that it seemed unlikely I would learn anything new, even now. I was wrong.

"Edward de Mordaunt was a friend to my brother when we were…alive. He betrayed us both."

"Did you kill him?" Jack asked.

Quin shook his head. "I didn't become aware of the betrayal until my death. When I reached Purgatory—"

"Purgatory!" cried several voices at once.

Quin arched a brow at me.

"I never told them," I said sheepishly.

"Why not?" Jack exploded.

"Jack," Hannah warned. "Give her a chance to explain."

"There is no explanation," I said with a shrug. "I knew what reaction that news would receive and I wished to avoid any prejudice."

"Prejudice!" Langley spat. "There is no prejudice in excluding someone from Purgatory from my house."

"Has Quin done any harm to anyone here?" I shot back. "No. He has saved us, many times. Being from Purgatory doesn't mean he's a bad person. It means he has a chance to redeem himself and wipe the slate clean."

"Why were you sent to Purgatory?" Hannah asked.

Quin's gaze flicked to me. "I killed someone who didn't deserve to die by my hand. It was a mistake." He put up his hand to ward off any more questions along that line. "De Mordaunt is a shape-shifting demon."

That certainly got us back on track. We all gaped at Quin. "My God," I said on a breath. "How…?"

"He's not full-blood. He's descended from a demon on his father's side. The demon escaped to this realm and

41

consumed the body of Gilbert de Mordaunt in France. It kept his form and lived as him for the rest of his life."

"He landed in England along with William the Conqueror," I said, recalling the details. "He was granted lands here after years of service to his new king."

"Gilbert de Mordaunt wrote the book."

"The book of spells?" Sylvia asked.

"Not just spells. It contains other information about the different realms, portals and supernatural. I believe it's the only one of its kind. "

"And Myer no longer has it," I said heavily.

"Wait a moment." Hannah sat forward on the sofa, her teacup raised halfway to her mouth. "If the de Mordaunt line contained a demon, doesn't that mean Lord Alwyn is part demon?"

"It seems the demonic traits have been bred out," Quin said. "Otherwise he would have used his abilities."

"Thank God," I muttered. "Imagine the danger he would pose if he could harness fire or shift form."

Sylvia lowered her teacup to the saucer. "Or possessed superior physical strength."

I shivered.

"All of this I learned from the Purgatory administrators after my death," Quin went on. "I died before de Mordaunt. Upon his death, he was sent to Purgatory too. The administrators of the Waiting Area couldn't determine if his earthly crimes were sufficient for him to be sent to the dark place, so he was given a chance to redeem himself through the Purgatory trials. He chose not to participate."

"What do you mean?" Langley stretched the ends of his crimson smoking jacket over his paunch, but they wouldn't connect. "How can one choose not to be redeemed?"

"Everyone has a choice." Quin's eyelids lowered. "Almost everyone."

"Why would someone choose Purgatory over redemption?"

42

"It's better to exist in Purgatory than be sent to the dark place."

"He thinks he'll fail the trials," I whispered. The horror of it chilled me. "His soul must be black indeed and he knows it."

Quin frowned. "I believe so."

"You mentioned sending him back to the dungeons," Hannah said. "Is that where he lives?"

Quin nodded. "The dungeons in Purgatory hold those spirits who don't wish to participate in the trials. He must have escaped."

"Why in God's name would Myer bring someone as dangerous as that back here?" Sylvia asked.

Nobody had an answer to that.

A thought occurred to me. "De Mordaunt wasn't in spirit form. He was real, like you."

"Aye," Quin said darkly. "And I don't know why."

"There are too many unanswered questions," Langley said. "I don't like it."

"Agreed. If you'll excuse me, I must speak to the administrators."

He blinked out. Just like that, he was gone. I was used to spirits coming and going suddenly, but not Quin. In the past, he'd stayed for days once he was here, and always said goodbye first.

But, of course, this was different. He needed answers only the administrators could give.

I poured myself another cup of tea and waited. We all waited. The others talked quietly among themselves, but I didn't participate. I was worried about what Quin would find in Purgatory upon his return. Chaos? Answers? Would he be allowed to come back?

Time dragged. Every tick of the clock on the mantel sounded loud, every creak of the house had me casting my eye to the door.

"Uh, Cara?" Sylvia cleared her throat. "Do you know if we must summon him again for him to reappear?"

43

"I...I'm not sure." I felt somewhat foolish. There was so much of Quin's past and current existence that I knew nothing about. If I'd been giving myself advice, I would have told myself not to fall in love with such a mysterious man. It seemed like something only foolish girls would do and I hated to think of myself as silly.

Just then he reappeared, causing me to jump. Sylvia gasped but covered it with a cough.

"Well?" Langley barked.

"Myer was taken to Purgatory from one of the demon realms and requested the administrators' help."

"Help with what?" I asked.

"They would not say."

"And they gave him help in the form of de Mordaunt?"

"They offered all the spirits the chance to accept the task and use it as a trial. Pass the trial and crossover to a contented afterlife. Fail and be damned forever. De Mordaunt was the first to take up the offer. The administrators gave him a solid form for the task."

"Why did de Mordaunt accept it if he hasn't accepted any other trials in all this time?" Jack asked.

"I don't know."

From the way Quin's eyes flashed, I wondered if de Mordaunt's reason had something to do with him, his presence here and the connection we had with Myer. "I will see you again," de Mordaunt had said before he left. There was something between Quin and de Mordaunt. Perhaps de Mordaunt saw this as an opportunity to get at Quin.

"I see the administrators allowed *you* to return," Langley said.

Quin gave a curt nod. "They asked me to watch and intervene if something goes wrong."

"It seems they don't trust de Mordaunt either," I muttered.

Sylvia threw up her hands. "Then why did they let him come at all?"

"Because every spirit deserves the chance to redeem himself," I told her. "Even sinful ones. It is only the purely evil that are sent to the dark place."

"I don't like that they're testing de Mordaunt's soul here, on us."

"Nor do I," Quin murmured. "Does anyone have a suggestion for where Myer would have taken de Mordaunt?"

"My guess is London," Jack said. "He's not someone who has ventured far in his lifetime, except to come here and the portal from time to time."

"Then that's where I'm going." Quin strode toward the door.

I sprang up and went after him. "It's late. If they ride all the way, they won't reach London until tomorrow evening. You can rest here overnight and catch the train in the morning and still beat them."

He stared at me a long time, steely resolve glinting in his eyes. All previous softness toward me had vanished. He was worried. He finally nodded. "I will stay here tonight."

Good. Because I planned to speak to him alone. And tomorrow, I would go with him to London.

45

CHAPTER 4

Dinner was a somber affair, during which few words were exchanged. I had the distinct feeling that everyone had many questions to ask of Quin, but refrained. Knowing he was from Purgatory *had* changed their attitude toward him. It wasn't that they seemed to fear him now, but rather their manners didn't allow them to ask the questions on their lips—whom did you kill and why was it a mistake?

Perhaps I was ruder, or perhaps my closer connection to Quin gave me greater allowance, but I decided to confront him on the issue again. Later. Alone.

"The train departs at nine," Sylvia said, breaking through the silence. "Are you going with him, Jack?"

Hannah's fingers tightened around her knife and fork, but she did not tell her husband he couldn't go. Jack opened his mouth to speak, but Quin got in first. "I don't need assistance. I will travel to London alone."

"I'm coming," I said.

That earned me glares, but only Quin spoke. "No, you're not."

"Not to help you send back de Mordaunt," I assured him. "I have people to see in the city. I was leaving Frakingham tomorrow anyway."

Hannah snorted softly.

"Who?" Sylvia asked, a challenge in her voice. "Emily and Jacob aren't even there."

I wasn't so sure I liked this forthright Sylvia anymore. She seemed to enjoy saying what she thought a little too much. "People who are not Emily and Jacob."

"The only other person who has written to you here has been Mr. Faraday."

Quin stilled beside me.

"Yes, well." I cleared my throat. "I've decided to pay him a visit. He may have remembered something helpful from the time he was possessed. It happens, you know. Sometimes victims can recall pieces from their memories. Their minds are not always completely overtaken by the spirit. Perhaps he can tell us the name of the medium who helped the ghost of Holloway possess him." I bit my lip to stem my rambling, despite warming to my excuse. Nathaniel Faraday *might* have something more to tell me. But best of all, I could spend several hours with Quin as we traveled to the city together.

"You will not put yourself in danger," he said in that tone of voice that invited no argument.

"Not on purpose, no."

"You never do it on purpose, Cara, yet danger seems to find you nevertheless."

I met his narrowed gaze with my own, then tossed him my most dazzling smile to disarm him. "That is hardly my fault."

His eyes crinkled at the corners and a smile tugged at his mouth. "You're a mischievous imp," he whispered when the chatter resumed around the table.

A mischievous imp who wasn't giving up.

I retired early and listened for his footsteps along the corridor. He was only a few minutes after me. I waited a little longer before treading softly toward his room. I knocked on his door and he opened it, not a flicker of surprise on his face at seeing me there.

He crossed his arms and presented a solid wall of man to block my entry. "You should not have come."

"I couldn't help it. It's what we mischievous imps do."

He scowled again but did not move aside. I stood on my tiptoes, reached behind his head, and pulled him down for a kiss. His resistance melted away and he kissed me back, circling his arms around my waist.

Then I was suddenly jerked inside. He broke the kiss, but I was pleased to see that his face was flushed and his breathing ragged, like my own. "Anyone walking past could have seen," he growled.

I refrained from once more telling him that I didn't care about my reputation nowadays. He seemed not to be hearing the message and I didn't want to argue with him tonight.

I shut the door. His scowl resumed and he crossed his arms again. I advanced on him and he backed away. His forehead smoothed and he looked decidedly more anxious.

"Stay there," he said, sounding like a medieval knight not used to his command being disobeyed.

I blinked innocently. "Afraid of me, Warrior?"

"Aye," he said on a breath. "And afraid of my reaction to you if you draw nearer."

I continued my advance. Every step toward him sent him one step back, as if I were a cat and he my prey. He bumped into the bed and promptly sat on the mattress.

"*I'm* not afraid of *you*," I told him.

His gaze shifted away. I caught his chin and forced him to look at me again.

"I'm not afraid of you," I said again, more serious this time.

His Adam's apple jerked with his hard swallow.

"Nor will I think you anything but a good man when you tell me what you did to land yourself in Purgatory."

48

"I did tell you. I killed…a man who didn't deserve to die by my hand."

The hesitation wasn't lost on me. "Who did you kill?"

His jaw tightened beneath my fingers. I softened my grip and stroked the tension away until I felt him relax again. He placed his hand over mine but did not try to remove it.

"Was it your wife?" I whispered.

His wide gaze locked with mine. My breath caught. My heart stopped. For one dreaded moment I thought I'd said too much, crossed a line that he'd drawn for himself.

"Do you…think *that* of me?"

"Of course not, but you've given me so little information. Aside from de Mordaunt, she is the only one you've spoken about with any sourness in your voice." I sat beside him and folded his hand on my knee. "Whenever you speak of her, you don't sound as if you liked her very much. But I thought if you had…killed her, then it must have been a terrible accident, because I know you wouldn't hurt a woman on purpose. Tell me about her."

I thought he would brush me off again, like he always did when I asked too many questions about his past. But this time he gave a single nod. "It's time you knew."

I let him gather his thoughts and waited for him to begin.

"I loved her, at first. She was beautiful, and I was young and naive. I believed she loved me in return. I learned before my death that she hadn't been faithful to me throughout the entire marriage."

How could a wife not be faithful to a man like Quin? He was kind and handsome, strong and capable. Why would she want to look at other men when she had him in her bed? It wasn't something I felt comfortable telling him, so I simply squeezed his hand and hoped he understood.

He gave me a flat, grim smile. "I didn't kill *her* when I discovered the name of her most recent lover." He removed his hand to scrub it through his hair. "I killed him."

"Who?"

"My brother, Guy."

Dear God. It was no wonder he was wracked with guilt. And no wonder he didn't think himself worthy of moving on from Purgatory. Killing one's own kin was a sin indeed and brothers were particularly close. In Medieval times, a brother was a man's greatest ally in battle, a staunch supporter in uncertain, violent times. Or he ought to have been. Guy had betrayed Quin by sleeping with his wife, and Quin had dealt him the ultimate punishment.

"Go on," I urged him.

Deep shadows haunted eyes that watched me closely. "You do not look at me as if you think my crime a heinous one."

"I have the feeling there is much more to this story."

"It's long and twisted." He blew out a long, slow breath. "I should have known there was something wrong. We were about to head into battle in the Holy Land. We stood together that morning, our squires dressing us in our mail shirts and preparing our weapons. He was very quiet. We all knew the battle would be difficult and we would likely be defeated. When I asked him if he was considering what lay ahead, he confessed instead. He said he'd always loved Maria, but she'd always spurned him, mocking him with her conquests of me and other men. It was just like her to use her beauty to manipulate and I had no reason to disbelieve him. Usually she merely teased him, but the night before we left England, she took him to her bed for the first time. He claimed he was too weak to resist.

"I was angry. At the time I thought Maria faithful, despite her flirtations. I didn't think she'd ever taken another to her bed...and...my own brother..." He cleared his throat. "I was angry at them both when he told me, but she wasn't there, so I took all my anger out on Guy. We fought in our own camp, without weapons. The king himself broke us apart. No one else dared come near."

"Did de Mordaunt see all this?"

"Aye. He relished our fighting. I should have known then that he had a part in it." I was about to ask for an explanation when he put up his hand. "I'm leaping ahead. The fight. The king separated us then we had to go into battle. It was difficult and we lost many good men to the infidels. It was becoming obvious that we needed to withdraw. As I waited for the order to be given, Guy fought his way to me. We'd both lost our horses by then. He apologized and begged forgiveness, but I refused to give it. I was furious. With the battle frenzy upon me, my anger was too powerful for me to overcome. I turned my sword on Guy. He defended the first blow. As I went to strike him a second time, he lowered his sword. He died instantly." He jerked his head to the side, as if turning away from the memory.

"You weren't expecting his capitulation," I whispered.

He closed his eyes. "It was his way to make amends."

"Oh, Quin. I'm sorry for you. No man should have to bear his brother's death on his shoulders. But it was an accident. You know that, right? You never meant to kill him."

His nod was slight but it was there.

"Is that what you meant when you said it was a mistake? That you hadn't meant to kill him, only fight, but the administrators in the waiting area didn't quite know what to do about it?"

He shook his head. "It's more complicated than that. Guy's death is not considered a mistake, but the event that led me to kill him was. Guy only *thought* it was my wife he'd bedded. Her body was taken over by a shape-shifting demon who seduced him."

I gawped at him. The startling twist in the tale had rendered me speechless.

"It wasn't actually my wife," he clarified, mistaking my silence for confusion. "The demon shifted into her form, thereby killing her."

"Edward De Mordaunt," I managed to whisper.

He nodded. "He witnessed Guy's death on the battlefield but had been too far away to stop me. He came to me, screaming like a madman, accusing me of being a murderer. I was already feeling guilt and loss, and I didn't disagree with him. I must have told him why I'd done it; I don't recall. He explained that Guy hadn't betrayed me, that I'd killed him for nothing. I didn't really understand what he was telling me, so he decided to prove it. He changed into the shape of the nearest infidel to show me what he could do.

"I was stunned. I knew nothing of demons or the supernatural then. I thought he was the devil himself come to punish me for the crime I'd committed against my brother. De Mordaunt was stronger than a man ought to be, his movements too fast to be natural. I realized he must be telling the truth and that he'd dampened his speed and ferocity until that point to hide what he was."

"Did he…love your brother? The way Bollard loves Mr. Langley?" My face flamed. It was one thing to think of Bollard and Mr. Langley as being more than friends, it was quite another to think of two men together in a sexual nature. It wasn't an image a respectable young woman was supposed to conjure.

"I don't know if theirs was that kind of love. After his display, de Mordaunt changed back to his usual form again. He was still angry, but there was pain in his eyes too. He told me he loved Guy and wanted him to enjoy the object of his desire before going into battle—Maria. He said he knew of Guy's love for her and her spurning of him. On that last night in England, he came to Guy in the night, using her form."

"That's cruel beyond words," I said. "To use her body to encourage a man to betray his own brother. That's not love, that's…madness."

"Aye, de Mordaunt was—is—mad. I think Guy's death made him worse. He wanted me to suffer for killing him. He didn't know how much I was already suffering. It was he who told me of Maria's infidelities, in an attempt to prove to me that the seduction wasn't Guy's fault but hers. 'How can a man who loves a woman as deeply as he loved her turn

that woman away when she offers herself to him?' That's
what he told me."

He'd been staring down at his hands, balled into fists on
his knees, but now his gaze lifted to mine. "On that, I agree
with him," he rasped. "It's nigh impossible."

It was his way of telling me to stay away. I did not think
losing my virtue to the man I loved was a sin, but he would,
and he already carried enough guilt. I didn't want to add
more.

"You died in that battle," I prompted him.

He nodded. "I lived a moment or two more after de
Mordaunt confessed. I could not think clearly. With
everything he'd said playing on my mind, and with my heart
sore over what I'd done…my reactions slowed. An infidel
cut me down from behind."

That's how he'd got the two long scars on his back. I
traced them through his shirt, but pulled my hand away
when he drew in a shuddery breath of desire. I must not
tempt him.

"If your intention wasn't to kill Guy, why were you sent
to Purgatory? Couldn't they see that your soul wasn't bad?"

"The administrators in the waiting area couldn't overlook
my crime. It was still a grave sin. They decided Purgatory
would give me a chance to redeem my soul. Once there, I
was asked if I wanted to perform a trial. I refused."

"Because of the guilt you felt."

He nodded. "I wanted to remain in the dungeons as
punishment, but they assigned me warrior duties instead."

"Because *they* didn't blame you for killing Guy. It wasn't
really your fault, after all. It was de Mordaunt's."

"And it was their fault that he was on our realm at all." At
my arched brow, he added, "Edward's ancestor, Gilbert de
Mordaunt, was a soul in Purgatory when he discovered a way
to escape and come here, to this realm, and live again. Once
here, the administrators could not get him back. There were
no warriors then. Gilbert lived peacefully and had children;

they had children and so on. Four generations later, Edward was born with strong shape-shifting powers."

"So Edward's crime came about through their negligence," I finished for him.

"It was a supernatural crime caused by the administrators' error. In light of that, I have been given special consideration and privileges. I can be a warrior forever."

"That's remarkable. I had no idea the administrators could make errors. It sounds so...human." A thought occurred to me. "What happened to Edward de Mordaunt after your death? Why was he sent to the Purgatory dungeons? It seems like he ought to go straight to Hell for what he did to Guy and you. And Maria."

"Despite his ancestry, and being in possession of Gilbert's book, Edward didn't know that shifting shape into another living person would kill them. He had never read the entire book. Nor did he seduce Guy out of maliciousness. It was born of love."

"He was certainly malicious toward you! And Maria too."

"Souls aren't sent to the dark place for ignorance or inconsiderateness. Only the blackest souls burn in Hell. His wasn't deemed black enough, but it wasn't pure enough to move onto a better afterlife either. So he was sent to Purgatory for the trials."

"Yet he chose not to perform any and redeem himself."

"Until now."

"I think the administrators should take a good long look at their policies. That man—demon—is dangerous."

"When I take him back, I'll tell them you said so."

Was he teasing at me? It was difficult to tell with his eyes, hooded as they were.

"You've been in Purgatory a long time for a crime that wasn't your fault, Quin. But you no longer feel guilt, do you? Isn't that why you wanted the book? So you could leave?"

"Aye. The time I was summoned by the monk from the abbey showed me what real evil is. That was no war that I interrupted. Countrymen murdered one another at the whim of their king."

"There are some dark times in this nation's history and the dissolution of the monasteries is one of them. A tumultuous era followed. Is that when you decided you wanted to leave Purgatory and move on?"

"Aye. It was like a cloud lifted from my eyes. I began to understand the difference between true evil and what I'd done. I never intended to kill my brother, but I'd felt immense guilt until then. I did deserve my punishment, Cara."

"To a point."

He nodded. "I decided it was time to move on. To forgive myself. I asked to face a trial, but the administrators would not let me go. They said my work was too important and I could not be spared."

"That's not fair! They promised you the job only for as long as you wanted to do it."

He merely shrugged. "It's difficult to argue with them when they've made up their minds."

"You should ask again."

"I have."

"Beg them."

"I don't beg."

I pressed my lips together. "Quin, you must continue to petition them. Surely they can see how wrong they are."

He heaved out a sigh and leaned his hands behind him on the bed. "I've stopped asking."

"Why?"

His gaze slid to me.

"Oh." I swallowed the lump in my throat. "So you can come here and see me again."

He pushed off from the bed and strode to the window. I got the feeling he needed to get away from me. "It's time for me to ask again."

"Time for us both to move on, you mean?"

He said nothing.

If he moved on, we would be forever apart, until my death. I tried not to think about the finality of his decision. I *did* want him to enter his afterlife. But I would miss him immensely.

"You were prepared to use the book once," I said. "Gilbert de Mordaunt wrote it all down in there, how to escape and live here, everything. He succeeded. Couldn't you?" I glanced around the room, half expecting lightning to strike or flames to burst up from the floor as punishment from the administrators for my suggestion. Nothing happened, but the air in the room seemed to thicken and weigh heavily between us.

Quin stared out the window even though there was nothing to see in the dark. "I learned about the book from Myer twenty-two years ago when I was summoned here. I overheard him telling the others what it contained. However, it wasn't until I saw the de Mordaunt family crest that I realized Gilbert de Mordaunt had written it."

I remembered the hunt for the book, using other old texts and some ingenuity to find it. I'd been ill at the time. Quin's presence had saved my life.

"I waited for an opportunity to come here so that I could retrieve it, and your illness presented me with the best chance. My only chance. I've since learned that I would have been a fool to use the book to live here again."

Part of me wondered if he was only saying that because I'd refused to give it to him at the end and he didn't want me to feel guilt for withholding it. "Nothing happened to Gilbert," I said.

"How can we be certain?"

I let the matter drop. We were getting nowhere, and he would never blame me for thwarting his only chance at living again. "Thank you for answering all my questions, Quin. I know it wasn't easy to lay everything out for me. I'm sorry to stir up old and awful memories."

He leaned back against the window frame. He crossed his ankles and arms and regarded me levelly. "I wanted you to know it all. I thought keeping it from you would protect you." His gaze slipped away. "Or protect my reputation in your eyes."

"Your reputation is safe with me, Quin."

He unfolded his arms and leaned his hands on the windowsill behind him. His thumb flicked at a flake of peeling paint. "Now that I've answered your questions, will you answer one of mine?"

"Of course. What is it?"

He continued to finger the paint flake until it came away. It fluttered to the floor near his feet. His thumb stilled. "What will you tell Faraday when you see him?"

I opened my mouth to say that I wasn't going to see him, but stopped myself. It was the excuse I'd given at dinner and if I didn't continue with it, he might order me to stay at Frakingham. "About what?"

"About your…interest in him."

"I have no interest in him beyond his first-hand experience of possession."

"You used to."

"That was before."

"You might rekindle those feelings if you spend more time with him."

I studied him, trying to read his mind, but his face was blank, his eyes shadowed. "Perhaps," I said, thinking of the easy friendship I'd shared with Nathaniel. That was all it was—friendship. There had been no passion. I knew that now after experiencing it with Quin. "I didn't enjoy the awkwardness between us when I last saw him. I hope he has had time to think about the paranormal, and come to realize its existence. Perhaps that's why he wrote to me. Perhaps he wants to learn more."

Quin grunted. "Do we have to discuss him?"

"You brought him up!"

"I wasn't expecting your enthusiasm."

He was jealous of Nathaniel. I bit my lip hard to hide my smile. Reveling in his jealousy did seem wrong, but I couldn't help the thrill it brought me nevertheless.

He stalked across the room to the door. "Good night, Cara." He jerked the door open. "We both need our sleep for the journey."

"Good night, Quin. Sleep well." I paused in front of him and stood on my toes. I kissed his lips lightly.

He rocked back on his heels and blinked at me. He seemed caught between taking me in his arms, and kissing me thoroughly, and pushing me out the door.

I made the decision easy for him and left. There would be no tempting Quin tonight. Or ever.

CHAPTER 5

Concentrating on my book on the train journey to London was far too much to ask with Quin sitting opposite me, his knees bumping mine. The angles of his face fascinated me; so smooth, yet hard too. The muted sunlight from the cloudy day filtered through the window and painted deep shadows beneath his cheekbones and below his downcast eyes. He was reading a newspaper; unlike me, he apparently had no difficulty in concentrating.

Although he'd brought the old newspapers from the attic, he'd also bought a current one from the newspaper boy in the village using money Jack had given him to cover his expenses in London. It was that one he was reading now.

"Anything interesting in there?" I asked, leaning forward.

He nodded and kept reading.

I switched seats and sat beside him. He shifted to make room, but our thighs remained touching. It was an intimate position, one that would have raised eyebrows if anyone else had been in the berth with us. I put some space between us, aware of not trying to tempt him. That got him looking up from the paper and directly at me.

"I can restrain myself," he said.

My face heated. "As can I." I nodded at the paper. "Are you reading that article on the missing museum artifacts?"

He nodded. "It's intriguing. The police inspector in charge seems more competent than Weeks. He has interviewed suspects and knows how the vagabonds broke in."

"He has probably done more, but that is the only information he's given the reporter. He wouldn't want to reveal too much to the public, and the thief, before apprehending him."

"I wondered if that were the case." He nodded, as if satisfied the entire constabulary wasn't all as foolish as Harborough's Detective Inspector Weeks. He studied the newspaper again and seemed to forget that I was there, until he spoke in a quiet voice. "If I were a modern man, this is what I would choose to do."

"Be a policeman?"

He narrowed his eyes at me. "Are you mocking me?"

"No! I...I didn't know you'd thought it through. Living here, I mean."

He straightened the newspaper with a snap and continued reading. "It may have crossed my mind."

I laid a hand on his arm. "Quin—"

"I shouldn't have mentioned it. It's an impossibility."

"I know." I removed my hand. "I'm not sure I picture you as a policeman anyway. A soldier perhaps, but that could simply be because that's what you've always been."

He regarded me out of the corner of his eye. "I was never given a choice. In my time, we did what was expected of us."

"It is somewhat the same today. There are more choices, but one must still do as one's gender and circumstance dictates. As a woman, I cannot join the police force, for example, and Samuel had to break away from his parents in order to marry Charity, although they've mended the rift now."

"I commend Gladstone for it. Your friend Sylvia should do the same if she cares for Dawson enough."

I sighed. "I think she does. She just needs the courage to follow her heart. I'll speak to Tommy about her while I'm in London."

We both turned back to the newspaper article. "Perhaps a private inquiry agent," I said after a moment.

"A what?"

"It's somebody who investigates where the police have failed or refuse to believe a crime has been committed. You could specialize in supernatural investigations." I tapped my lip, warming to the idea. "You could be the first paranormal inquiry agent in England. Perhaps the world."

"Cara." The misery in his eyes was like a slap across the face.

I shook off my thoughts. Why had I been thinking along those lines anyway? All it did was make us both sadder. "I'm sorry. My enthusiasm got the better of me."

He nudged my arm with his elbow. "Perhaps it's something you could do instead. You did tell me you were restless about your future."

"A woman private inquiry agent would find it difficult to attract custom. Society may have come a long way since medieval times, but not *that* far."

"What if you asked a gentleman of your acquaintance to help? You could work together, with his name on the calling card."

I arched a brow at him. "And do you have a gentleman in mind?"

"Faraday."

"Nathaniel? But he doesn't even believe in the supernatural."

"*You* could make him believe. You have remarkable powers of persuasion where men are concerned."

I searched his eyes, but there was no humor in them. He shifted his gaze away. "Quin, do not push me toward him. I can never like him in that way and you know it."

"I know no such thing."

"Last night you were jealous of him."

"I was not."

I snorted. "You didn't want to discuss him. What has changed?

"I decided to be practical and think only of your future." He returned to reading his newspaper, his jaw rigid. "As you ought to do."

***

We parted ways at Jacob and Emily's Eaton Square house after a brief argument in the hansom cab that drove us from the station. I wanted to know what Quin's plans entailed, and he refused to tell me. I pestered, cajoled and tried to sweet talk him into telling me. He remained as unyielding as a rock.

I slammed the door shut in my frustration and marched up the front steps to the townhouse. I only glanced back when the cab didn't drive away immediately. He stared at me through the window, his expression unreadable, until he finally gave the signal to drive off when Watkins, the butler, opened the front door. I watched the hansom turn the corner, heading in the direction of Claridge's, where Quin would be staying, then instantly regretted saying goodbye on an angry note. Indeed, we hadn't even said goodbye.

The Eaton Square house staff hadn't been expecting me, and my sudden arrival threw them into turmoil, despite my pleas that they shouldn't go to any trouble. There was only the housekeeper, butler, cook, one maid and one footman in residence, the others having gone with Jacob and Emily, but it was more than enough for me. With veiled admonishments that I should have given them notice, my room was soon made ready and tea brought up with some honey cakes.

I informed the maid who helped me change outfits that I would be out for dinner and Cook needn't bother to prepare anything for me.

Her lips pinched. "You've received an invitation, miss?" She knew none had arrived for me and clearly disapproved of my going out alone in the evening.

"I'll dine at a chop house. Oh, and tell Watkins not to wait up. I'll take a key and let myself in."

That caused her eyebrows to shoot up her forehead.

"I have friends to call upon. Miss Evans and her fiancé, Mr. Gladstone." I wasn't sure why I felt compelled to make up a story for her benefit, but it would hopefully stop her gossiping. I would hate for such gossip to reach Emily's ears. My niece would only worry.

"Will you require the footman to accompany you, miss?" the maid asked.

"No, thank you."

More lip pursing. I ignored her and succumbed to the hair pulling in silence as she rearranged it. She helped me dress in a simple royal blue and cream gown with a matching jacket then pinned a small hat to my hair.

With Emily and Jacob having taken their carriage, I caught a hansom cab to Clerkenwell. I alighted at the school, a large and imposing edifice that dominated the street. Scrawny tenements cowered beside it, clinging to its walls like a child to its mother's skirts. Lines of washing flapped overhead in a breeze that brought a waft of sewage to my nostrils.

I felt dozens of eyes following me as I headed up the steps and knocked on the school's door. A maid let me in and scurried away to fetch Charity and Tommy while I waited in a sitting room that was sparsely but neatly furnished. There wasn't a speck of dust on any surface, but I supposed that was to be expected in a school that taught the domestic arts—among other subjects—to orphaned children. I waited, listening to rhythmic hammering coming from somewhere in the depths of the vast building. Some minutes later Charity glided into the room, a warm smile on her lips.

"Cara!" We embraced one another. I'd missed my friend these last few weeks. We needed her quiet elegance at Frakingham. She was such a calming influence on everyone, although she probably wouldn't agree. "We didn't know you were back in London."

"I just arrived."

"Please excuse that infernal banging. Our new science laboratory is coming along nicely but the noise is rather trying. Did you catch the train down?"

"Yes, with Quin."

"Quin!" She caught my hands and searched my face. "Why is he here? Is everybody at Frakingham all right?"

"It's quite a story, but everyone is well. Or as well as can be expected with Sylvia pining for Tommy."

The man himself entered the sitting room at that moment, the slight flush to his cheeks the only indication that he'd heard me. He sketched a brief bow. I took his hand in mine and kissed his cheek in return.

"You are being far too formal for a friend, Tommy," I admonished him.

The color in his cheeks rose further. "You're well, Miss Moreau?"

"Cara. And yes, I'm well. Has your arm improved?"

The arm hanging loosely at his side lifted a few inches. "I've regained some movement." But not nearly enough to work, he might have said but didn't.

"The exercises have helped somewhat," Charity said cheerfully. "But it will take time."

Tommy shrugged his good shoulder, as if the functioning of his arm didn't matter, but I knew it was a show of bravado. For an active man such as himself, losing the use of his arm was a distressing hindrance. He would find work difficult to come by. It was another reason he needed to return to Frakingham House—he had secure work there as Jack's assistant.

"And everyone at home?" Tommy's swallow was audible. "Are they well?"

I liked that he still called it home, despite everything. "They are, but there have been some interesting developments since you were there."

The color drained from his face, and I quickly reassured him once again that nobody was hurt. "Myer returned through the portal, bringing a fellow with him by the name of Edward de Mordaunt. He's known to Quin."

"So you summoned Quin too," Charity stated for me.

"Sylvia summoned him only moments before they appeared." At mention of her name, Tommy's gaze sharpened and locked with mine, as if he could dig more details out with his stare. "She was worried that Jack and I were about to go into the portal to fetch Myer back."

"And were you?" Charity asked.

I thought it best to skirt that issue and her lecture. "We didn't, and in the end, nobody needed to fetch Myer. The problem is, the fellow he brought with him is not only part demon, he was sent to Purgatory for misdeeds committed in his lifetime."

I relayed what Quin had told everyone at Frakingham, leaving out the details of our private discussion. Although I suspected neither Charity nor Tommy would judge Quin unfairly for the things he'd done in his past, I knew he wouldn't want them to know.

"Has Quin gone to Myer's house now?" Tommy asked, glancing toward the window.

"I don't know," I said. "He wouldn't inform me of his movements."

"Perhaps I should find him—"

"Tommy," I chided gently. "He doesn't require any help."

His fist curled on his lap. "If it weren't for this bloody arm!"

"I know. Don't agitate yourself."

"I am not agitated! I'm useless." He got up and strode around the room, his long legs taking him quickly from one end to the other and back again.

Charity shrank into her chair and eyed him warily. She'd probably never seen him like this, and she didn't like confrontation, particularly with men.

"You are not useless," I told him.

"I am. Hopeless. This…" He punched his limp arm. "*This* is hopeless. I'm no good to nobody." Whenever he became upset, his accent changed from his carefully cultured one to the street slang of his youth.

"Even if you were able bodied, Quin wouldn't want your help," I said. "He doesn't want to draw any of us into warrior business unless it can't be avoided."

"It's not just that," he snapped. "The servants at Freak House need overseeing. I should be there to make sure that turd of a butler is putting the silver away in its proper place and not pilfering it."

"It wasn't your job to oversee the servants," I said. "Not in the days before you left anyway."

"And Jack needs my help," he said, ignoring me.

"True."

"And Sylvia…" He stopped pacing and studied his shoes. "I should be there for her."

Now we got to the crux of the problem, finally. "You will be, when Mr. Langley comes to his senses."

"And when will that be? I'm sick of waiting, Cara. I'm grateful to Charity and the other teachers for allowing me to stay here, but it's not where I want to be. I want to be with Syl and my friends."

"You will be."

"I won't. It's hopeless." He began pacing again.

I sprang to my feet and stepped in front of him. He tried to step around me so I grabbed him by the arms. "It is *not* hopeless. You're both alive, despite the best efforts of some evil creatures and spirits. Where there is life, there's hope."

"Cara's right," Charity said. "It could have been so much worse. We are all very lucky to be where we are today. Do not give up on being with Sylvia."

"I'm not. I haven't." He heaved a deep sigh and blinked up at the ceiling. "I just can't stop thinking about her. I wish I was there instead of here."

"Then it's time to stop thinking and wishing, and *do* something instead," Charity said.

"What do you mean?" we both asked.

"Self-pity is unhealthy for your soul. As is inaction."

"Are you suggesting that I act?"

"Doing something is always better than doing nothing."

I tended to agree with her. Not knowing where Quin had gone, and what his plans entailed, was tying my insides into knots. Knowing that he would leave this realm again when his task was complete made me feel altogether ill. We had parted on a sour note earlier, and I desperately wanted to wipe that from our slate. But even more than that, I wanted to find a way for him to be here, on this realm, alive.

According to the book, it was possible. Gilbert de Mordaunt had done it. Since he wasn't here, and nor was the book, I had two options—Myer and Edward de Mordaunt. They knew where the book was. If I could get my hands on it…

I felt a little giddy as I made my decision. I wasn't yet certain how to go about approaching the two men but I knew I had to. Doing nothing was driving me to madness. Even if I failed, I would know that I had tried. I still felt somewhat guilty for not giving Quin the book, like he'd wanted, when we found it. Clearly there were no repercussions, as I'd expected, or Gilbert would have suffered some awful fate.

"Cara?" Charity asked. "Why have you got that funny little smile on your face?"

I schooled my features and laid my hands flat on my stomach, where it felt like a thousand butterflies had taken up residence. "I just remembered something I had to do tonight."

"Is it something Mr. Beaufort would disapprove of, as your guardian?"

"Probably."

She groaned.

"Should we be worried?" Tommy asked.

"Of course not." I patted his arm. "Just because Jacob would disapprove doesn't mean Emily would. She's far more liberal minded."

Charity stood beside Tommy, presenting a united front to me. "As long as it's nothing dangerous," she said.

I kissed her cheek then squeezed Tommy's hand. "I must dash. Goodnight."

I turned to give them a little wave from the doorway only to find them both scowling at me.

***

I dined alone in the ladies' dining room at The London Restaurant on Chancery Lane then returned to the Eaton Square house and begged the maid for the use of her clothes.

"Whatever for, miss?" Her impertinent question had her instantly biting her lip in contrition. If the housekeeper had overheard the way she'd questioned me, she would have been given a severe talking-to. As someone who also had trouble holding her tongue on occasion, it didn't bother me.

"A social experiment I wish to perform this evening," I told her airily. "Nothing of a clandestine nature, I assure you. Besides, it's not as if you need your uniform tonight. You're already dressed in your bed clothes."

She looked down at her nightdress, as if she had only just realized she stood before me in nothing else. "Are you sure it will be returned before I rise in the morning, miss?"

"Of course. I'll sneak in when I get back and lay it on that chair there."

"I get up early, miss. Usually when the master and mistress are away I can sleep until dawn, but with you here, I must be up to do the blacking and polishing before you rise."

I suspected that was said to make me feel guilty for being there. "It will be returned well before then." I held out my hands. "May I have it, please?"

She fetched her neatly folded dress and apron and passed them to me.

"It's fortunate we are of a size," I said.

She didn't look as if she thought it were fortunate. She looked as if she expected me to return it torn and dirty. I thanked her and left before she changed her mind. I dressed in my room then snuck out without the rest of the staff noticing. It wasn't yet nine, but dusk blanketed the city, allowing me to walk in the shadows to Berkeley Square. I stood across from the Myers' house for several minutes, forming my plan and observing. Several lights were on upstairs, but nobody came or left the building. If Myer and de Mordaunt had been riding since the day before, they ought to have just arrived in the city. They would be exhausted, something which could work in my favor.

I glanced around at the small park behind me, half expecting to see Quin shadowing a tree or shrub, but the dim street lighting revealed nobody. He could be well hidden, or he might not be there at all.

I headed down the narrow mews lined with stables and carriage houses, with rooms above for the drivers and stable hands. Most were quiet, the only sounds coming from deep masculine voices from the rooms above, or the shuffling of horses' hooves in the stalls below. The third one, however, had some activity. A yawning youth mucked out an empty stall with a half-hearted effort.

"Excuse me," I asked the boy in a French accent.

He jumped at the sound of my voice, even though I'd spoken quietly so as not to startle the horse. He blinked at me then rubbed his eyes. "Who're you?"

"I have a message for Mr. Myer. Is he at home this evening?"

He propped the stall door open with his elbow and eyed me up and down. "I never seen a darky girl before."

I bristled. "Mr. Myer," I prompted. "Is he at home? Is that his horse?" I thickened my accent, but I probably shouldn't have sounded as if I were demanding an answer from him. A servant girl would be less authoritative, even a French ladies maid. "My mistress wishes me to deliver a message to him directly, so if you could please tell me if he is inside the house."

"Mistress, eh?" He snorted. "No lady has ever tried to give him a message before."

"There is a first time for everything, as you English say."

His tongue darted out between his lips and he licked the lower one. His gaze settled on the bare skin at my throat. "Aye, there is."

It was harder to get answers from this fellow than Quin. "He is inside then, is he not?"

"Maybe." He came out of the stall and the door swung closed behind him. "What I want to know is, are you that color all over?"

For goodness' sake. He wasn't going to give me answers, only trouble. I went to walk away but he grabbed my arm. "Not yet," he said.

"Unhand me or my mistress will hear of your behavior. She is a great friend to Mrs. Myer's, as well as your master." I hoped invoking the name of the more formidable Edith Myer would frighten him more than mention of Everett Myer. Fortunately it did. His fingers sprang apart and I edged away.

He snorted softly. "Bloody French. Think you better than the rest of us."

The clip clop of hooves came from the entrance to the mews. We both peered into the dark lane where two riders approached.

"Bloody hell!" the lad scurried back into the stables. "The master's back! Get down here!"

Muttered curses and thumping feet sounded above. I flattened myself against a wall, thankful that my dark hair and clothes allowed me to disappear into the shadows. The two riders came into view and I knew it was Myer and de Mordaunt without seeing their faces. The big frame of the medieval soldier and the tall, lanky one of the modern

MY SOUL TO TAKE

gentleman were a giveaway. They wore different clothing than when they'd stepped out of the portal, dressed in riding cloaks and gloves but no hats.

A second youth and an older man barreled down the stairs and bowed to Myer. The first lad took the horses through to the stalls while the second filled a trough with water from a bucket.

"Go tell the house staff that the master's back," the older man ordered, nudging the lad's shoulder. The boy scampered off toward the house. The man welcomed his master back. "You've been missed, sir. Everyone's been worried."

"Thank you, Jenkins. My wife?"

"Er, I s'pose she missed you too, sir."

"I mean is she home?"

De Mordaunt's gaze darted around the stable interior and I stopped breathing. He didn't see me, thank God. Myer's gaze was less alert. Exhaustion dragged at his eyes, and his shoulders sagged. His legs were still in a bow shape from riding and he rubbed his lower back.

"She's not in, sir," Jenkins said. "She went out earlier."

"The carriage is here."

"Aye, sir. She walked." From the way Jenkins didn't look at his master, he clearly thought this odd behavior for a married gentlewoman calling on her friends. Or perhaps, like me, he knew Edith Myer didn't have friends to call upon.

Myer merely grunted. "Good."

Good? He didn't want to see his wife? Perhaps he didn't want to explain about de Mordaunt. I could understand his apprehension. Her presence always made me feel somewhat anxious too. I could only imagine what it would be like to live with her. On the other hand, Myer had his hypnosis to fall back on when necessary, and he had used it on her too.

"I'm too tired," he went on. Too tired for what?

Myer turned to go, jerking his head at de Mordaunt for him to follow. They drew very close to me, but walked on without looking my way.

"When will she return?" I overheard de Mordaunt ask.

"How the blazes would I know?" Myer said. "It seems I've been gone for days."

"I knew where my wife was at all times."

"Even when you were away?" Myer snorted.

They disappeared out of the mews and I crept after them, keeping to the shadows. I wanted to speak to them about the book but I hesitated. Together, they worried me. Separately, I suspected I might have stood a better chance. At least with Myer. Of the two, he was the least dangerous. I thought.

They climbed the front steps and the door opened. A footman welcomed them in and shut the door again. Lights blazed from all windows, and I imagined servants racing back and forth downstairs, throwing jackets over their nightgowns as they prepared a supper for their master and his guest. Now was my best chance.

I headed down the short flight of steps to the service door. It was unlocked. I let myself in and steeled my nerves. A maid turned out of a room ahead, her back to me as she hurried along the corridor and up the service stairs, her arms full of linen.

I followed her, grabbing a lit lantern off the wall hook at the base of the stairwell. I made sure to keep her in my sights until she headed through the door on the third floor.

I listened to her receding footsteps then ventured out. The stairwell door opened onto a main passageway. Up ahead, I caught a flash of dark skirts as the maid entered a room. Most London townhouses of this size had the same layout, so I knew we were near the master and mistress's bedrooms, not the guest chambers. The maid must be making up Myer's bed.

I slipped into the corridor then crept into another room. It was a small sitting room, probably for Mrs. Myer's use. I listened at the door, but the house was vast and the voices distant. They were distinctly male but I couldn't make out any words.

The maid emerged from the room a few minutes later and disappeared into the service stairwell again. I checked along the corridor and, seeing no one, slipped into the bedroom she'd just prepared for her master. I glanced around and wondered where best to wait. I didn't want his valet to see me and, since all gentlemen had a valet to help them undress, I decided to hide behind the heavy curtain until Myer was alone. It was somewhat scandalous—very well, *extremely* scandalous—but these were extenuating circumstances.

The thick brocade fabric settled around me and I waited, listening to the thud of my heartbeat. I could no longer hear voices. Indeed, I could hear nothing of the rest of the household. Only a sort of clinking sound coming from…outside?

I pressed my face to the closed window and looked down. I gasped. Someone was climbing up the wall! I'd seen only one person do that, using pipes and vines to haul himself up. Quin. Except this time the window he needed to get through was higher, closed, and there were no vines. If he fell…

It didn't bear thinking about.

On the other hand, if he made it up, he would see me in Myer's bedroom and order me to leave. I didn't want an argument or my plan to be foiled.

I needed to make a decision, and quickly. Help Quin inside, or get out before I was discovered.

CHAPTER 6

I unlatched the window and opened it an inch before slinking away from my hiding place and out into the corridor again. Voices approached and there was no time to sneak back to the service stairs and disappear from view. Besides, I wanted to speak to Myer, not hide. All I had to do was get him alone.

Except it wasn't Myer and his valet's voices I could hear. It was Myer's and de Mordaunt's.

"I don't know when she'll return," Myer said with exasperation. "No one does." He seemed to be talking about his wife again.

De Mordaunt responded, but his accent made him difficult to understand at a distance. It seemed thicker than when we'd first met. Perhaps he was tired too and reverting to his more natural speech pattern.

"Your room is down there," Myer said. "It's the master's suite and should suit your needs."

"You do not sleep there?"

"I prefer to sleep as far away from my wife as possible."

De Mordaunt snorted.

Panic slammed into my chest. I wasn't in Myer's room. It was de Mordaunt's and he was coming my way! I warred with myself and quickly decided it was too late to chase after Myer. I would have to speak to de Mordaunt instead. At least he would be on his own. Perhaps he would not present a danger to me. After all, I wasn't a danger to him. He would see that instantly. Wouldn't he?

Myer's footsteps receded and de Mordaunt's approached. I stepped out of the shadows, and he stopped short. His eyes narrowed and he angled himself closer. I lifted the lantern so he could see my face.

His lips parted and his gaze darted up and down the corridor. Looking for Quin?

"I am alone," I whispered. If Quin had climbed into the bedroom, he might be able to hear my voice if I spoke at my normal level.

"Is that so?" he growled. "Where is your dog?"

"Not with me."

He cocked his head to the side, regarding me. The light from my lantern picked out the hard gleam in his eyes and leant a cruel edge to an already sharp face. "Why are you here?"

"I need the book. I'd like to borrow it."

He blinked in surprise. "The book? You do not ask why I am here, Miss…"

"Moreau. No, I do not. That is your affair, and Myer's."

"And St. Clair's?"

"He says your visit is sanctioned by the administrators."

He glanced up and down the corridor again. "Then he will not try to send me back?"

"You should ask him that, not me."

He seemed to consider this a moment. Then he said, "Why do you want the book?"

"I'm a spirit medium, Mr. de Mordaunt. I've been told the book contains information about the supernatural, including the origins of people like me. I wish to know about my ancestry and why I am what I am." I shrugged, doing a good job of feigning ignorance, I thought. "Is it so strange to want to know your heritage?"

I hoped that appealing to his own strange heritage would help develop a connection between us, and encourage his sympathy, but his eyes continued to bore into me aggressively. "Liar."

I swallowed and opened my mouth to protest, but shut it again when his lips curved into a slick smile. He took a step toward me and I inched backward. "Pardon?" I squeaked.

"Myer told me what you are and why you are a medium. If he knows about your tribe, then I suspect you know too."

"That's a rather big leap to make."

"Is it?" He took another step closer and I took another back.

He reached out and caught my chin in his hand. I flinched as his fingers dug into my skin. He leaned in, his face so close that it blurred. His breath reeked. His eyes gleamed. "Why do you want the book?" he snarled. "Tell me the truth, this time."

I tore myself away and pressed back into the wall. My hands shook, and a chill raced up and down my spine. "I wish to know all the secrets contained within its pages." Not wholly a lie this time.

He grunted a laugh. "I'm sorry to disappoint you, but I do not have it. Nor do I know where it is."

I licked dry lips. The action drew his attention. He pressed his own lips together and his gaze heated.

"But I might know the information you seek." He reached out, but instead of grasping my chin again, he gently touched my lower lip with his fingertip. "Ask me."

Bile burned my throat at his touch. I swallowed it down. I could bear his touch in exchange for answers. "Your ancestor, Gilbert de Mordaunt, came from Purgatory and lived here. How?"

His gaze flew to mine and his hand recoiled. He began to laugh, a bitter, twisted sound that set my nerves on edge. "You wish to know for St. Clair? So he can exist again?"

"Keep your voice down," I hissed. Quin was most likely just on the other side of the door.

"Do you know what he did?" His voice wasn't quiet. "Do you know why he's in Purgatory?"

"Yes," I whispered. "I know."

The door crashed back and a shadowy figure flew out of the bedroom. Quin stood between de Mordaunt and me, his sword in his hand.

De Mordaunt stumbled back, but recovered before he fell.

He bared his teeth. "St. Clair." He spread his arms wide. "Are you here to destroy me?"

Quin's fingers flexed around his sword hilt. He didn't speak, and although his back was to me, I knew he was furious from the set of his shoulders.

De Mordaunt chuckled. "Go. Take your lovesick fool with you. I have no need for her when there are prettier girls in the house."

Whip-fast, Quin smashed his fist into de Mordaunt's jaw, sending the other man reeling back into the wall. De Mordaunt recovered and hurled himself at Quin, but Quin put up his blade and stopped him with the flat edge pressed into the other man's throat.

"You hurt anyone on this realm and I will hunt you down and kill you." Quin's voice was low, quiet, but the menacing tone was unmistakable.

He took my hand and dragged me away, his gaze on de Mordaunt until we rounded the corner. He dragged me down the stairs, catching me round the waist when I stumbled. The butler gaped at us as we passed and I mumbled an apology as we headed out the door.

Quin did not stop. He marched me up the street. I had to run to keep pace or risk him dragging me again. His rigid shoulders and hard jaw invited no arguing and certainly no stopping. Once we'd entered the next street, and I was sure nobody followed us, I tried to break through his steely exterior.

"No response about me not being the prettiest girl in the house?" My joke fell flat, but it did get a reaction. He spun me round and forced me against a wall of a house on the corner.

He slammed his hands onto the bricks on either side of my head and leaned in until we were nose to nose. "What were you doing?"

I tried to dampen my racing heart, but it was no good. While I wasn't afraid of him, I was uncertain of how he would act. He was, after all, a medieval man who'd been locked away in Purgatory for hundreds of years. It was possible he'd just been acting the gentleman all along. I swallowed. It seemed I was a *little* afraid.

"That is my affair," I told him quietly. "And I do not appreciate you trying to bully me into telling you."

His lips thinned. "What. Were. You. Doing?"

I bunched my fists in my skirts. If he wasn't going to listen then I wouldn't say anything. I lifted my chin and waited for his next tirade to begin.

"He could have hurt you."

"He didn't."

"It was foolish and dangerous."

"Much like scaling three levels to a locked window."

He slammed the flat of his hand against the wall near my ear. "Enough, Cara! You're not listening to me. That man has a cruel streak. If I hadn't interrupted—"

"I would have handled him, Quin. I can deflect a man's interest."

"And if not? He despises me. What do you think he would have done after he found out about us?"

I ducked under his arm and stalked away. I was very aware that if he had wanted to keep me there, trapped against the wall, I would not have been able to escape so easily. "I do not have to answer you or do as you say," I tossed over my shoulder.

Next thing I knew he grabbed my shoulder and spun me round to face him. I would have lost my balance if he hadn't grasped my arms and held me up. He was still looking as ferocious as a swarm of bees. "I heard you," he snapped.

"What?"

"I heard you ask him for the book. For the information in it."

"Then why did you ask me what I was doing there?"

"I hoped you would answer me yourself instead of lying."

"I haven't lied. I merely avoided telling you the truth."

"Stop it, Cara. This is not a game and you are not to endanger yourself for me." He shook me. "Do you understand?"

"Quin," I began, meeting his gaze with my own determined one. This required some delicacy if I were to diffuse his temper. "I will not give up. I will fight for you and your life, even if you don't want me to."

He let me go and straightened to his full height. It was difficult to see in the darkness, but I think his eyes softened a little, although his body was still ramrod straight. "You must not endanger yourself for me. Do not go near de Mordaunt or Myer."

"Myer knows where the book is, even if de Mordaunt doesn't."

The lamplight picked out the flash of his eyes in the dark. "And how am I meant to live with myself if something happens to you because of me?" he ground out through a clenched jaw.

There was nothing to say to that. He was right. That's why I hadn't wanted him to know what I was doing. If he was kept in the dark and something had happened to me, he wouldn't have to shoulder that guilt too.

I suddenly felt drained. Arguing with him sapped my strength and stretched my emotions to breaking point. I wanted to hold him and be held by him, and share sweet words, not harsh ones. But he still looked forbidding enough that I decided to keep my distance. Hot tears of frustration burned my eyes. I turned my back to him and walked off, letting them flow while he couldn't see.

I didn't hear him following, and it wasn't until I reached Eaton Square that I realized he had been walking several paces behind the entire time. Not even his footsteps echoed in the crisp, quiet evening air, while my shoes were as loud as a horse's hooves.

My tears had dried up and I felt ready to face him again and apologize, but when I paused at the house's front steps, he didn't approach. In fact, he'd gone. I searched up and down the street but there was no sight of him.

I sagged against the iron fence separating the footpath from the basement service steps. My heart ached and I almost began crying anew. Quin might stay mad at me for the remainder of his stay, and part of me couldn't blame him. I had ruined his chance to spy on de Mordaunt and given him cause to worry over my safety. I had ruined everything that was good between us.

Yet I wasn't entirely sorry. None of those things mattered as much as finding the book and using it to keep Quin here.

***

Samuel's message arrived while I ate my breakfast. The maid had delivered it to my room and stayed to arrange my clothes for the day. She didn't utter a word about her uniform being exactly where I said I would leave it, or about my nocturnal wanderings. Perhaps, like me, she wanted to forget the entire evening had happened at all.

Charity informed me that you and St. Clair are here in London, Samuel's message read. *I will hand over my investigation to you. I have located the Hatfields' butler from that time. His name is Duffield, and he is residing at the House Of Charity, 1 Greek Street, Soho. He might recall something important.*

No need to define "that time". He knew I would understand his meaning.

Thankful to have something other than Quin to focus on, I quickly finished eating and dressed. I dashed off a note to Nathaniel Faraday before my departure, asking him to meet me at the Eaton Square house later that afternoon. It was time to get our meeting over with and put an end to any awkwardness that lay between us and any affection on his part. It was best to do it as quickly and efficiently as possible so that no doubts could linger.

I hired a hansom to take me to Soho Square, a small open area amid a chaotic network of streets and lanes. Like Clerkenwell, where Charity's school was located, Soho housed some of London's poorest residents in crooked, crumbling buildings that looked as if a strong sneeze would blow them over. The faint odor of filth and foulness lingered in the inert summer air. Wretched faces lifted as I passed, and children scurried toward me like rats when they saw me reach into my purse. I pressed a few coins into grimy palms before approaching the door of number one.

The House of Charity seemed too spectacular and grand for the slum, until one remembered that Soho once accommodated London's rich. The entrance hall was flanked by two sitting rooms for the use of the residents who weren't out looking for work. A handful of ancient women bent over needlework in the women's room, while three elderly men read the newspaper in the other. A fourth dozed in an uncomfortable looking chair in the corner. I approached the men's room and asked after Mr. Duffield. A man with a crooked back shuffled over and offered to show me to Duffield's room.

"He's too ill to leave the bed," he told me.

A large woman with thick black eyebrows and a beaked nose blocked the entry to the main stairs. "It's all right, Mr. Manners. I'll escort the lady to see Mr. Duffield."

"Right you are, Mrs. Forbes."

I thanked the fellow as he shuffled off and introduced myself to the unsmiling Mrs. Forbes. "I wish to speak to Mr. Duffield," I said. "He's unwell?"

"He cannot get out of bed. It's his legs."

"I see. Then perhaps you will show me to his room."

"It isn't *his* room, Miss Moreau." She picked up her skirts and lifted them just enough to climb the stairs without tripping on the hem. I followed suit and kept apace. "He shares it with other poor men of good reputation."

"You offer a wonderful service here, Mrs. Forbes. I commend you for your charity. Am I to understand that Mr. Duffield has no family who can take care of him?"

"He has no one. Most of our elderly residents are alone and unable to work anymore, despite a lifetime of commendable service. Mr. Duffield used to be a butler for a grand family, you know."

"A noble profession."

"The most noble. He would have been well taken care of, if his master and mistress hadn't unexpectedly died."

I wondered if she would share any details of their deaths with me but she did not. She indicated that I was to walk ahead of her through a door leading off the first floor landing.

"He could not find other work after their deaths?" I asked.

"No." Her brusque response invited no further questions. "May I ask why you wish to speak to him?"

"It's a private matter," I told her.

Her beaky nose twitched and wrinkled. "In there." She nodded through the door. "Seventh room on the left." She walked off without a glance back.

I entered the long dormitory and passed the high partitions that separated the space into smaller "rooms," as Mrs. Forbes had called them. I counted down to the seventh on the left and entered the cubicle. A man of almost the same pallor as the linen lay on the bed, his closed eyelids covered in spidery red lines. A washstand, chair and small table were crammed into the space between bed and partition, but it looked clean and comfortable enough. A bible occupied the narrow shelf, but there were no other items nearby.

"Mr. Duffield?"

His eyes opened and the cloudy orbs wandered before finally focusing on my general location. "Y-yes? Who are you?" He tried to sit up and I rushed to his side to help him.

"My name is Miss Cara Moreau. I wish to speak to you about the Hatfields."

His jaw slackened, but still his gaze didn't quite focus on me. He was blind, I realized. "Miss Moreau? Do I know you?"

"We haven't met, Mr. Duffield. May I sit?"

He nodded and I sat on the chair, smoothing my skirts over my lap. "Forgive my humble home, if you will. I live in reduced circumstances now." A little color infused his cheeks, and although it was from shame, it made him look more alive and a little younger.

"It's quite all right. I know things would have been different if Mr. Hatfield had lived longer."

"You knew the Hatfields?" He frowned. "You sound too young to have been a friend to them."

"I know of them and their unfortunate end. That's actually why I'm here. I have some questions for you."

"About the Hatfields?"

"Yes. What were they like?"

"Mr. Hatfield was a gentleman, a good businessman and a fair employer. A humble fellow cannot ask for more."

"And yet he made no provision for you?" It was overstepping the boundaries of politeness, but it did seem odd that a long-time butler to the household would end up in the reduced circumstances he now found himself in.

"He made no provision for me in his will," he said tartly. "That's the problem, Miss Moreau. He thought he would outlive me, I assume. He was younger than I." He spoke matter-of-factly, in an accent that was more cultured and perfect than Jacob's.

"You couldn't find another position after his death?"

"My eyesight was failing me, even then. I should have been let go but he kept me on. A good man, Mr. Hatfield was. A very good man." He sighed heavily and leaned his head back against the bedhead as if it were too heavy to keep up.

"Mr. Duffield, there's no easy way to ask my next questions, so I'm going to come right out and ask them. What can you tell me about the deaths of Mr. and Mrs. Hatfield, and the maids?"

He lifted his head and stared in my general direction. "You know about the girls?"

"It was mentioned in a newspaper article."

"True, but not at first. They were rather forgotten, poor things. Olive and Jenny, their names were. Nice girls. Good girls, and sweet companions to Miss Hatfield."

"Edith? Edith Hatfield, now Myer?"

His face clouded and he nodded. He looked toward the light coming through the window. I thought he would say more, but he seemed to be lost in remembering.

"Tell me about Edith," I prompted. "What was she like?"

He smiled. "She was a lively thing. What she lacked in beauty, she made up for in spirit."

It was a similar story told by Lady Preston, Jacob's mother. She had also claimed Edith was a terrible flirt as a young woman and liked the company of gentlemen. I decided not to ask Duffield about the flirtations. I gathered from his warm response that he had liked the girl, and he might not take kindly to me disparaging her with gossip.

"But something changed," he said, his face sagging once more. "It happened before her parents' deaths, though, not after. Strange that, don't you think, Miss Moreau? I always thought it odd that she would retreat into herself *before* that bleak day. It was as if she'd seen what would happen and felt the loss before it occurred."

Surely Edith Mayer wasn't a seer; there would have been some indication before now. Unless she'd been hiding her abilities from us all this time.

"Go on," I said, barely able to hide my eagerness. "Was she particularly close to those two maids?"

"Oh yes. She confided in them all the time. Indeed, it was they who first brought the strange change in Edith to my attention. They came to Mrs. Urcott and me—that's the housekeeper—and told us Edith wasn't quite herself. She didn't want anyone to help her dress or comb her hair anymore. She didn't want the girls near her at all."

So what was she hiding all of a sudden? A disfigurement? A pregnancy? Had she been raped? I shuddered at the thought.

"Did she no longer treat them as confidants?" I asked.

He shook his head. "The only times she emerged from her room was to ask questions of us about her parents." He shrugged. "As I said, strange."

"What sort of questions?"

"She wanted to know how much her father was worth." He lifted his milky eyes to mine and I felt sure he could see me. "She wanted to know who would get his fortune upon his death."

I gasped. "She was told that she was an heiress?"

"It was common enough knowledge. I don't know why she needed to ask. It hadn't been kept secret from her."

Then her question was odd indeed.

"Apart from that, she hardly spoke to anyone in the house anymore. Not the maids, her parents or callers. She spent all day and night locked in her room, reading everything she could get her hands on. All of it non-fiction, but there was no pattern to her reading. She read everything in her father's library—and it was extensive—geography texts, history, economics, science. For someone who had hardly ever picked up a book except for the penny dreadfuls, it was very odd. She wouldn't emerge from her room for anyone, not even her gentlemen callers."

"Were there many?"

"Oh yes. Her father was one of the wealthiest men in the country and his daughter was his heir. Every bachelor in Britain, and some from the Continent, tried to woo her. They were like darts and she the target. Their visits were something she used to delight in. She would always change into her prettiest clothes and have one of the girls fix her hair and pinch her cheeks until they were pink as a rose. Then she suddenly stopped caring. She wore her hair differently and no longer cared for fashion or her figure. It was most unlike her."

"What about Mr. Myer? Was he one of her visitors?"

"He was the most persistent. He never gave up on her. She ignored him at first, of course, like the others. Mr. Myer was nobody in particular and his income only modest, his prospects limited. He wasn't even handsome, and she did enjoy the company of the handsome ones the most."

"Yet she married him."

"She did." He shrugged. "Persistence pays off, I suppose. After she retreated to her room—and this is before her parents' deaths, you understand—he still visited every day. She never emerged to entertain him, or accept his flowers and other little gifts he sometimes brought her. Not then. The only time she did speak with him was after her parents died. Shortly after, as I recall. He never stopped visiting, even throughout the tragic days following their deaths when everyone else sent their condolences but avoided coming to see her. He did not. Indeed, their first conversation afterward was very long and held in private. He sat with her for hours in the library and we weren't permitted to enter. She locked the door. It was the first time they'd ever been alone. That's when he proposed and she accepted."

"He caught her at a time when she needed someone," I suggested.

"Perhaps. Or she was simply too numb and heartsick to refuse him. She certainly wasn't herself in the days leading up to their deaths, and after."

"Their marriage saw Myer become wealthy overnight. Extraordinarily so."

"It did." He gave no indication what he thought of that.

"What do you think happened to the Hatfields and the maids, Mr. Duffield? Did they take their own lives as was reported?"

"No. Absolutely not! Why would they? They had everything to live for. They had money and influence. Their only worry was Edith with her silliness, and the men who only wanted her for her money. Hardly enough to warrant...that. They wouldn't have left her to fend for herself."

I patted his hand. "I believe you."

"You do?" He seemed surprised. "Thank you. I'm glad someone is finally asking these questions. They should have been asked many years ago."

"Why didn't you tell the police?"

"Tell them what? That Edith may have foreseen her parents' deaths? Or that the Hatfields never killed themselves? Why would they care what I thought? Nobody has asked my opinion until now, Miss Moreau. I assumed nobody cared."

"I do."

"Why?"

I hesitated, unsure how to proceed. "I'm a private inquiry agent and a client has asked me to look into the deaths." It was an outright lie and I hoped it wouldn't blacken my soul.

"Who is your client?"

"I'm afraid I'm not at liberty to say."

"Very well. I will respect your need for discretion. I am simply glad to impart what I know to someone willing to dig for the truth. Their deaths have been a dark spot in my life all this time." Another sigh deflated his entire body and hollowed out his cheeks even more. "It was a dark year, sixty-six. A very dark year."

"Thank you, Mr. Duffield. I have to leave now. Is there anything I can get you?"

He gave me a flat smile. "I am well taken care of here."

I saw myself out and was deep in thought when I encountered Mrs. Forbes again at the base of the staircase. I gave her some money for Mr. Duffield's lodging and food, which she accepted without thanks or a smile. It almost didn't matter where the money went. I was too pre-occupied to care.

Despite having all my questions answered, I was only marginally better off than before. I was more certain than ever that Myer had pursued Edith for her fortune, and was ready to believe that he'd had a hand in the Hatfields' deaths to secure their daughter. But I was beginning to wonder if Edith herself had poisoned them.

Mr. Duffield's words kept spinning around and around in my head. He'd repeatedly called her change of behavior before her parents' deaths odd. Her reclusiveness was "unlike her, " and her questions about things she should know "strange. " Indeed it was, but only if Edith Hatfield had been herself.

It was entirely normal behavior if she'd been possessed.

The idea grew on me as I walked through the streets of Soho. I hardly noticed where I went, only that I was heading in the direction of Belgravia. The more I thought about it, the more I thought my idea had merit. Possession explained it all, including the theory that both Myer *and* Edith had conspired to kill her parents for the inheritance. But who had possessed her body and why? And was she still being possessed even now, over twenty years later?

It was an extraordinary notion, but one I couldn't shake. I needed to speak to someone about it, and since Samuel was the one who'd sent me to Duffield, I decided to catch the omnibus to his home. There was one other reason why I wanted to visit Samuel—I wanted to ask him if he would hypnotize Edith Myer and compel her to answer my questions.

CHAPTER 7

"Bloody hell," Samuel muttered when I'd finished telling him what I'd learned from Duffield. "Possession."

I hadn't got as far as to share my suspicions with him; he'd come up with the idea of possession on his own. I was relieved that he agreed with me and that I wasn't jumping to conclusions. "I think so too."

"What does St. Clair think?"

I sipped my tea, taking my time to look around the sitting room and not at him. "I don't know. I haven't see him today."

"You're not investigating this together?"

"He's busy watching de Mordaunt and Myer."

"Of course. Administrators' business."

I set down my teacup. "I have a request to make of you, Samuel, if you don't mind."

He arched a brow. "This sounds ominous."

"I want to ask you to hypnotize Mrs. Myer."

He stroked the handle of his teacup with his thumb, his gaze intent on the liquid inside.

"I know it's a lot to ask," I said. "And I know you don't like hypnotizing people without their permission."

"Charity wants me to refrain, and I don't want to go against her wishes."

In other words, he wasn't against the practice, but he would do whatever his fiancée asked of him. He loved her deeply, and upsetting her would upset him. "Talk to her first and press upon her the need for such action," I told him. "I'm sure she'll understand."

"I will try."

"If you tell her what Duffield told me, and our conclusion that Edith is likely possessed, she'll agree. It's not like you'll be hypnotizing *Edith*, only the spirit in her body."

He seemed to warm to that idea. "I think she'll agree to it if I put it like that."

I was about to take my leave when I had another thought. "I think Mr. and Mrs. Myer conspired to kill her parents. Or the ghost possessing her did, I should say."

"It's very likely."

"That makes them allies, of sorts."

"Yes." He leaned forward, his eyes blazing with curiosity. "Why, Cara? What are you thinking?"

"I've overheard snippets of Myer's conversation with de Mordaunt. They seem to be waiting for her to return home. It's as if Myer brought de Mordaunt here for something that involves his wife. I wonder what it is."

"Perhaps he needs to silence her. If she decided to babble about their crime, he would be in a lot of trouble."

"But why, after all these years, does he need to keep her quiet when she is as guilty as he is?"

"Perhaps the possession of Edith Myer has ended and she's her original self again. Perhaps she has memories of the time she was possessed and knows what Myer did. She might have threatened to go to the police and have him arrested."

"True. But telling the police of Myer's involvement would implicate her too. She cannot claim innocence because she was possessed at the time. They'd lock her up in Bedlam asylum and throw away the key."

He nodded. "You're right. So the question is why is he after her *now*?"

"And why does he need the involvement of a supernatural fellow?"

"The administrators from Purgatory have sanctioned de Mordaunt's presence here, correct?"

I nodded.

"So whatever Myer and de Mordaunt are up to, it's probably nothing that will cause harm to any good soul, or they wouldn't have agreed to the scheme."

"Hmmm. I'm not sure I believe Myer to tell the administrators the truth," I said. "They might think him up to one thing when he is, in fact, attempting to do something else."

Samuel stroked his lower lip. "Myer cannot be trusted, but to think that he's had a purpose for wanting to open the portal and get his hands on the book all along is quite a stretch of the imagination. I thought him quite the idiot, to be honest. A zealot, but a foolish one."

"We all did." I stood and thanked Samuel. "Speak to Charity, and let me know when you're ready to hypnotize Edith Myer."

"That's all well and good," he said, also rising. "But we have to find her first."

"Perhaps she returned home late last night or early this morning."

"If that's the case, we may be too late. Myer and de Mordaunt have likely got to her and done whatever it is they intended to do by now."

A sobering thought. "I'll find Quin and see what he knows. Then I must return to Eaton Square." I checked my pocket watch. "I've asked Nathaniel Faraday to meet me there to discuss his possession a little more. He might have remembered something."

"He came to see me recently." Samuel had been walking me to the door, but I stopped and stared at him.

"Nathaniel? What for?"

He smiled. "He wanted to talk about you, as it happens."

I lifted my chin. "Oh? What did he want to know? And what did you tell him?"

"I mentioned nothing about you being a medium." He rested a hand on my arm and steered me back into the sitting room, away from the door where the servants might hear our conversation if they walked past. "He wanted to know your situation, so I gave him the brief version of your life, leaving out the medium aspect. Is that all right?"

I nodded. "I don't keep my upbringing a secret."

"He then asked me questions about the supernatural. Many questions. He wanted to know everything I knew."

I eyed him closely. "It sounds as if he believes."

"He seemed to. He was insatiably curious. I directed him to George Culvert and suggested he ask to borrow a book or two. Just something general, as an introduction."

"A good idea. It will save a lot of questions. Thank you for telling me. I'm at least a little more prepared for our meeting later."

"Are you? Cara, he might not want to ask *you* questions about the supernatural. His interest in you lies elsewhere."

I sighed. "I know. Forewarned is forearmed."

He laughed and shook his head. "He seems like a decent fellow. You could do well with him."

"He's not for me, Samuel. You understand."

He sighed and put out his arm for me to take. "I do, and that's why I won't advise you to take any offer Faraday makes seriously."

I stood on my toes and kissed his cheek. "Thank you, Samuel. You're a good friend."

He grunted. "Just don't tell Beaufort I sided with you on this matter. Emily may be sympathetic, but I doubt he would be. His preference for you would be Faraday over St. Clair."

Unfortunately, I suspected he was right.

***

I didn't expect to find Quin at Claridge's Hotel, but I had the cab wait for me outside while I enquired within. The concierge informed me Quin had left early that morning and not returned. I drove on to the Myers' house, but I couldn't see him lurking in the park opposite. The footman told me that neither Mr. nor Mrs. Myer was at home.

With no idea where anyone could be; I continued to Eaton Square. The cab drove off and I was about to head up the steps when a large, dark figure lurched in front of me. Thick fingers grasped my upper arm, digging into my skin.

I gasped and tried to pull away, at the same time peering up into the face of...

"Lord Alwyn!" I stopped struggling. The earl's grip was too strong, and surely I was in no danger from him while standing outside my home in full public view. "What do you want?"

A dollop of ash dropped from the cigar dangling between his lips and landed on his jacket lapels. He didn't seem to notice. "You did something to me." His snarl was as vicious as any guard dog's on the scent of an intruder. "I don't take kindly to *girls* who try to get the better of me."

"Did something to you?" I echoed. He knew he'd been hypnotized, but that didn't mean I should admit my friend had been the one to do it.

"Don't play the fool with me, little bitch." White foam frothed at the corner of his mouth. "Myer told me I'd been hypnotized. He removed it, and now I remember everything."

I swallowed. He'd been hypnotized because he wanted me to give him the book—which I didn't have—and threatened to harm my loved ones if I failed to deliver. In the time between announcing his threat and Samuel applying the hypnosis, my father had died. We'd never been entirely sure if it was coincidence or not.

"What do you remember, Alwyn?" I refused to address him as "my lord" or acknowledge his status in any way. This man was *not* my superior, no matter what his title suggested.

"I remember that you owe me a book."

"I still don't have it."

"I know. Myer told me after he removed the hypnosis."

"When did he come to see you?"

"This morning. He's looking for his wife. During our discussion, it became clear my memories had been tampered with. I knew it must be you, bitch."

I arched a brow. "Did Mr. Myer find his wife?"

His eyes narrowed to slits. "You may not have the book, Miss Moreau, but you do have something else I desire."

"What could I possibly have that you want?"

"Money."

I snorted. I was hardly rich. Jacob was, and he gave me a generous allowance while I was in London, but I doubted it was enough to satisfy the expensive tastes of the brute before me. He was a notorious gambler who liked to play and win big, but it also meant he lost great sums too. Money he couldn't afford to lose.

He chomped down on his cigar, his fat lips stretching into a cruel smile. "Is that a no, Miss Moreau?"

"Of course it is. I don't have any money."

His grip tightened and I winced as pain spiked down my arm. "You can get it."

"And if I don't?" Despite the defiant lift of my chin, my insides were somersaulting and my mouth went dry.

Alwyn's face drew closer to mine. He puffed a ring of smoke in my face, making my eyes water and my throat clog. I refused to cough. "I can ruin your reputation in this city. You'll never make a good marriage after I tell them you frequented gambling dens like a common whore."

"It was only one den, and I wasn't dressed as a whore, I was dressed as a boy."

"You've spent your nights whoring yourself to that foreigner, St. Clair. I'm surprised Beaufort let it go on under his nose."

"Go ahead, Alwyn. Tell the world. I don't care." It was the truth, but I worried that by shrugging off his threats I was pushing him to even more dangerous depths.

He jerked his head at the front door. "Then how fortunate that your family is out of the city. Safe."

I swallowed bile. I'd been right, but knowing that held no comfort. "Jacob would see you hang if you touch anyone in his family. If he let you live that long."

His grin returned, crueler than ever. "You have other friends in the city, I believe."

Did he know where to find Charity and Tommy? Samuel could take care of himself, and them, if he had warning. I had to get word to him quickly.

I tried to pull myself free but Alwyn wouldn't let go. He only grinned wider. "That's it, little bitch. Fight me. Show me some of that fire I know you possess." He removed his cigar and I had the horrible thought that he was going to kiss me with those fishy lips of his.

I leaned back as far as possible and scanned up and down the street. If I called out, would anyone come to my rescue? There were a few passersby on the other side, but none particularly close, and most were nannies pushing perambulators. I couldn't imagine them wanting to interfere and confront a man the size and stature of Alwyn. On the other hand, Jacob's butler and footman were inside the house. If I screamed loud enough, they would come to my aid.

I opened my mouth to shout, but a strong voice carried to me on the breeze. "Remove your hands, sir!"

"Nathaniel!" I cried, as both Alwyn and I turned toward the figure striding toward us. I felt as if I should warn him, but what did one say about a prick like Alwyn? "Careful, you don't want to be associated with me or he might kill you" seemed inappropriate for the public place we found ourselves in.

"Cara," Nathaniel said upon reaching us. "Are you all right?"

I tried to pull away again but Alwyn wasn't letting go. He plugged his cigar back into his mouth and glared at Nathaniel.

"Leave us," Alwyn growled.

Nathaniel bristled. "Unhand her now."

"Or you'll do what, you pathetic turd?"

Nathaniel's fist slammed into the side of Alwyn's face. Alwyn's feet remained planted on the pavement, but the force sent his upper body back with a jerk. His grip loosened enough that I could pull free.

Nathaniel flexed his fingers. "Or I'll do that."

Alwyn recovered and fisted his hands at his sides. His great hulking frame straightened to his full height. He was a giant, with the girth to match. Nathaniel may have been tall, but he was slight by comparison. Alwyn could pummel him with one of those ham fists of his.

I stepped back again to put some distance between us, then bellowed, "Watkins! Outside! Now!"

Alwyn's top lip curled back, the cigar still pressed between his teeth. "You haven't heard the last from me." He strode off just as Watkins opened the front door. He and the footman both emerged and trotted down the stairs.

"Miss?" the butler asked.

"It's all right now. Thank you, Watkins. But do not, under any circumstances, allow Lord Alwyn into the house." I pointed at the retreating figure as he rounded the corner. "Ever."

"Yes, miss. Understood."

"Thank you, Watkins."

"Would you like tea prepared for you and your visitor, miss?"

"Yes, thank you. We'll be in the sitting room."

He bowed and headed back inside with the footman. I turned to Nathaniel. He seemed to be in shock, his mouth slightly agape, his eyes huge. It probably wasn't every day that he punched a gentleman while standing on an exclusive London street.

"That was impressive," I told him. "Thank you for your timely rescue."

He closed his mouth and bowed. Upon straightening, he offered me his arm and we walked up the stairs together. Another glance back up the street confirmed that Alwyn was indeed gone.

"Glad to be of service."

"I didn't picture you as a pugilist."

"I learned how to fight on my recent jaunt to Melbourne. It can get a little rough there in the evenings." He tugged on his lapels, straightening his jacket, and eyed me with concern. "Are you all right?"

"Quite well, thank you." I didn't tell him that my insides were still feeling somewhat wobbly and my heart raced. "Your timing was perfect."

"Who was that man and what did he want?"

"Lord Alwyn."

"A lord!" His eyes grew even wider. "Bloody hell. What have you gotten yourself into?"

I sighed. "It's quite a tangled story. Untangling it will require some time."

"I have time."

I watched him out of the corner of my eye and kept my voice low. "It involves the supernatural."

He didn't flinch, wince, pull a face, curl his lip or do anything that indicated he thought me mad. "Then I am all ears."

He delivered me to the sofa in the sitting room and took up a chair opposite. I kept alert for any sounds of the staff approaching but heard no footsteps. "You sound as if you believe now," I told him. It would help if I knew how much he knew and what he believed in. There might still be some things outside the realm of his knowledge, and just because he said he believed, it didn't mean he didn't have doubts anymore. He could be pretending for my sake.

"I've spoken extensively with George Culvert. He's quite an interesting fellow."

"And very knowledgeable."

He nodded, watching me closely. To see my reaction? But why? "Cara…" He leaned forward, resting his elbows on his knees. "I must apologize. I'm deeply sorry for doubting you. I regret my hasty dismissal of what you said a few weeks ago. Not only was it poor manners, I know now how naive I was."

I smiled warmly. "It's all right, Nathaniel. You were very confused at the time. You'd lost a considerable part of your memory and there I was, telling you all sorts of strange things. No sensible person would have believed me. You have no need to apologize."

He drummed his fingers together and seemed to be considering his next words carefully. Finally he lifted his gaze to mine and his fingers stilled. "I know you're a medium."

A hiss of air escaped my lips. "Samuel said he kept that information from you."

"Culvert told me."

"Oh."

He raised his hands, palms flat in surrender. "I'm sorry, Cara. I didn't put any pressure on him to reveal your secret."

"It's not a secret," I said quickly. "Well, perhaps it is, but not a very well kept one. All my friends and family know, and I don't keep it from those with an open mind who need my help with a spirit matter."

"Ah. So you think of me as closed-minded."

"No! Well, yes. You didn't take particularly well to learning about possession."

He winced. "True. But I hope I can make it up to you. I hope you can see that I'm willing to accept the strangest, most fantastical things you want to tell me." He smiled sweetly. "Please forgive me, Cara."

"There's nothing to forgive."

The footman brought in tea and cake. We didn't speak as he poured, and the silence felt…odd. Not strained, but not comfortable either. Perhaps it was because Nathaniel was looking at me in *that* way. A way I wanted only Quin to look at me.

Quin. Where was he now? And was he still angry with me?

The footman finally left, and I handed Nathaniel his teacup. He accepted it with another smile and a rather intense gaze that had my face heating.

"I want you to know that I don't mind," he said.

"Don't mind?" I frowned. It took me a moment to pick up the threads of our conversation again, and when I did, I blinked at him in surprise. "That I am a medium?"

"It adds to your unique charm."

I would have thought I possessed enough uniqueness simply from my coloring and having lived in another country on the other side of the world for the last eight years, but it would seem my being a medium was what made me odd in his eyes. Well then. I wasn't sure whether Nathaniel ought to know I found his opinion a little offensive or whether to accept it gracefully and swallow my pride. I supposed he was being as gentlemanly as possible about it.

"As long as you don't do that possession business like she did."

"Pardon?"

"The woman who possessed me. I mean, the woman who helped the spirit to possess me."

"Does this mean you've remembered something?" We'd wondered if a man could be a medium, even though all the texts had specified that only women were.

"Not everything. I cannot see her face, for example, but I do recall her voice. It was definitely a woman's voice."

"Perhaps she kept her face from you, so that you couldn't identify her when you became yourself again. What was her voice like?"

"Not high and silly, but not deep either." He shrugged. "It wasn't a particularly pleasant voice."

"Would you know it if you heard it again?"

"I don't know. I'm sorry. I'm not much help."

"It's all right. But there is a woman whose voice we might like you to hear."

"Who is she?"

"Mrs. Edith Myer."

"Myer again!"

I nodded. "She's Everett Myer's wife, and we've reason to believe she's possessed, or was."

"You don't say. Can a possessed woman also be a medium?"

"I don't know. If she is a medium, or was, she kept it a secret for a long time. Not even a whiff has reached Emily's ears—or mine—and we've been seeking other mediums for years."

"I think you need to tell me everything you know about the Myers. They seem to be involved in the supernatural up to their necks."

"Are you sure you want to hear it? It's quite a tale."

"I won't succumb to hysteria, Cara, if that's what you're afraid of."

I smiled. "I suppose not. You've proven your mettle after your display with Alwyn outside." I sipped my tea to wet my tongue for the long explanation I was about to give. "I think we've managed to piece together past events that are affecting what the Myers do today," I said. "In sixty-six, Edith's wealthy parents and two maids died suddenly. They were poisoned, and it was treated as suicide, or possibly murder-suicide, by the police. The matter was laid to rest. Shortly before that event, Edith had begun acting strangely. As the butler said, she wasn't quite herself. Shortly after the deaths, Edith married Myer. We now have reason to believe that both Everett Myer and the possessed Edith conspired to kill her parents so that she could inherit the family fortune."

He blew out a long breath. "Extraordinary. Is there more?"

"Oh yes." I couldn't keep the triumph out of my voice. "Quite a bit. We've suspected Myer of something for some time, we just didn't know what. He has a long history of acting suspiciously and recklessly when it comes to the supernatural. He first came to Quin's attention when——"

"Whoa!" He held up a hand. "Slow down. Quin is your friend, St. Clair, right? The foreigner?"

I sucked air between my teeth and hoped Quin wouldn't get mad——madder——at me for revealing his secret. "He's an otherworldly warrior who travels between realms to…fix things that have gone wrong. If he's summoned, that is."

He shook his head and blinked somewhat dazedly. "Interesting. Go on. How did Myer come to his attention?"

"There's a portal at Frakingham Abbey, near the house. It allows people and…other things to travel between realms. It's usually closed but there is a spell that will open it. That spell was uncovered and given to the Society for Supernatural Activity, of which Myer was merely a member then. He's now the master."

"When was this?"

"In sixty-seven." Oh. My. "Sixty-seven," I whispered.

"The year after Edith's parents were murdered. Is that significant?"

"I don't know." I tried to recall the exact dates on the newspaper articles, but I drew a blank. They were in Quin's possession. I would need to look at them, but I wasn't sure if that would help me fit any more pieces of the puzzle together. "I wonder if Myer joined the society before or after he met Edith."

"Why is that important?"

"It may not be. If he was a member of the society *before* he met her then that means he already knew about supernatural phenomena, and possibly had a direct hand in her possession somehow, maybe by knowing the medium who did it. But if he wasn't a member, and only joined *after* they married, then it may prove that he had nothing to do with her possession."

"A good point."

"What does interest me is that his visit to Frakingham in sixty-seven is the earliest reference we have to his zealousness. I find the timing extremely coincidental."

"What happened during that visit to Frakingham? Did he open the portal?"

I laid out the details for him, telling him that Myer had desperately wanted the book and believed opening the portal was the only way to get it. Unfortunately he'd released demons that killed his colleagues. "Quin had to come and get rid of them."

"So he's quite strong then, St. Clair?"

"Very."

His lips flattened. "Your eyes light up when you talk about him, Cara."

I thought about protesting, but all I said was, "Oh." I stared down at my teacup and, no longer thirsty, set it on the table near the sofa arm.

"I imagine it's thrilling having someone like that around."

I bit my lip and didn't dare look at him. "He can't always be around. He returns to his realm when his task is complete."

"He does?"

"It's just that he's been kept busy here lately. We've seen a great deal of one another."

He was suddenly kneeling before me, his hand covering mine on my knee. "I can see that you are...intrigued by him."

"It's rather more than that."

He cleared his throat. "Cara, I think...I hope you know why I'm here."

"I think I do." I tried to remove my hand, but he wouldn't let it go.

"St. Clair is not...a viable option."

"Thank you for stating the obvious," I bit off.

His lips tightened, and I thought he would get up and leave, but he seemed to be making a conscious effort not to. "When your affections for him wane, I'll still be here."

I arched both brows. "Wane?" I would have laughed except I didn't want to hurt his feelings. "Nathaniel, if you believe that what I feel for Quin will simply fade over time, then I must tell you that you aren't as in love with me as you think you are."

It was his turn to arch his brows. "I beg to differ."

"If you were, you would *know* that such feelings are not trifling. They're solid and permanent. They're not going anywhere."

His eyes lowered to our linked hands and his cheeks infused with a blush. "That's quite a declaration. I hope he knows how lucky he is. And I hope you know what you're doing, Cara, but I can't help but think you're throwing your life away."

He went to remove his hand from mine, but I caught it with my other, trapping it. I was about to tell him that I wasn't throwing away my future, but had decided to embrace spinsterhood and do something worthwhile with my remaining years in this realm.

But Quin took that moment to walk in. He stopped short in the doorway. His gaze flattened at the sight of Nathaniel kneeling before me and me holding his hands. A muscle throbbed in his jaw.

He turned and walked away.

CHAPTER 8

I leapt up and squeezed past Nathaniel. "Quin! Wait!" I had to lift my skirts and run to catch up to him before he strode out the front door. Watkins hovered nearby, attempting to blend into the surroundings.

Quin stopped and I caught his hand. But now that I had him, I didn't know what to say. His hard eyes gleamed like polished gems, but he didn't look at me. Tension stiffened his shoulders and bunched the muscles in his jaw. He pulled his hand free of mine. It was such a small reaction, yet it brought tears to my eyes.

"Leave us, please, Watkins," I said.

The butler bowed and exited toward the service area at the back of the stairs.

I took Quin's hand again, and this time he didn't try to pull away. "Quin, I whispered. "Look at me."

He didn't.

I was about to touch his face when Nathaniel joined us. Quin pulled away from me again and took a step back. My heart sank.

"I'm going," Nathaniel said shortly. "I can see I'm only getting in the way here." He dipped his head in a bow to me. "Take care, Cara. If you change your mind…" His gaze shifted to Quin.

Quin crossed his arms and glared back at Nathaniel. It seemed he had no difficulty making eye contact with *him*. Not that I wanted him to make that sort of eye contact with me. He looked as if he wanted to punch Nathaniel in the nose.

Nathaniel proved he was made of stern stuff. He didn't cower but squared his shoulders. "You ought to know that a fellow named Alwyn was here. He threatened Cara."

Quin dropped his arms to his sides and a shadow passed over his face. "You…removed him?"

Nathaniel inclined his head. "If I were Cara's—" He huffed. "I think it's in Cara's best interests if she leaves the city for a while. She's not safe here while Alwyn is making threats."

I bit my tongue to stop myself telling him I didn't need his advice, but I'd injured him enough. He had helped me get rid of Alwyn, and for that, I was grateful.

Before I could tell him so, however, Quin said, "Faraday."

Nathaniel paused on the threshold. "Yes?"

"Thank you." Nathaniel gave him a flat smile and nodded. He turned to go, but Quin continued. "I'm sure Cara will wish to call on you again when all this over."

I was too shocked to utter a single word. I simply stared at him. The door clicked closed and I realized that Nathaniel had left and I hadn't said a proper goodbye.

I clamped my fists on my hips. "What was that for?"

Quin said nothing but he was at least looking at me now. His expression was unforgiving and fierce, but I was feeling fierce myself. I certainly wasn't going to retreat.

"You can't give him hope like that," I snapped. "It's not fair on him."

C.J. ARCHER

Watkins emerged from the service area and Quin turned that glare on him. The butler gulped and scurried away again.

Quin grabbed my hand and drew me up the stairs. My long skirt made stair climbing at speed quite impossible and I stumbled. He caught me and slowed his pace until we reached the third floor, where my room was located.

"If you required privacy, the sitting room would have been adequate," I told him.

He pushed open my bedroom door and directed me inside with a little shove. "Pack. Now."

He shut the door between us, me on the inside, him outside. I re-opened it. He stood there, his face a picture of barely contained rage.

"Stop it, Quin," I snapped. "You're being...medieval."

He stepped toward me, and I put my hands up, warding him off. I wouldn't put it past him to pick me up, carry me inside and pack for me. Perhaps that was more barbarian than medieval but, at that moment, I wouldn't have put it past him.

He heaved in a breath and let it out slowly. "Cara." His voice was a little less commanding, but it seemed to take some effort for him to soften it. "Will you leave London?"

"Not yet."

He leveled his gaze on me. "Please."

"Quin, I appreciate you asking me and not descending to caveman tactics, but I can't leave yet. There's too much to do here."

A beat passed. Two. "Then you leave me no choice."

He turned but I caught his arm before he walked off. "Where are you going?"

He gave me another one of his steely, don't-ask glares.

"No, Quin. Do *not* confront Alwyn."

He said nothing, but at least he didn't wrench himself free.

"Anyway, you would have to find him first. You know how difficult he can be to locate." Still no response, other than the glare. "There are only a few people in the city right now that I care about who would be on his list to…harm. Samuel, Charity and Tommy will be all right, once I send word. And you…" I swallowed. "You will be with me, where I can keep my eye on you."

I grinned, but that only turned his glare more withering. My smile faded. Jokes and reassurances weren't yielding results, so it was time to resort to the bald truth.

"What would you do with him if you found him? I doubt threats would work. Anything more…final…would be worse for you." I pressed my hand to his chest, over his heart. It thumped against my palm. "Your soul must be protected, Quin. You cannot kill a man in cold blood, only self-defense. If you do, you may never get out of Purgatory."

He groaned, the vibrations rumbling through my palm. "I'm not getting out anyway. I spoke to the administrators again today. They restated their decision to keep me in my current role as warrior."

"What? Why?"

"They say I'm competent."

"Then stop being competent!"

He grunted.

"I won't accept their decision," I said. "They cannot do that to you. Every soul should have a chance to cross or—" I bit my lip and lowered my hand.

"Or stay here using the spell from the book?"

I shrugged. Perhaps if I didn't go on, he would simply give up asking.

"Cara?" Or perhaps not.

"I need to warn Samuel about Alwyn. Are you coming?"

For a moment I thought he would order me to stay in the house but, after a brief hesitation, he said, "Since I can't find Myer or de Mordaunt, I might as well escort you."

"Thank you. That would have been quite gallant if you hadn't said it in that bad-tempered voice."

He grunted.

"Or grunted."

We walked to Samuel's house and I managed to extract more than a few reluctant words from Quin about where he'd been that morning. Indeed, by the time he finished telling me how he'd searched for Myer and de Mordaunt all over the city before the trail ran cold, he seemed to have gotten over his bad temper. He was almost himself again, except that he was more alert than usual, as his gaze darted in all directions. Searching for Alwyn, I supposed, even though the threat hadn't been to my person but those I cared about.

"I believe they're trying to find Mrs. Myer," I told him.

"I too believe that."

"Do you know why?"

"No."

"I have a theory."

That earned me a surprised look and his full attention. "Go on."

I told him how I'd gone to see Duffield, the Hatfields' old butler, and all the things I'd learned from him. "It's possible that Edith is—was—possessed," I finished. When he didn't respond immediately, I added, "Perhaps."

"It's a good theory."

"Thank you."

"It would mean she's in danger from them."

"Yes," I said quietly. "She knows too much about the deaths. If the possession recently ended, she may have threatened to go to the police so Myer has decided to act."

"It would have been foolish of her to warn him of her intent to tell the authorities."

I frowned. "True. She doesn't strike me as a foolish woman. On the other hand, it's possible I haven't met the real Edith Myer, only the spirit possessing her."

"If this is a recent threat to him, why has he been searching for the book and trying to get through the portal for years? His interest in both is not recent."

"Also true. Damnation. I don't think my theory is standing up too well. Oh, that reminds me, did you notice the dates on those newspapers? The ones about the murders?"

"April 1866."

"About a year before Myer opened the portal that first time."

"Is that significant?"

"I don't know. It does seem coincidental that these events all happened around the same time. The deaths, the opening of the portal, Myer's new interest in the supernatural. Bloody hell. I wish I could think of a reason *why* it was significant."

His gaze slid to me. "You have a foul mouth for a gentlewoman."

"That's because I haven't always been a gentlewoman. You should have heard the things I said when I was younger."

His lips twitched into an almost-smile. Good. It seemed his anger was almost entirely gone. I slipped my hand into the crook of his arm and squeezed. Some of the tension in his body eased, but he continued to scan his surroundings as if nothing had changed. We were on Grosvenor Place, a busy thoroughfare used by the well-to-do heading in and out of Mayfair on horseback or in gleaming carriages. The day had clouded over and rain threatened to add to the pall that continuously hung over the city. I didn't particularly like the confines of London, with its endless grayness and overcrowded streets. Perhaps, when all this was over, I would move to the country. Somewhere close to Frakingham and my friends. And the portal.

Unless I could get Quin here on a permanent basis.

"Even if Mrs. Myer isn't in danger, she will have answers," he said.

I nodded and pulled myself back to the present situation. "We must find her first."

***

"I was on my way to see you, Cara," Samuel said when we met him out the front of his house. He'd been about to climb into his carriage when he spotted us. He nodded at Quin. "St. Clair. Good that you can join us again."

Quin shook Samuel's offered hand. "We bring worrying news with us."

I relayed my meeting with Alwyn and watched as Samuel's eyes grew dark and troubled. "Thank you for the warning. I'll go the school now and bring Charity here. Tommy too."

"She can stay with me."

He shook his head. "She stays where I can see her until the danger is removed."

Removed? How did he plan on *removing* Alwyn? I didn't dare ask. Samuel was usually a gentle, calm soul; except for when Charity's safety or happiness was threatened.

"We'll come with you," Quin said, holding the carriage door open for me to climb in after Samuel.

"Wait." Samuel pinched the bridge of his nose and leaned out. "I almost forgot. The reason I was coming to see you is that I needed to tell you about Edith Myer's secret house."

"Secret house?" I echoed. "If it's such a secret, how did you find out about it? Oh, yes, of course."

His gaze slid to the footman standing a few feet away to check that he was out of earshot. "I hypnotized the Myers' driver. He's being paid extremely well to keep the knowledge to himself. The man is very loyal to her."

"Loyal to her money, you mean."

"A woman can own property without her husband's consent?" Quin asked. "Or am I being medieval again?" His anger with me must have dissolved completely if he was mocking himself.

"Any property she owned before marriage is turned over to her husband's control upon their wedding day," I said. "But if he isn't aware of it, he can't do anything about it."

Samuel gave us the address of the house in the suburb of Camden Town.

"That's not a particularly good area," I told Quin. To Samuel I said, "Have you been there yet?"

He shook his head. "I thought St. Clair should go. This is his affair."

"And mine," I said, unable to keep indignation from my voice.

Both men regarded me levelly.

"Be careful," Samuel said. "The school!" he ordered the driver. "And quickly."

We watched him go then set off toward the main road where we would find a hansom cab to take us to Camden Town. I needed to walk fast to keep up with Quin.

"Don't you dare try to leave me behind," I told him.

He slowed down. "I've come to realize that you're the type of woman who cannot be left behind." Was that a sigh at the end of his declaration?

"Good. I'm glad you've modernized your thinking in that regard."

"That doesn't mean I won't try, from time to time."

I tilted my head to look up at him. Was he joking again? "Is this one of those times?"

"If it were, I wouldn't tell you and give you the opportunity to sway me from my position."

"Oh good."

He slanted his gaze toward me. "Good?"

"You've just admitted that I'm capable of swaying you. I'll keep that in mind for future reference."

He forged ahead, but not before I managed to see the small smile tugging the corners of his mouth. He muttered something I couldn't quite hear, but sounded like "Imp." I smiled to myself and walked faster to keep up.

***

"There are spirits here." I peered at the two ghosts lounging against the brick wall of a warehouse. They resembled figures from an artist's charcoal sketch, not merely because of their hazy ghostly form, but also because of their blackened, charred clothing and skin. "They must have died in a fire."

111

Quin assessed the warehouse building as we drove past. "The brickwork is blackened above the top floor windows and the roof appears new."

"Poor souls. I wonder if I ought to speak with them and help them cross."

"You think you can do something for them?"

"Perhaps."

He didn't respond, and I thought the conversation at an end until he spoke as we drove around a bend into a residential street. "You have a good heart, Cara."

The quiet earnestness in his voice surprised me. I blinked at him, but he was still looking out the window. "Thank you."

"It draws you into trouble."

"Sometimes." I thought it was more my unwillingness to give up and walk away that did that, but perhaps he was right. "Not always."

He finally turned to face me. Small lines rimmed his eyes. He looked exhausted, and worried. He probably hadn't slept all night, keeping watch at Myer's house. "Promise me you won't place yourself in dangerous situations."

"Does speaking to Mrs. Myer count?"

His lips flattened, as if he didn't appreciate my attempt at humor. "I can protect you today. But after I'm gone—"

"Don't." I turned my shoulder to him. "I don't wish to discuss that eventuality. It only ends in us arguing." And a sadness welling so deep inside me that it felt endless.

He sighed, but didn't push the conversation. Besides, the driver was pulling to a stop outside a row of modest three-story brick houses; they had once probably been yellowish but were now stained gray thanks to decades of soot. The houses themselves were quite a good size, but from the many people wandering in and out of the doors, I wondered if they'd been subdivided into apartments. It was odd to think of one of London's richest women holed up in a poor tenement, grousing with her working class neighbors.

"Any sign of de Mordaunt or Myer?" I asked.

"None." He stepped onto the pavement and offered me his hand.

I took it and allowed him to help me down the step. He paid the driver and he drove off. I wasn't sure if we should have let him go just yet.

Several of the grim children's faces eyed us as we approached the door of Mrs. Myer's house. I smiled at them but they did not smile back until I handed them a shilling each. Quin knocked but there was no answer.

"Is the lady who lives here home?" I asked a doe-eyed little boy with no boots and filthy feet.

He shrugged. "Dunno, miss, but I can find out for you."

"Can you? That would be a great help."

He held out his hand and I placed another shilling in his palm. I expected him to go and ask his mother in one of the neighboring houses if she knew where Mrs. Myer was, but he simply walked up to the front window and tried to open it.

"Locked," he said to me.

"Aye," Quin said with a wry twist of his mouth.

The boy held out his hand again.

I arched my brow at him. "You want more money for telling us nothing of particular use?"

"No, miss." He looked offended, but did not retract his hand. "I want another coin for breaking this glass and going inside to check."

"No! You cannot break into someone's house!"

The boy sighed and lowered his hand. "Suit yourself, miss."

Quin gave the lad a coin from his pocket as he passed.

"What was that for?" I hissed when the boy walked off, taking his friends with him.

"Ingenuity and audacity. The child could go far if those traits are encouraged."

"Or he could end up in jail."

Quin's eyes merely gleamed with amusement and it softened my attitude a little. He would make a wonderful father. Would have, I corrected myself. It couldn't happen now.

A blur at the edges of my vision caught my attention. I turned toward it and stared into the pale face of a ghostly little girl dressed in a nightshirt. Her damp hair was plastered to the sides of her face, her eyes and cheeks sunken. The legs sticking out from the nightgown were as thin as twigs. I guessed her to be about ten years old, but it was difficult to tell with children who had died of disease. She gasped when she realized I'd seen her and scurried backward on bare feet.

"Wait," I called out.

Quin straightened and stepped forward, perhaps thinking I'd seen Mrs. Myer. I placed an arm in front of him. The girl already looked frightened, and I didn't want him to scare her even more.

"I can see you," I said more quietly, adding what I hoped was a reassuring smile. "I'm a spirit medium."

When she stared at me blankly, I grew worried that she may not know she was dead. I was trying to think of a sensitive way to tell her when she spoke.

"The lady in that house is out," she said, pointing a boney finger at Mrs. Myer's front door.

"Oh. Thank you. Do you know her?"

She seemed to consider this question, then gave a shrug. "A little. I live there." She pointed at the adjoining house, her gaze turning wistful. Through the open window, I could see a woman bent over a baby's crib, another three children gathered around her skirts, all younger than the ghost. The girl's family.

"When did you last see her?" I asked.

"Today. I think." Another shrug. "She's a strange one, my ma says."

"Strange? In what way?"

"She's uncommonly strong."

That almost had my eyebrows shooting off the top of my head. I hadn't expected such a description. "Strong?"

"Ma saw her fight a man."

I blinked at her. "A man?"

She nodded. "I heard her tell Da when they thought I was asleep. The lady came here at night, just walking with no light, Ma said. The thief attacked her with a knife." She indicated the pavement at her bare feet. "Right here, it was. She got away, real easy. Too easy for a mere woman, Ma reckoned."

Could the spirit possessing Mrs. Myer be that of a man? But if that were so, he would still be limited by the body he occupied. A woman's weaker body couldn't suddenly become strong, even if she were possessed by the best pugilist in the country. Could Mrs. Myer simply be a woman with uncommon strength, as the girl said? She was a tall woman, with a broad, unfeminine figure, so it was possible she was stronger than average. But to fight an armed thief with nothing but her fists was quite a stretch.

"Thank you," I said to the little girl as her ghostly form fizzled like a faulty gas lamp. "That was very helpful. Is there something I can do for you? Do you wish me to tell your mother that you're content?"

She didn't look content. She looked anxious as she glanced toward the open window of her house. "Lady…"

"Yes, child?"

"Will you tell me what to do now?"

Her question surprised me. Hadn't she already been to the waiting area and talked to the administrators? Surely they had informed her of her options. "You should go to that bright place, the waiting area, and they will take care of you. They're very nice and will see that you're well looked after."

She shook her head. The solemnity in her eyes worried me. "I can't. They told me to wait here, but I don't know if I'm supposed to go inside or stay outside."

I glanced at the house. "Why are you supposed to wait?"

"To collect my baby brother."

I stared at her as all manner of things went through my head, until I realized she wasn't here to bring harm to her brother, but collect his soul. Sorrow punched me in the chest and tears welled and hovered on my eyelids. The baby in the crib was about to die and his big sister, also recently deceased, had been sent to help the little one.

I bit down hard on my wobbly lip, but it was several moments before I'd composed myself enough to speak. Quin came to stand beside me, his arm at my back, his hand resting on my hip. He didn't know what had made me sad, but he knew that I needed his solid, silent support at that moment.

I was about to tell the girl she could choose to wait wherever she wanted, when the baby's faint, wispy spirit floated out the window and into her arms. While I battled my tears, the little girl gave him a smile as he gurgled up at her. They were gone before I could gather myself enough to speak.

The mother's quiet sobbing stretched my frayed nerves further, and I could no longer hold in my tears. I watched her shuddering shoulders before I thought of something to do; perhaps the only real thing in my power to do, as a stranger.

I removed the purse from my reticule and sneaked up to the open window. I set the purse down quietly on the inside ledge, just out of view of the street while the little family still had their backs to me. It contained fifteen or so pounds, enough to cover the costs of two funerals, with a good sum left over to keep the family out of poverty for a while. It was my entire allowance for the month from Jacob, but I was glad to give it. It wouldn't ease the mother's sorrow, but it would hopefully ease the financial burden.

I rejoined Quin and took his offered hand. "She's not home," I told him, switching back to the task we'd set out to accomplish. "But there's something interesting you should know."

"The only thing I want to know this moment is if you are all right." His thumb stroked my knuckles and his eyes searched mine.

I nodded and squeezed his hand. "I will be."

"Come," he said, gently. "We'll talk over there in the shadows." He led me by the hand across the road and into an empty lane. The stench of urine assaulted my nostrils and I breathed through my mouth. Quin directed me to stand against the wall and I angled myself so that my shoulder propped me up rather than my back. My bustle was too big to make that position comfortable.

He cupped my jaw and circled his other hand around my waist, splaying his fingers at my back. His eyelids lowered and he leaned in. The delicious scent of him replaced all foul ones. His breath brushed my mouth. His warm lips kissed away the tracks my tears had left. I put my arms around him and closed the remaining gap. His lips kissed their way to mine, and I held him harder, fiercer, not wanting the sweet moment to end. The hand that cupped my face moved to the back of my head, teasing a groan from me as my muscles relaxed. I sank into him, relishing the hardness of his body beneath our layers of clothing and cursing the strict confines of the bodice that kept me from feeling more.

The tenderness of the kiss was quickly replaced by a hungry urgency. A need built inside me, an aching, throbbing need that swelled until it threatened to consume me. I dug my hands through his hair, grateful that he wore no hat so that I could stroke the soft locks. I opened my mouth and darted my tongue out, tasting, exploring, all the while wishing there was some way I could get even closer to him.

A snort from behind Quin had my heart leaping into my throat. "Whore," a woman's voice muttered before her footsteps receded from the lane's entrance.

Quin broke the kiss and pressed his forehead to mine. Our breaths came in ragged gasps and our hands moved to link together at our sides.

Then he pulled away altogether and turned his back to me, so that he was facing Mrs. Myer's house across the street. I wanted to press my fingers to the back of his neck, but refrained. His body still rose and fell with his heavy breathing, but his shoulders were rigid.

I couldn't stand the awkwardness that blanketed us. It shouldn't be like that. It wasn't right. "Quin," I began, but stopped, unsure how to go on.

"I know," he said thickly. "But we cannot. It's better to accept it now than let it go further."

I didn't agree, but I knew I couldn't sway him. He was too much of a gentleman, and had far too much self-control to take my virtue, either here in a stinking lane or in a soft bed in my Eaton Square bedroom.

"Damnation," I muttered.

His shoulders seemed to lose some of their rigidity at my curse, but he didn't turn around to face me. "What did the spirit say about Edith Myer?"

I sighed and pushed aside the lingering desire rattling my nerves, and focused on why we'd come. "She said Edith was very strong. She fought an armed man and won."

He swung round, his eyes huge.

"We've seen her wandering about at night before," I said, remembering the first kiss Quin and I had shared, outside the Myers' house one evening. Mrs. Myer had interrupted us. Regrettably.

He shook his head slowly. "It doesn't seem like possession."

"No. It doesn't."

Our gazes locked and I knew we had both had the same thought. "Demon," we said together.

CHAPTER 9

"Do you think it's possible?" I whispered. The notion that a shape-shifting demon consumed the original Edith Myer— Edith *Hatfield*—and had been using her form for more than twenty years...it was almost unfathomable. To what end?

"It's possible," Quin said. "It's the only explanation I have. If Edith had suddenly appeared on this realm, I would have considered the possibility that a different sort of otherworldly creature came here and assumed an identity. But she existed in human form and was known since birth."

"And her character was reported to have changed. Of anyone alive, the butler Duffield knew her best." It was fortunate he *was* still alive. Perhaps the demon that had killed Edith's parents and maids didn't know that the other servants knew her well too. That and his poor eyesight might have saved him.

"Do you think Myer found out and that's why he asked for help from the administrators?" I asked. "To send her back? No, that doesn't make sense. Why not just ask *you* when you came here in sixty-seven, then again more recently?"

"Because he didn't know me or what I was in sixty-seven. He was still inexperienced with the supernatural. Besides, we had so little time to speak then. I performed my duties and returned."

"While he was recovering from the shock of unleashing demons that killed his colleagues."

"And more recently..." He shrugged. "I can only suggest that he was anxious about seeking the right sort of help."

"The right sort?"

"If he wanted to keep his own involvement in the Hatfields' deaths a secret, he wouldn't want to speak to me, a warrior for Purgatory. He might have been worried about what the administrators would think and do to his soul."

"But the administrators will know what he did."

"If the demon performed the murders, and Myer was merely duplicitous, it's not enough to blacken his soul. If he'd asked me for help, however, I would have forced him to divulge why. De Mordaunt wouldn't, nor would the administrators. They leave such choices up to the individual."

It seemed imprecise to me. Shouldn't someone who hired a killer, for example, be considered as guilty as the killer himself? On the other hand, it did explain why de Mordaunt hadn't been sent straight to Hell.

"I find it more likely that Myer wanted to bypass dealing with Purgatory altogether," Quin went on. "It would be safer for his soul if he went to the realm Edith's demon is from. Hence his need to find the book and use the knowledge of that realm contained within its pages."

"Do you think he jumped into the portal on the off-chance he would land in the right realm?"

He merely shrugged. "He couldn't know that the administrators of the different realms and final destinations all talk to one another."

I had the ridiculous notion of a large meeting room where a group of old men with white beards sat around a circular table, an agenda of business before them. Quin gave me a curious look as I suppressed a bubble of laughter. "He's acting like a man with something to hide," I said.

"He is. Mayhap the deaths weigh on his conscience, even now."

"Yes. Perhaps. Even so, what does he want de Mordaunt to do? Send Edith back?"

"Possibly."

"After all this time? When she hasn't harmed him?"

"Perhaps she didn't know what he's been trying to do until yesterday."

I had another thought. "Myer had an amulet. Samuel's father stole it from him and used it to summon a demon, bringing about his own death when he couldn't control it. Why didn't Myer just use that on her, to send her back, when it was still in his possession?"

He thought about it for a moment. "Perhaps he tried. It's possible the demon that consumed Edith Myer was a *tikama*, a royal guard. They're given special powers that make them immune to amulets."

"But not blades forged in their realm?"

"No."

Quin turned back to the house. He leaned one shoulder against the wall and crossed his arms over his chest. "She's the one who helped Holloway's spirit possess Faraday."

"Shape-shifting demons can be mediums too?"

"Some. It's rare, but if she can shift shape *and* communicate with spirits, it means she's extremely powerful. It explains why she was chosen to be a *tikama* in the first place."

I blew out a breath. "I wonder what else she's capable of."

He said nothing to that. His pose might look casual, but I noticed the tension in his jaw and across his back. He was worried and trying not to show it. "She didn't want Myer to get the book, so she had Holloway's spirit keep him from it deliberately."

That explained why Holloway, in possession of Nathaniel's body, didn't let Myer anywhere near the book, when he easily could have, when we had it in our hands. Holloway was directed to hinder Myer's search for the book, not help as we'd thought.

"She wanted that portal destroyed," I said. "She was vehement about it." Her odd behavior when she'd told us to destroy it should have sent off more alarm bells than it had. She'd never been one to show any interest in the paranormal until then. Before that, she would scoff at her husband's hobby. Then, when the discovery of the book was imminent, she'd changed tactics.

Why had none of us seen it? The others were going to be very surprised when we told them.

Quin pushed off from the wall and stepped back, further into the shadows, taking me with him. I glanced past his shoulder to see Myer and de Mordaunt approach the house. Myer lifted his hand to knock on the door, but de Mordaunt jerked him back by the elbow. He applied his shoulder to the door and, despite the onlookers who'd stopped to watch, forced it open.

He entered the house while Myer waited outside and kept watch. De Mordaunt reemerged a few minutes later, alone. He strode to the middle of the street and, hands on hips, looked left and right. A cart had to swerve to miss him, sending the empty barrels crashing against the tray's left side barrier.

"I think it's time we spoke to them," I said.

Quin's gaze slid to mine.

I waved in the direction of Myer. "If he wants to send her back, we can offer to help. He should at least know that we won't work against him."

"I am not disagreeing with that part," he said.

"Then what?"

"*We* won't speak to them. *I* will."

"It's only talking." I looked past him and smothered my triumphant smirk. "It seems you won't have a choice. They had the same idea as us."

Myer and de Mordaunt advanced toward us, but it wasn't until Quin stepped out of the shadowy depths of the lane that they spotted him. Myer stopped suddenly, eyes wary, but de Mordaunt hardly paused. He slipped a blade out from his sleeve in the time it took to blink. Like Quin, he'd dispensed with the sword in public.

Quin withdrew his own dagger and settled into a fighting stance. The two men circled one another, snarls on their lips like two dogs preparing to brawl.

"No," I said, moving closer.

Quin put his arm out to stop me and de Mordaunt took the moment of distraction to lunge. Quin jumped back, knocking me over. My shoulder slammed into the wall and I winced as pain tore down my arm.

Quin's lip curled and he struck out at de Mordaunt, missing him by a hair as de Mordaunt swayed out of the way. He chuckled and prepared to lunge again.

"Stop it!" I struggled to my feet. Myer came to my aid and assisted me to stand. "Stop fighting. We're on the same side." I hoped. When de Mordaunt's knees bent slightly, preparing to lunge again, white-hot anger coursed through me. "Myer, call off your dog! This is *not* the way to send her back."

A wheeze escaped Myer's parted lips. "You...know?"

I switched my glare to him and skewered him with it.

He swallowed. "She's right. We may need their help."

"I don't need anyone's help," de Mordaunt snarled through clenched teeth.

He didn't alter his stance. Nor did Quin. I stepped between them and spread my arms out, one toward each opponent. "Calm down or we'll get nowhere."

Quin scooped me around the waist and hoisted me out of the way. Doing so meant that he was vulnerable and exposed to de Mordaunt. We both were.

De Mordaunt chuckled. "Soft."

Quin's gaze switched to me. I liked to think I didn't quaver, but my heart momentarily leapt into my throat. He looked like he wanted to lock me in a room somewhere to keep me out of danger.

"That was foolish," he hissed.

"He isn't going to harm us," I whispered. "Not when he needs us."

My conviction did nothing to soothe the ire crackling through Quin's body. I extricated myself from his grip and addressed Myer.

"She's a demon, isn't she?"

Myer's gaze flicked to de Mordaunt then back to me. He nodded.

"How did you know to find her here?" I asked.

"When she didn't return home I wondered if she had somewhere else to go. I hypnotized her maid first, but she didn't know Edith's whereabouts. It was only this afternoon that I realized the driver might have taken her somewhere."

"You hypnotized him too?"

He arched a brow. "Did Gladstone?"

I nodded toward the house. "We arrived a short time ago and learned that she wasn't in. Our methods for discovering that information were a little more subtle than yours."

Myer's lips flattened. He looked at de Mordaunt, but he and Quin were still eyeing one another with murderous intent.

"What are you planning on doing to her?" I asked.

Myer scrubbed his thick sideburns. "First, you tell me what you know."

"We know she's a demon who came here over twenty years ago and took Edith's form. She killed the people who knew the original Edith best—her parents and the maids." I held my breath. "You both did."

He took a step back as if I'd pushed him. He swallowed hard, and even in the waning light and deep shadows, the whites around his pupils were visible. "I didn't...it wasn't me!" His voice squeaked on the last word. He cleared his throat and wiped the back of his hand across his mouth.

I said nothing, hoping he would fill the silence and explain out of a desire to clear his name.

"Miss Moreau, you must understand…she was the driving force behind the plot to…get rid of them. I wasn't expecting that. But once it happened, it was too late to back away. I knew I would have been implicated in their deaths if I spoke out."

If he suspected that, then he wasn't innocent at all. Not in my book. He had something to hide. Perhaps he didn't have actual blood on his hands but metaphorically speaking, he did.

"Did you know what she was from the beginning?"

He shook his head. "Not until after we married."

"Why did she marry you?"

"She—the demon—was confused when it first arrived here. I'm still not certain if Edith was chosen specifically or it was her poor luck. She was at a ball, you see, at a country estate."

"Frakingham?"

"Windamere Manor."

"Windamere! That's Lord Wade's house." The same Lord Wade who'd held Hannah captive in his attic when her aptitude for fire became apparent—and dangerous. The same Lord Wade who fathered Jack Langley. Windamere wasn't all that distant from Frakingham, but the two great estates had little to do with one another. It wouldn't take long for a fast demon to leave the portal at Frakingham Abbey and travel to Windamere. A confused and hungry creature could do it in a day. I shuddered to think of the damage it had wreaked along the way.

Another thought struck me. One that chilled me. "Is…is she Jack's mother?"

He shook his head. "She's the demon that Jack's mother came here to find and return to their own realm. Jack's

125

mother was…diverted, by Wade and her pregnancy, before she could succeed."

And her death. "Jack's mother was sent to hunt down the other demon—Edith's demon—because of the crimes committed there, wasn't she?"

Myer held up his hands. "I didn't know that, of course. Not then! If I had…"

"Tell us what happened when she—it— arrived at Windamere."

He lowered his hands to his sides. "It saw Edith outside in the garden. With a gentleman." It was difficult to tell in the fading light, but his face seemed to flush. "She was quite the flirt in her youth. The demon waited for the suitor to leave then…you can guess what happened."

I could. The demon shifted into her form, killing her in the process. The old Edith Hatfield ceased to exist and the new one was now in control of her body. It was such a horrid process, and I couldn't quell the shiver that crawled down my spine at the thought.

"The demon continued to live as Edith, albeit reclusively, for a little while."

"So I heard."

He frowned. "From whom?"

"Never mind. Go on."

"I continued to visit her house during those weeks, although she refused to see me. Her other suitors became less enamored when she wouldn't see them, but I was more determined. Despite her singular lack of encouragement, I visited every day. Her parents confided their concerns to me, speculating that she'd become ill. Or worse."

"Worse?"

"That she'd been…compromised at the ball and was hiding away until she knew whether her condition would show."

Oh. *That* sort of compromised.

"She wasn't impregnated, however. She was merely…not herself. It was around that time that she began to ask questions about her parents, her inheritance and rights."

"She became aware of the vast wealth at her disposal if she removed her parents."

He nodded. "The demon was very intelligent but not particularly subtle. The maids began to wonder why she was asking but they were also not very clever. The legalities of inheritance laws were above them. Edith came to me next. I was the only person outside the household she had access to. It wasn't that she trusted me; it was more that she had nobody else to ask. By then, she could pass as the real Edith, albeit somewhat changed in character. The demon had learned to live as a human. I had no idea. She asked me all sorts of questions about women's roles in English society, the law, economics… Her questions were endless. I answered them as best I could."

"Did you guess that she was planning to murder her parents?"

He swallowed. "I…had some notion, just before it happened."

I took that to be a definitive yes, and that he was unwilling to implicate himself in the crime. "At what point did you suggest marriage?"

"We had a long discussion one day, at the end of which she told me she wanted her father's vast wealth for herself. I told her the only way to secure it and ensure some distant cousin didn't get it was to marry. She said she didn't like the thought of being subject to a husband's will. I joked that she ought to choose a weak fellow, one she could easily manipulate." His laugh was high and nervous.

"Did she know you could hypnotize at this point?"

"Good God, no. It was several months before I revealed that. Not until I…grew concerned that she was something non-human."

"She threatened you?"

His swallow was loud in the still air of the lane. "Not quite. But once I learned her secret, she looked as if she would remove me on more than one occasion."

"Why didn't she, do you think?"

"I suspected I wasn't a big enough threat to her. By then she could easily pass as human. She must have decided she wanted to stay here and continue to be Edith. She became involved in bank affairs and wielded some power through it. I think she decided that removing me would only bring close scrutiny. Scrutiny she wanted to avoid by then."

"But *you* wanted to remove *her*," Quin said, speaking for the first time since Myer had begun his story. "You wanted to reopen the portal."

Myer nodded. "She told me that she was a rogue demon the first time I hypnotized her. After that, I became concerned that I might be in danger because I alone knew about the murders. I thought it best to get rid of her, by sending her back to her realm."

"But she never hurt you," I said.

He looked down at his feet. "She wasn't a good wife."

I wanted to tell him he'd made his own bed and now had to lie in it, but if he spoke the truth, he hadn't known Edith was a demon upon their marriage. Nobody should be forced to lie in *that* bed.

"You were worried that she would implicate you in the deaths of her parents and those maids," I suggested.

He inclined his head in a nod. "That crossed my mind, yes. I could be in a great deal of trouble if suspicions were raised. It was in her power to point the authorities in my direction. Our relationship was...uneasy from the beginning, and I suspected that one day she would grow tired of me and end my life."

"Why not just hypnotize her into *not* doing that?"

"I tried, but I'm not sure it ever worked." He frowned again, this time harder. "Hypnosis seems to be somewhat erratic on her. I suppose it's something to do with her demonic nature."

I nodded, thoughtful. "I believe Jack isn't affected, and he is only half demon."

"Demons have different capabilities," Quin said. "Jack's and hers won't necessarily be alike."

I saw de Mordaunt move out of the corner of my eye. He simply shifted his weight and leaned back against the wall, no longer looking as if he expected Quin to attack. He did, however, keep him in his sights. The powerful figure and sharp eyes reminded me that he too had demon blood. I wondered if he had any special capabilities, aside from shape-shifting, or if they'd been bred out of him. His connection to the full-blooded demon that had taken over Gilbert de Mordaunt's body was a few generations in his past.

"I delved further into the supernatural after learning of her true nature," Myer went on. "It became my passion. I found out about the book and the portal, but had no idea where either were located until Lord Frakingham brought that torn piece of paper to the society."

"In sixty-seven," I said.

"In sixty-seven. You already know how that excursion went."

We did indeed. Two men from the society had been killed by the demons that had escaped through the portal when Myer opened it. Demons that Quin had sent back when summoned.

"I experimented with summoning another demon, hoping that bringing one here from that realm would get word back there. But that was a spectacular failure."

Quin blinked at him. "You summoned a demon here as an *experiment*?"

Myer touched the tie at his throat. "Langley didn't tell you?"

"I knew," I said. "The others told me about the first demon Tommy and Jack had to fight off. You couldn't control it."

"Yes, well. It was a learning experience. After that episode, I decided the book could help me. I thought the best solution would be to send Edith back through the portal, but I had no idea how to open it when that piece of parchment went missing."

"When you did open it, you jumped through it instead."

"I would have opened it sooner if you hadn't kept the book from me," he growled.

Quin bristled at the accusation flung at me. "If you'd told me what you needed to do, I could have helped." He pointed his chin at de Mordaunt. "Why him?"

"I wanted help, but not from any...sources that might condemn my soul for actions that weren't my fault."

"You mean for your involvement in killing the Hatfields."

His lips flattened, but he didn't deny it. So his involvement had been more than he'd implied. Perhaps it had been his suggestion to kill them after all, as we'd originally thought. I decided not to pursue the issue. If we wanted answers, we had to keep him on our side and willing to talk.

"I only thought to speak to the authorities on the demon realm. But they sent me to the Purgatory administrators when they couldn't understand me."

"You're lucky they didn't shred you into a thousand pieces." Quin didn't sound too glum about the prospect.

Myer wiped the pad of his thumb over his top lip, swiping at the beads of sweat there. "The Purgatory administrators gave me him."

All eyes shifted to de Mordaunt. He held Quin's steadily.

"I didn't know he had a grudge against you." Myer held up his hands, his eyes once more huge as he watched the two fierce warriors glare at each other. "Surely his presence cannot be blamed on me."

I had to agree with him. Myer was a fool and untrustworthy, but he hadn't asked for de Mordaunt and couldn't have known his connection to Quin.

"She knows where I've been." Myer stared toward the house, now shrouded by dusk's blanket. "She'll kill me when she sees me. We have to get to her first."

"Wouldn't she have tried to kill you already if she suspected?"

"Not with my guard dog at my side."

De Mordaunt snorted. "I am not *your* anything."

Myer edged away from him.

"Do you know she's a spirit medium?" I asked him. "It's one of her demonic talents."

"I wondered after you told me about Percy Harrington's spirit possessing that other banker. It seemed too coincidental *not* to be her."

"Did she kill him too, do you think?"

He shrugged. "I don't know. She may have, once she learned she would inherit the Harrington fortune too. But if so, it would seem they came to some sort of agreement after his death."

"She helped him possess that poor fellow, and used him to continue his sick ways with young women." Poor Charity came to mind, but her indomitable spirit had seen that Harrington's soul suffered for his crimes against her and the others.

"I do believe he held some sort of affection for Edith," Myer mused. "It's the only explanation I can think of for his thorough dislike of me during his lifetime."

"And for telling us that you went through the portal. He didn't have to do that."

He shifted his weight. "How did he get out of Hell to do so?"

"It's a long story, but there were some problems while you've been away. Thanks, I might add, to you."

"Me?"

"Aye," Quin growled. "Your actions released evil spirits into this realm."

Myer waved his hand. "That wasn't intentional."

"That isn't the point!" I spat. "Mr. Myer, you need to begin taking responsibility for your actions. Better yet, stop performing such dangerous and irresponsible acts altogether."

He held up his hands, attempting to calm me. But I didn't want to be calm. I advanced on him, my hands on my hips. He cleared his throat. "Once Edith is gone, I'll keep my interest in the supernatural to purely academic studies," he said. "Not, uh, practical ones."

"Be sure that you do."

I asked Myer a few more questions about the reception he'd received in the demon realm, and how he'd communicated with them. It seemed the communication had been the problem, and not wanting to deal with the alien figure in their realm, they had called on the Purgatory administrators for help. I only half listened as Myer enthused about the things he'd seen in the other realms, his current problems momentarily forgotten.

They weren't forgotten by Quin or de Mordaunt. The two men stood on either side of the lane like sentinels, watching the street for Edith, although I suspected Quin was keeping de Mordaunt in his sights too. Darkness had descended while we'd been talking, punctured only by the candles visible through windows and the two hissing street lamps. The light from the latter struggled to reach our laneway entrance and certainly didn't illuminate the entire length of it.

My stomach protested at the lack of food. I'd hardly eaten all day. Hopefully no one else had heard it. Correction: I hoped *Quin* hadn't heard it. He might use my hunger as an excuse to get me to leave. I was surprised he hadn't told me to make my way home already. I suspected it was too late now. He wouldn't want me wandering around the dark city alone, nor would he want to leave his post to escort me. He'd been assigned to watch de Mordaunt, and it was one task he wouldn't want to fail.

Thinking of his warrior duties reminded me of the book and getting him out of Purgatory. I tapped Myer's shoulder, startling him. I pressed a finger to my lips and indicated he should follow me into the further reaches of the lane. He hesitated and gave me an arched look that I pretended not to see.

I glanced at Quin's broad back then headed into the inky blackness lurking in the depths of the lane. Myer followed.

"What is it?" he asked. We were far enough away from the two men that we couldn't be overheard, but even so, he kept his voice low.

"Where's the book?"

He hesitated. "You don't want St. Clair overhearing you ask me that?"

I kept silent, hoping that would encourage him to talk.

"Understandable," he said, answering himself. "He and de Mordaunt are alike and I know what *he's* capable of."

"They are not the same," I hissed.

"Their predicaments are. I believe de Mordaunt took this trial because he knew I had the book and he wants it for himself. To escape Purgatory," he added as if clarifying for me. "It contains information on how one can leave and live here."

"I know. His ancestor accomplished such a feat and wrote the book."

"Is that why St. Clair seeks it too?"

"He's not seeking it." I didn't tell him Quin had once sought the book, to use the information to free himself, but I'd stopped him. Or that we'd since swapped our positions and I now wanted to use it to bring Quin here and he'd refused.

"De Mordaunt is," Myer whispered. "I promised it to him in exchange for his help."

I gasped then covered my mouth, but Quin didn't move from where he stood near the entrance to the lane. "Why did you do that?"

"He was the only one of those vile Purgatory spirits who offered to help me, and only then in exchange for the book. Don't worry," he added. "I'm not a fool. Unbeknown to de Mordaunt, I gave the book to the administrators for safekeeping."

I groaned inwardly. If the administrators now had it, I'd never get my hands on it. The situation was becoming more and more hopeless. I would never find a way to keep Quin here.

"Don't tell him, or he might..." He swallowed. "It might go badly for all of us. He's a rogue as it is. I don't know why he's even in Purgatory. He should have been sent straight to Hell, if you ask me."

I knew what he'd done to Quin during their lifetime—tricking him into taking the life of his own brother—but did Myer? "What has he done?" I asked.

"Nothing. Yet. But the threat of violence clings to him as badly as the smells in this lane."

"Do you know what the administrators have done with the book?" I wasn't sure what the administrators looked like, or if they even had a physical presence. Could they even hold onto an object from this realm?

He never had a chance to answer. Down by the entrance, both Quin and de Mordaunt stirred. Quin glanced over his shoulder and, seeing me further back with Myer, began to move toward us. I came forward and met him halfway down the lane. De Mordaunt was already moving across the street.

Edith Myer was returning to her secret house. And she wasn't alone.

CHAPTER 10

"Hold." Quin put his fist up in a military style signal, stopping Myer and me behind him. "De Mordaunt, get back here."

"You hold," de Mordaunt tossed over his shoulder. "I'm no coward. Myer, come."

"Er, I think I'll stay here until it's all over."

"Wait!" I called to de Mordaunt. "Don't do anything violent. We need to *talk* to her. And we don't know who those people are with her. They might be innocents, or perhaps other demons with superior strength."

De Mordaunt didn't break his stride or bother to respond. He wasn't as accepting of a woman's interference as Quin. I watched him watching de Mordaunt. His fingers gripped his knife, and I knew he had others hidden in his clothing and strapped to his body, including Jack's otherworldly blade. Still, I knew he wished he had his sword with him.

"Let him go," Myer said from behind me. "He might succeed. Besides, he's already dead. What can she do to him now?"

I waited to see if Quin would answer, but he was too intent on de Mordaunt ahead. Edith and the three men with her had already rushed inside after inspecting the broken door.

"He's mortal in this realm again," I told Myer. "His body is, anyway. If it dies, his soul will return to Purgatory and it'll be back to the dungeons for him, having failed this trial."

"That doesn't sound so bad."

Perhaps not for someone who'd willingly spent centuries in those dungeons without requesting a trial. I suddenly felt less anxious and far more willing to let de Mordaunt confront Edith without us. Without Quin.

I sidled closer to him, but resisted the urge to wrap my fingers around his arm in an attempt to keep him with me.

"What's she doing?" Myer squinted into the dark street as shapes moved on the other side of the fractured door.

De Mordaunt covered the remaining distance with a few long strides but stopped outside the doorway. Hands on hips, he appeared to be studying the shapes.

"She has barricaded herself and her new friends inside," Quin said. "Since the door was smashed in."

"Not *my* doing," Myer protested.

"Your dog, your responsibility."

Myer looked as if he would protest again when Quin moved off. "Stay there, Cara." He had only taken a few steps when he hesitated and glanced back at me. "I mean it."

He didn't wait for my nod. He jogged across the street and joined de Mordaunt, who was still pounding on the piece of furniture that had been dragged in front of the door.

Myer clicked his tongue. "What are they doing? Just break the bloody window and climb in!"

"And walk into a potentially fatal situation?"

"We just had this discussion, Miss Moreau. They're dead. You would save yourself a lot of worry if you accepted that fact."

My heart lurched at the harsh truth but I kept my eyes on Quin. He and de Mordaunt seemed to be having a heated discussion, their growls and the occasional snapped word reaching us but not the entire conversation.

"I am coming to get you!" de Mordaunt suddenly shouted at the house. "You think your pathetic efforts will stop me?"

He pushed against the barricade, causing something to crash and wood to splinter. It would appear the blockage wasn't quite stable, and the blockage wasn't quite stable.

Faces appeared at windows up and down the street, some holding candles and lamps aloft to see what the fracas was about. Someone called out for them to keep their voices down. In the house next door, where the little children had died, a child peeked over the windowsill, only eyes and hair visible. That window was closest to Edith's house. Should anything go wrong...

I bunched up my skirts to clear them from my boots. "Come with me," I ordered Myer.

"What? Why?"

"You need to hypnotize some people."

"No, no, no." He flapped his hands, warding me off. "It's far too dangerous over there."

I grabbed his arm and hauled him after me. He didn't put up too much of a fight, and I suspected he was curious to speak with his wife. With her inside, and Quin and de Mordaunt outside, the situation seemed secure enough. For now.

But I wasn't taking any chances with that child. We walked along the street on the far side then crossed and approached the neighbor's house from the opposite direction to Edith's. We still needed to get closer to speak to the child, but hopefully we could advance undetected.

Thumps followed by the cracking of wood reached my ears. De Mordaunt was attempting to kick in the barricade. Quin hung back, his eyes skyward. No, he wasn't looking at the starless sky, he was watching the upper windows. Someone could easily drop a heavy object onto their heads from up there.

I shoved Myer's shoulder and nodded at the child, still visible through his own window. Myer sighed and the child heard it. He stood—it was definitely a boy of about six or seven—and darted back inside when he spotted us.

"I tend to have that effect on children," Myer said. "They don't like me very much."

The child's mother appeared, her eyes swollen and red. She glared at us through the window then slammed it shut. She hustled the boy away and went to follow him, but my purse caught her attention. She picked it up and peered inside. She pressed a hand to her chest and then to her lips as they began to wobble. My throat tightened at her reaction and I almost smiled, despite everything. She swung back to face the window, catching me watching her. I stumbled back, bumping into Myer, and hurried away from her house.

"We didn't have to hypnotize the boy," I said, "but the others might be different." Up and down the street, people had emerged from their homes or openly watched through their windows. I doubted anyone would have fetched the police. Camden Town was the sort of district that took care of its own squabbles.

"I can't get to them all!" Myer cried. He peered up at the windows above Quin and de Mordaunt. "Besides, I need to be here. I may need to hypnotize *her*."

It was actually a good idea. If only she would make an appearance at one of those windows, he could try. All he needed was a moment or two. Hypnosis could work remarkably quickly.

A man's face and upper body appeared at one of the windows a second before he dropped a large earthen pot.

"Move!" Quin shouted as he leapt to his left. De Mordaunt jumped to his right, landing on his feet on the pavement. He hadn't even glanced up at Quin's warning. It was interesting that he trusted Quin enough to rely on him to watch his back. Or his head, as it were. They had once fought on the same side, many years ago, so it was understandable.

"I wonder who they are," Myer whispered, his gaze fixed on the upper floor. Quin and de Mordaunt hadn't spotted us yet, nor had the face at the window.

"Demons?" I suggested. "Escaped ones in a similar situation as your wife?"

"There are no other escaped ones. I learned that in Purgatory."

"Then they are probably spirits she gathered from somewhere and helped possess living bodies." I remembered the warehouse we'd passed around the corner with its burnt ghosts lingering out the front.

I needed to tell Quin and de Mordaunt. If they managed to get inside and had to fight, it would be horrific if they killed one of the innocent—possessed but very much alive—bodies.

I edged closer to Edith's house, not looking to see if Myer followed or not. Quin hung back a little from the doorway, perhaps mindful that his task was to watch de Mordaunt. Sending Edith back was de Mordaunt's trial; Quin was merely acting as reinforcement in case de Mordaunt failed.

"Quin," I called softly from the top of the staircase leading down to the basement.

He swung around, his brow scored with deep lines, and marched toward me. He grabbed my arm roughly and even in the poor light, his ice-cold gaze pierced me. "Cara, this is foolishness. Go!"

Anger rose at his tone. I wasn't so foolish as to place myself in the line of danger, and it wasn't out of some silly girlish fantasy to have him save me that I was there. "In case you haven't realized, I wanted you to know that the others with Edith are spirits possessing the bodies of the living."

"Are you certain?"

"No, but Myer says there are no other escaped demons on our realm."

"That we know of."

"True. But it's more likely she has encouraged those victims of the warehouse fire to possess the living. Don't hurt them. I don't want blood on our hands."

I didn't catch the word he muttered under his breath, but it sounded French.

Out of the corner of my eye I caught a movement at the upstairs window. Quin did too and he hustled me further away, into the middle of the street.

"Watch out!" I cried as a large pot was hefted onto the windowsill.

This time de Mordaunt was aware of the danger and leapt out of the way before my warning had left my lips. Steaming water cascaded from the tilted pot to the pavement below, splashing over his boots but not his body or head.

De Mordaunt let out a string of words in what sounded like several different languages. I didn't understand any of them, but from the way he spat them, they were probably curses unfit for a lady's ears. He resumed kicking at the barricade in between glancing at the windows above.

Something inside clanked to the floor, and there appeared to be a gap at the top of the barricade now. It was dark beyond. Silent.

"That's it!" Myer urged. I hadn't realized he'd come up beside me. "Kick the bloody door down and charge in!"

"He ought to break through soon." Just as I said it, the large dresser blocking the doorway moved a few inches. De Mordaunt stopped kicking and applied brute force instead.

A figure emerged from the top floor window. Edith. Her hair had come out of its tight arrangement and gray wisps hung around her blocky jaw and flat face. She glanced down at de Mordaunt below, and I opened my mouth to shout another warning at him when she produced a revolver. She didn't aim at him.

She aimed at us.

I didn't see her fire the revolver but I heard it. Quin flattened me against the pavement, his body protecting mine. The move was so swift I didn't have time to resist or even register what he was doing until the hard uneven stones of the pavement pressed into my back. The moment I registered that he'd probably saved my life, I was being picked up and tossed over his shoulder like a sack of potatoes.

He sprinted down the street, his arm clamping across my thighs, my bustle pointing heavenward. My hat fell off and tumbled away. It was the most ignoble position to be in, and not terribly comfortable either, but I didn't fight him. He rounded the corner and deposited me on my feet once more. Another gunshot cut through the shouts of the onlookers but we were safe.

Quin checked around the corner and was almost barreled over by Myer. He leaned back against the wall and bent over at the waist, panting heavily.

"She's...shooting...at...us!" he gasped out.

Quin looked as if he would dare another glance around the corner, but I grabbed his shoulder, stopping him. Our gazes connected. I shook my head.

He tucked loose strands of hair behind my ear then stroked my cheek. It was too dark to make out his expression or eyes, but I had a feeling it had softened now that we were safe.

"Why didn't she produce the revolver before?" Myer asked. He was still leaning against the wall, his lanky frame rocking in time with his deep breaths.

"Because she knows de Mordaunt and I are already dead," Quin said. "She wasn't aiming at us."

"No," Myer said, voice shaking. "She was aiming at *me*."

"Agreed. She did not produce the weapon until she saw you." Quin's curt tone wasn't accusing, only direct. "Stay away from him, Cara. I don't want you caught in the crossfire."

I nodded and folded my arms, rubbing them even though it wasn't cold.

Perhaps he hadn't seen my nod in the darkness because he added, "I can't do this if I know you're in danger. Do you understand me? Get away from here. From him."

I hated being chastised like a child but I knew that my vulnerability worried him. I wanted to tell him that I'd only come out of the lane to warn the boy, but I didn't think he'd care at that moment.

"I will," I assured him.

"Here." He flipped my hand over and placed a knife on my palm. I knew he had several more about his person.

"You keep it." I reached up my sleeve and withdrew the knife I'd tucked there. "I have my own."

His only response was a grunt, and I couldn't tell if it meant he was impressed, surprised, or still worried.

"Next time, I'll bring Jacob's revolver."

"There will be no next time."

A set of footsteps pounded down the pavement toward us. Myer yelped and moved behind Quin, but Quin shifted away so that he was in front of me.

"I do not like those weapons," came de Mordaunt's voice a moment before he rounded the bend.

Both Myer and I stepped out from behind Quin. "It's a revolver," I explained. "A gun. Sylvia fired one at you when you emerged from the portal."

"I know that. Stupid girl," he added in a mutter.

Quin slammed his fist into de Mordaunt's jaw, sending him careening into the wall of the building. De Mordaunt's head snapped back, smacking into the bricks with a sickening crack. Before he'd had a chance to recover, Quin dug his fingers into de Mordaunt's shirt at his chest. He stood nose to nose with him, the blade of his knife pressed against de Mordaunt's throat.

"Enough!" I tried to pull Quin away but he wouldn't budge. "She might be coming this way."

Quin backed off but did not sheath his knife. He watched de Mordaunt, his body taut, as if ready to pound the other man into the wall again. I wasn't sure if it was de Mordaunt's comment that he'd found offensive or merely his presence, but either way, Quin wasn't a man to be trifled with at that moment.

Behind me, Myer gulped.

"She left," de Mordaunt said, rubbing the back of his head. I assumed he could feel pain, like Quin, but was difficult to kill. He drew his hands away and studied the fingers. He tapped them together as if something sticky coated them. Blood? Perhaps he was surprised that he had any.

"How do you know she left?" I asked, risking another "stupid girl" accusation.

"I checked," was all he said, no hint of condescension in his tone. "The house is quiet. Everyone's gone. The back door was ajar."

"Blast!" Myer slapped his palm against the wall. When nobody moved, he added, "Well? What are you waiting for? Go and find her!"

"She could be anywhere," I said. "And she's armed. We don't want innocent bystanders getting shot."

"Can it do much damage?" de Mordaunt asked. "The gun?"

"It can kill you."

"Think of it as a small cannon," Myer told him, somewhat calmer but with a note of belligerence in his voice.

At de Mordaunt's silence, I added, "There were no cannons in the twelfth century either."

Myer sniffed. "Primitive."

Quin's hand gripped mine in the darkness. He stepped away, taking me with him. I didn't argue and didn't ask where we were going. I assumed he wanted me home, safe. I wasn't about to disagree with that. I wanted to be safe too. I only wished he would stay there with me.

"Wait!" Myer squeaked. "Where are you going?"

Quin didn't answer. "Home," I said. "I'll be there if you need me."

"But she'll come for me! She wants to kill me, now that she knows I informed the administrators and her realm's authorities."

"That is not our affair," Quin growled without slowing.

"How can you say that?" Myer's voice was high, afraid. "De Mordaunt, make him stay! We need his help."

De Mordaunt snorted. "*I* do not."

"You will have to help him though, won't you?" I asked Quin. "Or keep an eye on him, at least, to ensure he does his duty and only that?"

"Aye. But that isn't your concern."

"It most certainly is. Anything to do with you is my concern."

The hand that held mine squeezed. Then he let me go. I sighed.

"You'll be on the first train back to Frakingham in the morning," he told me as we walked quickly along the street toward a more major road. We wouldn't find a hansom cab after dark and the walk would be long. Part of me didn't mind—Quin was with me. Actually, it was a very large part of me that didn't mind. I hated thinking about being separated from him again. This walk might be the last time we saw one another.

I tried to swallow past the lump in my throat and suppress the tears stinging my eyes. I hated the hopelessness of his situation, and the overwhelming sense of loss that I already felt despite having him walk beside me.

I kept as close to him as my skirts would allow. He didn't seem to notice. His gaze scanned the street up, down, left and right. Every footstep, every scurrying rat, had him turning in that direction, his body tense and ready to spring. He still gripped his knife. I had to remember to give him the revolver when we got home.

We didn't speak again for some time. The evening air caressed my face and the exercise soothed my frayed nerves. It was nice simply to be near him, even though I suspected he was still in a temper, although perhaps not with me.

144

I knew the way back home. Living on the London streets as a child had given me an excellent sense of direction in the city, and I'd traveled most of the streets at one point or another. Nobody bothered us as we left behind working class Camden Town and skirted the eastern edge of Regent's Park. It wasn't yet late but most people were inside their homes. Only a few carriages drove past, and some pedestrians hurried back and forth, alert eyes watching their surroundings. Whether they were up to no good or simply worried about having their watches stolen, it was hard to tell. They all gave us a wide berth, perhaps sensing Quin was in no mood to be robbed of his possessions.

We made it all the way to Mayfair before I broke the smothering silence. If we were going to spend our last moments together in simmering anger... Well, I wouldn't.

"I hadn't expected her to use those spirits to possess," I said, starting with a topic that I knew he would respond to.

"No."

"But we should have expected her to use weapons."

"Aye."

I supposed his one word answers were better than nothing.

I slipped my hand into his, preparing to tighten my grip if he tried to pull away. He didn't.

His thumb caressed mine and he sighed. "You win, Cara."

"Pardon?"

"I cannot stay mad at you."

"Good. However, I wish to note that you have no reason to be mad at *me*. There was a child who needed to be warned—or hypnotized—to get out of the way."

"You could have let Myer to do that and stayed back in the lane, out of danger."

"Children are frightened of him."

"Then the boy would have retreated as soon as Myer faced him. Task accomplished." He spoke as if it were some military operation.

"Hmm."

"Hmm? Are you agreeing with me?"

I gave him another "Hmm." At least he was sounding much less moody now. Indeed, he almost sounded as if he were teasing me.

"If so, the following responses are more acceptable than 'hmm,'" he said. "'Thank you, Quin, for saving me.'"

"I don't think I like where this is going."

"'You were right, Quin. The lane was the safest place for me. I should have stayed there.'"

I rolled my eyes but he wouldn't have seen. He *had* been right, but that didn't mean I would play his silly game.

"'Next time I will obey your every word.'"

"Ha!"

He flashed a grin at me. "I knew that one would get a response."

I nudged him. Actually, I shoved him, but his step didn't falter. He responded by placing his arm around my shoulders and kissing the top of my head. His lips lingered and our pace slowed in unison until we stopped altogether. I circled my arms around his waist and lifted my face.

"You must be careful," he murmured against my forehead. "For me."

I rested my cheek against his chest and listened to the quiet, steady rhythm of his heart. "I am trying. I promise I didn't *plan* on leaving the lane."

His entire body seemed to sigh. His grip momentarily tightened before he pulled away. I refused to let go of his hand, however, and he didn't seem to want to sever that small connection either.

"You will get on the first train to Harborough in the morning, won't you?" he said.

"Yes. I never thought Frakingham would be the safest place for me, but it does seem that it is right now, what with Edith Myer roaming around London."

"And Alwyn."

I'd forgotten about him. Odd how he seemed like the lesser threat. I shook that thought away. It was the sort of thinking that could see him taking me by surprise and…

Quin must have detected my shudder through our linked hands. He pulled me closer to his side and pressed his hand to my lower back, above my bustle.

A little over an hour after leaving Camden Town, we arrived back at the Eaton Square house. The servants hastened to serve dinner in the dining room, and we both ate heartily with the footman and butler hovering nearby. Even afterward, when I wanted a quiet moment with Quin again, no amount of pointed looks in Watkins' direction made him leave. I supposed he was simply doing what he thought his absent master would want by ensuring my reputation was safe. It was somewhat frustrating, however, when it came to saying goodbye.

I lingered as long as possible in the dining room with Quin before walking slowly to the front door. We managed to put enough distance between us and the over-protective butler to have a private conversation, as long as we kept our voices low.

"What would you do if you were Edith Myer at this point?" I asked Quin.

"And I wanted to stay here?"

I nodded.

"I would destroy anyone who stood in my way—Myer, de Mordaunt, or a warrior from Purgatory tasked with sending me back if they fail."

I swallowed heavily. Destroy was such a final word.

"Then I would ensure the portal could never be used again so that nothing more could be sent through to take me back."

I chewed on my lower lip, thinking through the chain of events. "If you did it in that order, there's a danger of the administrators sending someone—or something—else through the portal *before* it's destroyed if they detect their warriors are…no longer able to serve them."

"So you would destroy the portal first?"

I nodded. "What would happen to you and de Mordaunt if the portal was destroyed and you were still here? Would you get to live here?"

He must have heard the hope in my voice, because his eyes softened. "No. We are dead. Nothing can change that. The administrators have granted us the use of these physical forms while we're here."

Granted. How kind of them.

"Destroying the portal would cut off our link to Purgatory, to the administrators, and we would simply cease to exist," he finished.

Simply? "But your spirits would remain, wouldn't they? I could communicate with you as I can with any ghost."

His hands twitched as if he would reach for me, but then he lowered them. "No. Only spirits who haven't crossed over from the waiting area can linger here."

My chest tightened. "Your spirit wouldn't return to Purgatory? Or move on?"

"It hasn't happened before."

It wasn't a no or an aye. Perhaps he didn't know. The hairs on the back of my neck rose as a chill seeped through my skin and settled in my bones. The thought of Quin ceasing to exist was horrible indeed. We couldn't meet up again in spirit form after my death if his essence was destroyed.

"If the demon thinks like us, Frakingham may not be the best place for you," Quin said.

"No. Perhaps not."

He took my hands. In the shadows near the staircase, Watkins stirred. I ignored him and focused on the caress of Quin's thumbs over my knuckles.

"Stay here until I send word," he said. "If she has left the city, you will remain at Beaufort's house. If she has not, you can go."

"And Alwyn?"

The shadows deepened in his eyes. "Will incur my wrath if he comes anywhere near you." He kissed the back of my hand, a very proper way for a suitor to bid his paramour goodnight. I wished for more. "Be careful, Cara."

"You too."

He opened the door but waited for Watkins to shuffle forward and see him out. "See that Lord Alwyn does not come inside."

"Yes, sir."

***

The morning dragged. I thought about visiting Samuel, Charity and Tommy but was afraid I'd miss any news from Quin. Not knowing how he fared was tying my stomach in knots, but knowing that I'd missed him if he came would be worse.

The pounding on the front door after luncheon had me leaping out of my chair in the sitting room. My sewing tumbled to the floor, but I was in too much of a rush to pick it up. I raced to the entrance hall, but hung back when I saw that it wasn't Watkins opening the door, but the footman.

"Did you check who it was first?" I asked him.

He blinked at me, his hand on the door handle. He didn't get a chance to respond. A hulking figure barged through and shoved him aside. The poor footman tumbled onto his rear. I almost went to aid him, until I saw who'd entered.

Alwyn bared his teeth and fixed wild eyes on me. "Come here, little bitch." He lunged past the footman and grabbed my wrist before I could flee.

He raised his arm, and I could do nothing more than turn my face as his massive paw came down and smashed into my cheek.

White hot pain burned one side of my face. My knees gave way. My vision blurred and everything went black.

CHAPTER 11

Voices filled my head. Loud voices. I opened my eyes, but winced as pain lanced my cheek and the bright light burned. I struggled to sit up. A pair of arms helped me. They were a comfort and I reclined into them, allowing him—they were definitely a man's arms—to hold me steady.

"Cara? Are you all right?"

"Nathaniel?" It came out slightly slurred. I squinted at him and tried to smile, but it hurt too much. "What are you doing here?"

A resounding crash and the shattering of glass had me spinning around, despite the pain. I gasped. Quin stood over Alwyn. The earl lay on the tiled floor, the hall table and mirror in pieces around him. His nose and lip bled and a dark bruise smudged his jaw, growing darker by the second. His eyes rolled up to the ceiling and he groaned. Nobody helped him as he attempted to sit up. Instead, Quin pressed his boot to Alwyn's chest, pinning him.

"Quin!"

He turned at the sound of my voice and removed his boot from Alwyn. "Cara." He closed the gap between us and knelt beside me. His hand hovered near my sore cheek before gently drawing a curl away from my temple. Pain darkened his eyes as he studied my face.

"I must look a sight," I said, trying to smile. God, even that hurt. I sucked in a steadying breath that would hopefully help me conquer the pain as well as mend my shredded nerves. It didn't work. I couldn't stop shaking.

Nathaniel's hand tightened on my arm. "Can you stand?" His voice was gentle, and his hands sure, as he helped me to my feet. They were not the hands I wanted touching me.

I withdrew my arm, but gave him a nod of thanks. I hazarded a glance at Quin, who'd also stood. His face was pale, the ridges of muscles in his throat hard and uncompromising. There was a stillness about him that seemed forced and unnatural, as if he were struggling against something. Not moving toward me? Why didn't he?

His gaze roamed down my length, lingering on my battered cheek, before finally meeting my own gaze. "You need to sit," he said. "And…drink tea."

"I'll bring some," said the housekeeper, standing back in the shadows of the staircase. Her footsteps hurried away.

"I think she needs a doctor more than tea." Nathaniel eyed my cheek. "The bone may be broken."

Quin's nostrils flared. "Of course. A doctor…" He cleared his throat.

I touched my cheek. It hurt but the pain was already lessening. "I don't think it's broken."

"Nevertheless, we'll fetch a doctor."

"I'll go, sir," said the maid. She skirted around Alwyn, her gaze glued to him, then raced out the door.

"Come into the sitting room." Nathaniel placed one hand on my elbow and the other at my back.

Quin watched from beneath lowered eyelids, his thoughts no longer visible to me. I wished it was his hands steering me, but he seemed to not want to touch me. It made no sense. What was he afraid of?

"Sir, what shall we do with him?" Watkins kicked Alwyn's knee, drawing a groan from the earl.

Quin arched a brow. "Cara? It's up to you."

"I want the law to deal with him as they would any common thug," I said.

"Take him to the kitchen," Quin ordered Watkins and the footman. "Tie him to a chair and fetch the relevant authorities. Be sure to report back after his hanging."

Watkins's eyes almost popped out of his head.

"We only hang for murder," I told Quin.

"Pity."

I allowed Nathaniel to help me into the sitting room. Quin didn't follow as Alwyn began to struggle, and Quin had to suppress him with another blow to the head. He seemed to relish the task and wasn't too gentle in dragging a dazed Alwyn off to the service area.

"Thank you," I said when Nathaniel sat me down on the sofa. He piled cushions behind my back until I waved him away.

He sat on the sofa beside me, a grim set to his jaw as he took my hand. "Are you sure you're all right?"

"I'm more shaken than hurt. This..." I waved at my cheek, "...will fade in a few days. I'm sure it's not broken."

"Yes, well. That fellow is a damned—" He pressed his lips together and didn't complete the sentence.

"What happened? I mean, you must have been nearby to arrive so quickly. You and Quin."

"I was coming to see you and had just turned into the street when I saw Alwyn on the doorstep. I was too far away to do anything, but I ran as soon as I realized he'd pushed his way in. Your friend St. Clair was coming from the opposite direction. He saw me running and realized something was amiss."

"Amiss?" I smiled at the understatement. My cheek didn't hurt quite so much with the effort this time.

He returned my smile. "We weren't fast enough to stop Alwyn from...doing that, unfortunately." His smile turned to a grimace. "I wish we had been."

"I must look quite a sight."

"You are as beautiful as always."

A blush crept up my throat. I thanked him, although his compliment made me feel more self-conscious than anything. I wasn't used to being called beautiful and I knew I was far from it at that moment. Nevertheless, he was sweet to say it.

"Cara, I'm worried about you."

"Oh, I'm quite all right now. Alwyn won't threaten me anymore."

"And all the other...troubles?"

"Will be resolved soon too, I'm sure. Quin is seeing to that."

His lips flattened. "Yes, he's very capable."

Quin took that moment to walk in. Neither Nathaniel nor I heard his approach. While he didn't scowl or otherwise give any indication that he'd heard Nathaniel, he must have. He didn't meet my gaze but instead hung back near the door, as if he were uncertain. I was about to invite him further into the room when the housekeeper entered, carrying a tray of teacups and a teapot. She set the tray down on the table near me, took one look at my cheek, and gave a sympathetic cluck of her tongue.

"Mrs. Beaufort will be most upset when she sees that," she told me.

"I'm sure," I said.

"Mr. Beaufort too."

"I would appreciate it if you kept the details to yourselves for the time being. Just until I've informed them." Not that I had any intention of doing so. Hopefully by the time I saw them, the bruising would have reduced.

"Sir?" She looked to Quin and jerked her head at my cheek.

That's when I noticed he was holding a cloth. He came into the room and held it out to me. I wished *he* would apply the cool, damp cloth to my face, but he simply continued to hold it out. I took it and pressed it gently to my cheek, careful not to wince as I did so for fear the gentlemen would grow anxious.

I waved to a chair. "Sit, Quin. Is Alwyn subdued?"

He remained standing. "Aye."

"Trussed up like a Christmas turkey, miss," the housekeeper said. "He doesn't look like a hoity-toity earl now, what with several bruises decorating his face."

Several? I eyed Quin. He looked away.

"Why did he come back here, do you think?" I asked.

"He claimed he couldn't find anyone else," Quin said.

I hadn't been expecting an answer, since Alwyn had seemed in no mood to talk to us. "He simply told you that?"

"No," the housekeeper said, far too cheerfully considering the situation. "*That's* why he's got so many bruises and cuts now."

Again, Quin looked away.

"I suppose Alwyn was referring to my family and friends," I said. "Everyone except Charity, Tommy and Samuel are out of London." I blew out a breath, very glad that Samuel had taken care of them. He must have housed them away from his home.

"Lord Alwyn had been drinking, miss." The housekeeper wrinkled her nose. "I could smell it on his breath."

"Thank you for the tea. Please see that the police are let in promptly when they arrive."

She left, and I expected Quin to finally sit but he didn't. "Thank you for taking care of Alwyn," I told him, lest he think I was judging him harshly for his treatment of the earl.

He simply blinked in response.

I accepted the tea that Nathaniel poured for me but couldn't hold the saucer, lift the cup and press the cloth to my cheek with only two hands. Quin knelt beside me and laid his hand gently over mine clutching the cloth. Our gazes connected and I saw deep regret lurking in them—regret that he'd not been there to stop Alwyn.

I rested a hand on his shoulder, hoping that gesture would do something to assuage his concerns. His eyelids fluttered closed, ever so briefly, and he drew in a long, careful and somewhat shuddery breath.

Nathaniel's teacup clanked loudly in his saucer. Quin's eyes opened and he set the cloth down on the table. "I have to go," he said, standing. "I'm still searching for Edith Myer."

"Yes, of course. Did you want something?" At his blank look, I added, "Your reason for visiting this afternoon."

"I came to see you." Again his gaze slipped to my cheek and the corners of his eyes tightened. "I should have come earlier."

I caught his hand before he walked off. I wanted to ask him if he'd return later, but I felt awkward with Nathaniel listening in. Besides, Quin had an important task to oversee; one that required his full attention. He couldn't afford to be distracted by me.

"Thank you again," I said, squeezing his hand in what felt like a ridiculously inadequate show of gratitude and affection. "Take care."

He heaved in a deep sigh, as if he'd made up his mind after a battle with himself to say something. Except it wasn't me he spoke to. He turned to Nathaniel. "Take care of her."

He left before I'd had a chance to catch my breath. I blinked back tears and willed my hands to stop trembling. I had to set down the teacup and saucer because they rattled too much.

"Cara?" Nathaniel said gently. "Will you be all right?"

"Yes," I whispered. "I'm a little rattled at the moment."

"Of course." He patted my arm. "Can I get you anything?"

"No, but there is something you can *do* for me. I want to tell Samuel Gladstone and my other friends what happened here. They need to know that the threat from Alwyn is over."

"I'll send the footman as soon as the police have removed Alwyn from your kitchen."

"Thank you." I leaned back against the sofa and shut my eyes. When I was finally alone, I would take a long bath.

***

I didn't get to have my bath until after supper. There was far too much to do beforehand. First of all the police arrived. While the constables removed Alwyn, the detective inspector interviewed witnesses. I'd managed to convince Nathaniel and the servants not to mention Quin's presence and felt sure they would comply. After all, Nathaniel knew Quin wouldn't be around much longer and it would look suspicious if he suddenly disappeared. He assured me he was keen to see Alwyn punished, and that meant keeping Quin a secret or the police might begin to have doubts. It also meant that Nathaniel received all the praise for thwarting Alwyn, much to his embarrassment. He made certain some of the praise was passed on to the male servants, which seemed to secure their silence on the matter of Quin. I was thankful there were only a few servants to keep silent and not the full number of staff. They were all loyal to Jacob and Emily, but it was still a rather important secret to keep.

I didn't see Alwyn get carted away, and I was glad of it. His presence was unnerving and the thought of him being in my house, where I was supposed to feel safe, would probably give me nightmares that night.

The doctor inspected my cheek while the police were still gathering details. He declared nothing broken, thank goodness, and prescribed a topical ointment. It was too late to send anyone out to buy a jar from the pharmacy by the time he left, but I resolved to get some in the morning.

It wasn't until after he departed that I realized Nathaniel was still there. He'd been following the inspector around, perhaps to ensure no one mentioned Quin to him inadvertently.

"Would you like to stay for dinner?" I asked, hoping he would say no. "The servants are out of sorts, but I'm sure they can put something together."

"No, thank you. I wouldn't want to inconvenience the household any more than they have been already. Besides, you must be tired."

Since I had just suppressed a yawn, I could hardly tell him I was fine. "Thank you for your help today, Nathaniel. I mean it. Not just earlier, when Alwyn came, but afterward. Your presence has been a comfort." It was the truth, I realized. Having him there had been of more benefit than I ever imagined. He ensured no one bothered me while the doctor visited, kept the servants busy and the police focused. Part of me wanted him to stay and keep me company into the evening.

My feelings surprised and troubled me. How could I think fondly of Nathaniel when I was in love with Quin? It must have been because Nathaniel was available. It wasn't *his* presence I specifically needed, just *someone*. As soon as Samuel and the others arrived, the need to have him there would disappear. Perhaps.

"Did you send someone to Samuel's house?"

"The footman. He said Mr. Gladstone wasn't at home, and left a message for him to be told of what transpired here. I'm surprised he hasn't come yet."

"I'm sure he will soon."

He frowned. "I hope not tonight. You need your rest, Cara. Doctor's orders."

"I know. I'm sure if Samuel gets the message tonight he'll leave his visit until the morning."

He seemed satisfied with that. For a moment, he simply stood in the sitting room, his weight poised on the balls of his feet as if he wanted to move, and quickly. A small line connected his brows and he looked uncertain. I thought perhaps he wanted to flee, but then he suddenly came to my side and sat down on the sofa.

"Cara…if you find yourself in need of…a friend, I hope you will consider me." His gaze lifted to mine and I suspected that "friend" had not been the first word on his lips.

I was grateful that it was the one he uttered, however. I took his hands in mine. "I already consider you a friend, Nathaniel." It wasn't quite what he'd meant, but it was all I could give him. "You've been wonderful, and I won't forget what you've done for me today."

His eyes searched mine, hopeful. Was he looking for a sign that I might one day call him more than friend? "But—"

"Nathaniel." I tightened my hold on his hands, then let go. "Please."

His smile was wistful. "Goodnight, Cara. I'll check on you tomorrow."

I watched him leave and was glad that he didn't look over his shoulder as he walked out of the room. While I was grateful for his company, and the way he'd taken care of me, I couldn't consider him a potential beau, and it would have shown on my face.

Quin was my only love and always would be. While I knew I could, and probably would, experience companionship with other men, there would never be anyone else who could set my heart on fire with just a single look. It was a precious and rare thing to experience desire, contentedness *and* companionship with one man, and I wasn't going to give him up without a fight.

Somehow.

When I finally sank into the warm water of the bathtub, which had been set up in my bedroom, I let the tears that I'd been holding in all afternoon flow. I'd always thought myself strong, after experiencing the darker side of humanity in my childhood, but one confrontation some eight years later had set me back and brought a well of emotions to the surface again. My life had become comfortable and mostly absent of fear and vulnerability. Even battling demons and evil spirits hadn't brought this reaction. Perhaps because Quin had been by my side at those times, and I missed him now. Desperately.

The soft click of my bedroom door opening cut off my tears. My heart leapt into my throat. *Oh God.* I opened my mouth to scream but closed it again when Quin slipped in.

"Bloody hell!" I hissed at him. "You scared the bleeding guts out of me!"

He gawped at me and it took me a moment to realize he wasn't shocked by my childhood gutter language but by my nakedness. I was still in the bathtub, my top half visible above the water. Perhaps shocked isn't the right word. He was certainly speechless for several moments but the sudden flare in his eyes wasn't from surprise.

Heat warmed my cheeks and I went to cover myself, but he quickly turned away to face the wall. "I, uh…" His voice cracked. He cleared his throat. "My apologies, Cara. I thought you were asleep."

"And you were going to sneak in and do what?"

"Nothing! Just…check that you were, er, sleeping."

"Quin, I'm quite sure that even in medieval times, that wasn't allowed."

"I can only apologize again. I wasn't thinking clearly." He shut the door and rested his hand against the frame. He bowed his head. "I was worried about you. I didn't think the servants would allow me to check on you if you were asleep, and I didn't want them to wake you."

"So you broke into the house?"

"It wasn't difficult. One of the rear windows was unlocked."

"On the ground level?"

"The second."

Good Lord, he was going to get himself— Oh.

My heartbeat slowed and my temper dampened. I felt foolish for admonishing him. Of course he hadn't been planning on doing anything wicked. He'd had dozens of opportunities already and hadn't done anything more than kiss me.

"Thank you for your concern," I said gently. "I'm all right."

"I thought I heard crying."

"You just said you thought I was sleeping."

"Ah." He cleared his throat again. "I…can't recall now."

I smiled at his back. Poor Quin. He seemed rather embarrassed. Not that he'd left yet me alone to dress. Not that I'd let him leave.

"Would you mind passing me that towel?" I asked.

"You want to get out?" His voice came out as a husky rasp.

My smile widened. "Yes."

"With me here?"

"Of course. You're not looking. Are you?"

"No!"

"You medieval men are such prudes. I wouldn't have guessed. Not that the history books mention anything about that side of things."

"What's a prude?"

"It means prim, demure."

He grunted. "I am *not* a prude."

"No? So you're not blushing over there as you stare at the wall?"

"Nor do I blush." He'd half turned his face so that it was in profile. I wondered if he was watching me out of the corner of his eye. "From what I've seen of this time, it's *you* who are the prudes."

Nobody could ever accuse me of backing down from a challenge. I stood. Quin turned fully to face me. There was certainly no shock in his eyes this time. The look he gave me could have set the copper tub on fire it was so hot. His gaze swept my length, but did not linger, and returned to my face. The dark intensity of desire swirled in their depths.

He lifted the towel off the back of the chair and approached me. He held it up and I stepped out of the tub and into the soft fabric. The act of wrapping it around me drew us close, trapping my arms at my sides. His arms circled me. My breasts pressed against his chest.

"Well," I murmured, tilting my face to his. "It would seem you're right. You're not blushing."

The corner of his mouth flicked up in an attempt at a smile, but it quickly vanished. His hands splayed at my back and I wished there was no towel, only skin. I dripped water all over the floor and his boots, but I didn't care. Nor, I was sure, did he.

He lowered his face to mine and breathed deeply, drawing my scent in. His lips kissed my bruised cheek, more soothing than any balm. He kissed his way down my jaw to my chin until finally he met my parted, waiting lips. My blood throbbed through my veins in response and drowned out the small voice suggesting caution. One of his hands moved to the back of my head, and he deepened the kiss.

He kissed me as if it was our first time, and our last.

With our bodies connected, I could feel the rapid, erratic pounding of his heart in his chest, and the tightness of his muscles as he restrained himself. It was a thrilling, searing kiss that blew away any lingering inhibitions I felt at being naked under the towel. I wanted to wrap my arms around him, touch his hair, his face, his chest, and I struggled against the confines of the towel.

He eased back but did not break the kiss entirely. "Don't move," he murmured against my lips. "If you touch me... I may be dead, but I'm still a man."

"I don't care."

He drew back completely and studied me. "I do." The ache in his words implied he almost wished he didn't.

"Surely there wouldn't be any consequences. You might be able to...perform...but your seed would be...er..."

"Unable to grow?"

"Precisely."

"I'm not willing to ruin you, Cara, no matter how willing *you* are."

161

I sighed and rested my forehead against his chest. It was a discussion we'd already had, and I doubted I would change his opinion. Not with words, anyway. And if I did, he might never be able to forgive himself. He was the sort of man who took responsibility even when events weren't entirely his fault.

He bent and kissed my bare shoulder. "I will go."

"Not yet. Can't you stay a while longer and...talk?"

He seemed to be considering that when the door handle rattled and the maid said, "Are you finished—"

"Wait!" I cried out, stepping away from Quin. "Don't come in yet! Stay there."

"Miss Moreau?" she said through the gap. "Is everything all right?"

"Yes! I'm just enjoying my bath too much to get out yet." I untangled my arm from the towel and dipped my hand in the water to splash it. "Would you mind making me some hot chocolate?"

"Of course, miss."

"Take your time."

The door closed and I wiped my wet hand down the towel. "That was close."

Quin's eyebrow quirked.

"All right, all right," I said on another sigh. "Perhaps ruining myself tonight wasn't such a good idea."

He rested his hands on my shoulders and stroked my collar bone. "Neither is talking. Goodnight, Cara." He kissed my forehead and headed for the door.

He gave me a sad smile then slipped out into the corridor.

***

A telegram from Frakingham thwarted the following day's plans. Not that I had any. I was alone and bored in the confines of the house. I even offered to polish the silver to keep my hands occupied and my thoughts from straying to Quin. Watkins refused, and seemed offended that I would want to do something as menial as polishing silver, so I spent the morning in the sitting room, trying to sew and worrying about Quin. Had he found Edith Myer yet? Even if he had, it could be some time before I'd know, as he wouldn't be able to tell me himself. He would have returned to Purgatory.

Jack's telegram was a welcome relief from my boredom. Until I read it.

Edith Myer here, it said. *Sylvia captured. Send St. Clair and the book.*

CHAPTER 12

Oh God, oh God. Poor Sylvia. She must be terrified. Was she hurt? Where was Edith holding her?

I gathered my skirts and raced to fetch a hat with a veil that would cover my cheek. I had to find Quin, even if I spent the entire day out looking for him.

I got no further than the bottom of the staircase when an urgent knock at the door startled me. My nerves were still somewhat jangly after the ordeal with Alwyn. I debated whether to answer it myself when Watkins sailed past me and opened the door.

"Samuel!" I blurted out when I spotted him on the doorstep. "Come in!"

Charity and Tommy entered with him and I hugged each of them in turn. They eyed me with concern. Or rather, eyed my cheek.

"Oh, Cara," Charity said, offering me another embrace. "You poor thing."

"Yes, yes." I waved away her sympathy. "There are more pressing matters to worry about than the state of my face."

Samuel grunted. "If I'd been here I would have thrashed Alwyn."

"There was no need. Quin did enough thrashing for everybody."

Samuel looked quite distressed that he'd not been here to help. I laid a hand on his arm. "You saved Charity from harm. Both of you," I added for Tommy's benefit. "Squirreling her away was the best thing you could have done under the circumstances. I had the servants and my two champions here to protect me."

"Two?" Charity echoed.

"Nathaniel and Quin arrived at the same time."

"Nathaniel?" Her small smile was meant as encouragement but I ignored it. Now was not the time.

Tommy's lips flattened into a grim line. "I should have come here as soon as Gladstone mentioned Alwyn's threat."

I touched his good hand. The other hung limply at his side. "Something has happened at Frakingham."

Tommy's face paled. "Sylvia?" he croaked.

I handed him the telegram. Charity and Samuel leaned in to read it. Charity gasped. She rested a hand on Tommy's back and gave Samuel a worried look. He returned it.

Tommy dropped the slip of paper and spun toward the door.

"Wait!" we all cried.

"I can't," he said. "I have to go there now. She needs me."

"The next train doesn't leave for Harborough until the morning," Samuel said.

Tommy stopped. His shoulders slumped. He pressed his thumb and forefinger into his eyes and groaned.

"We have to find Quin first," I said. If Edith Myer was at Frakingham, it meant Quin hadn't returned to Purgatory.

"How long will that take?" he snapped.

"I'm sure I'll see him today or tonight." Quin would visit me later, to see how I was. I was certain of it.

"I'll be on the first train to Harborough tomorrow whether he's there or not."

"He'll be there," I said as he strode out the door.

Jack's urgent request that we bring Quin wasn't going to present a problem. It was bringing the book that could be our downfall and see Sylvia harmed...or worse.

***

The berth in the first class carriage was uncomfortable; not only because it was a tight fit, with four long-legged males and myself, but also because of the tension between Quin and de Mordaunt. They sat opposite one another, their mutual hatred barely controlled as their glares became increasingly fierce as the journey stretched before us.

De Mordaunt had initially been reluctant to leave the platform, even as passengers streamed past him and climbed aboard. He eyed the steaming engine as if it would flick its forked tongue at him.

"Afraid?" Quin had muttered as he stood behind him, arms crossed.

De Mordaunt huffed and stepped through the door.

A satisfied smirk settled on Quin's lips.

"I seem to recall someone else being hesitant the first time he saw a train," I said, coming up beside him.

"Hesitant is not the same as afraid. I was merely curious as to its machinations."

I slipped my arm through his. "Try not to mock him. It'll be a very long journey if you two start fighting one another. Nor do I think the conductor will appreciate it."

"I'm not mocking. The man is a rat."

"Now, now. That's not very fair to rats."

He offered me his hand and I took it, but he didn't help me aboard. "Will you reconsider, Cara?"

"No."

"Not even if I say please?"

I shook my head. "I have to come. Sylvia needs me, and Hannah too."

"Sylvia has Dawson and Hannah has Langley. They don't *need* you."

I peered up at him through my veil and sighed. "*I* need *you*, Quin. I suspect this will be resolved soon, one way or another, and I want to be there when you leave."

It was true, but not the entire truth. I also wanted to be there in case Myer decided to go through the portal and retrieve the book. Whether the administrators would give it up easily was another matter entirely. I didn't see that they had much of a choice—the book belonged here, not in Purgatory. If I could get my hands on it somehow, I could use it to keep Quin in this realm.

It was a slim chance, but a chance nevertheless. When Quin had come to me the previous night, we'd eaten dinner at Verrey's in Regent Street, with Samuel, Tommy and Charity, and discussed the situation at length. Although Jack's telegram hadn't said it in so many words, we'd come to the conclusion that Edith was demanding the book in exchange for Sylvia's life. It was a somber thought that blanketed our little party all evening.

Samuel and Charity had decided to remain behind in London, while Tommy, Quin and I joined Myer and de Mordaunt. Quin had urged me to reconsider once we were alone, but I hadn't backed down, even when his temper rose. I was determined to go to Freak House too. He seemed more accepting of my decision this morning as we traveled to the station where we met the others. Even so, I withdrew my hand and stepped into the carriage quickly, in case he tried to block my entry.

I settled on the seat beside Tommy, and Quin occupied the space on my other side, with de Mordaunt and Myer opposite. The two otherworldly beings glared at one another and refused to move their knees to give the other space.

It was going to be a long journey.

The whistle blew and the stationmaster shouted at the people on the platform to stand back. The train jolted forward. De Mordaunt's fingers dug into the leather seat on either side of his thighs.

Quin grunted in what sounded like a smug laugh.

"It's more comfortable than horseback," I assured de Mordaunt. "And faster. We'll be there mid-afternoon."

He let go of the seat, but didn't acknowledge that I'd spoken. The man was an ill-mannered toad. I wondered if he'd been like that during his lifetime or if it was a trait he'd developed after his death, alone in his Purgatory dungeon.

"So, what is our plan?" Myer looked first at Quin then de Mordaunt.

"Kill her," de Mordaunt said with a shrug.

"Send her back through the portal," Quin said over the top of him.

Myer flicked his gaze between them. "Those are hardly *plans*. How do you propose to send her back, or kill her?"

"I cannot form that plan until we assess the situation," Quin said. "We'll do whatever we can to draw the demon away from Miss Langley without her being harmed." He spoke to Tommy as he said it, and Tommy gave him a firm, if somewhat grim, nod.

De Mordaunt rolled his eyes. "It would be easier if we disregarded the girl—"

"Disregarded!" I cried.

"Her safety is our priority," Quin said tightly.

Tommy sat silently in the corner, his cold glare on de Mordaunt's throat as if he were contemplating slicing through it with the knife I suspected he had tucked away somewhere on his person.

Myer nodded as he stared out the window. "Hopefully Miss Langley won't be harmed, although she's not the brightest girl. She mustn't be to have gotten herself kidnapped."

I laid a hand on Tommy's arm in the hope that would keep him calm. "At least she didn't aid a demon in committing all manner of awful crimes and then marry her," I shot back.

Myer turned a withering glare onto me that lasted so long I began to worry that he might hypnotize me and force me to apologize, or worse. Fortunately, he merely turned back to the window and watched the back fences behind a long row of houses whipping past.

"Women." De Mordaunt snorted. "The world would be a better place without their meddling."

"The world would be *empty* of human beings without us," I snapped. "Besides, is Edith even female?"

"Of course she is!" Myer spluttered. He flattened his tie and stretched his reddening neck above his collar.

"She must be a woman," de Mordaunt went on. "Look at all the trouble she's caused."

"It's not only women who cause trouble," Quin growled.

De Mordaunt's top lip curled into a sneer. "No?" He looked pointedly at me. "You're soft, St. Clair. You still fancy yourself champion of the ladies. If only your *wife* had fallen for it as easily as all the others."

Quin tensed but did not move. He had more control than me. If I'd thought I could best de Mordaunt, I would have thumped him.

"If only she hadn't encouraged Guy," he went on

Quin's hand curled into a fist on the seat between us. I inched my fingers closer until I was touching it. Tommy and Myer both stared out the window, pretending not to hear.

While Quin's eyes were hard, his lips had kicked up in one corner. It wasn't quite a smile, but it was unexpected. "If you want me to defend Maria's honor, you will have to do better than that."

De Mordaunt matched Quin's not-quite-a-smile with a more sinister version of his own. "Her honor isn't worth defending. Guy, however, was worth a hundred of you."

Quin held his gaze a few moments then lowered it. I frowned at the capitulation.

"They will be singing his praises in Heaven for eternity." De Mordaunt had turned a little toward Myer and his voice had become wistful and much less caustic. That surprised me. It seemed he had cared for Quin's brother and respected him; perhaps admired him. In my mind, that made it even more terrible that he'd orchestrated Guy's downfall by using Maria's body to seduce him.

"He was the best of men," De Mordaunt's voice softened further. "A fierce, courageous knight in battle, a master swordsman. I once saw him fell a dozen men on his own with nothing but a sword in one hand and a mace in the other."

Hearing of Guy's prowess only confirmed that he had *allowed* Quin to kill him on the battlefield. What a cowardly act. How could he not have known it would condemn his brother to a life—and afterlife—filled with guilt? I supposed he didn't suspect Quin would last long in battle—which he didn't—and knew nothing about the afterlife. Even if he had, he could never have suspected Quin would end up in Purgatory, condemned by the weight of that guilt.

I glanced at Quin. He stared back at de Mordaunt as if he were seeing something in him for the first time. I suspected de Mordaunt had never voiced his feelings about Guy before.

"He was the noblest, most loyal subject," de Mordaunt went on. "The king loved him above all others. Even more than you." He angled his chin at Quin.

Still Quin didn't speak. He seemed to be thinking, perhaps lost in the fond memories of his brother too.

"If he'd been given Maria's hand like he wanted— begged—she would not have betrayed *him*."

Quin stirred. "You knew her not at all if you believe that."

"I hope you rot in Hell for killing the man who meant more to me than mere friend," de Mordaunt snarled. "You do not deserve to be here, even for a day, an hour, enjoying the fleshly delights offered by the whores."

I slammed my arm across Quin's chest. He inched forward, but didn't push me away. "Don't," I whispered, leaning into him. "You'll be thrown off the train." I wasn't sure how anyone could get Quin to leave, but it wasn't worth the risk.

He sat there as rigid as a stone pillar, anger vibrating off him. It wasn't fair that de Mordaunt could get away with saying those things to him, and I felt somewhat guilty that he held himself in check because I wished it. When Quin remained silent, albeit seething, I addressed de Mordaunt.

"When Quin told me the story of what happened, I wondered why you did what you did. Of course, you couldn't have foreseen that Guy would give up his life to Quin out of remorse, but now I at least understand your motives."

"Guy give up? He wouldn't. He was too strong, too proud to lay down his life. He *liked* living. That prick murdered Guy." He nodded at Quin. "Out of jealousy."

"No. Quin wasn't the jealous one. Hurt, yes, but not jealous."

"What are talking about?"

"*You* were the jealous one."

"Of Maria?" He snorted. "Stupid girl, stay out of matters that don't concern you."

"This matter does concern me." I was aware that I was baring my teeth and I must look like a wild animal, with my face bruised, but I didn't care. If Quin wouldn't—couldn't—defend himself, then I would do it for him. "And I understand more than you think. You were jealous, but not of Maria and Guy's infatuation with her. You were jealous of Guy's love for his brother."

Quin's chest expanded with his sharp intake of breath. He was watching me openly, but I kept my gaze on de Mordaunt, his face twisted with ugly rage.

"You know nothing," de Mordaunt bit off before looking away. "You're only a woman, and a primitive one at that."

Quin's hand came down over mine, warm and reassuring. I blinked at him and he offered me a weak smile. His thumb stroked my knuckles and his left eyebrow lifted in question. I nodded. I was all right. De Mordaunt's words were just that—words. I could bat those away much easier than a fist.

Myer and Tommy both shifted uncomfortably, reminding me that we had witnesses. Neither of them knew the story of Quin's death, and I suspected I would tell Tommy and the others later, but not Myer. Some things should only be shared with trusted friends.

"Women are always causing problems," de Mordaunt muttered. I was about to tell him to stop voicing his ridiculous opinions when he added, "A *man* would not have allowed himself to get caught and used as a hostage."

Tommy leapt to his feet and slammed his fist into de Mordaunt's jaw before I had time to blink. De Mordaunt's head jerked back and hit the wall with a resounding thud. He slowly, slowly looked forward again and gave Tommy a slick, vile smile.

Then he lunged for him.

But Quin was faster. They clashed like two giants, their bodies slamming into one another. De Mordaunt tried to push Quin out of the way but he didn't budge. The close confines of the berth meant there was very little room for swinging fists or wrestling one another into submission. Quin, realizing this, grabbed de Mordaunt's shoulders and smashed his forehead into his nose. De Mordaunt sank onto the seat and his eyes rolled up into his head. Blood trickled from his right nostril. Quin stood over him. He may have been dressed like a gentleman, but he looked every bit the avenging warrior at that moment, as the hard planes of his face settled in determined lines.

The door slid open and the conductor took in the scene, his hand out to receive our tickets. He eyed Quin warily and swallowed loudly. "Is everything all right, ma'am?"

"Of course," I said. "Our friend suffers from nose bleeds. Mr. St. Clair here was just making him more comfortable." I touched Quin's elbow and he sat.

De Mordaunt seemed to have recovered quickly from the blow. He wiped the blood away with his sleeve and gave Quin a glare that could have pierced steel.

"Er, tickets, please." The conductor punched our tickets then backed out of the berth, sliding the door closed again.

"No more fighting," I hissed, mostly at de Mordaunt. "If you get thrown off the train, you'll have to find another way there. Do you understand?"

De Mordaunt simply wiped his nose again, smearing more blood on his jacket sleeve.

"He understands," Myer said quickly, a nervous squeak to his voice. "We haven't got time for tomfoolery."

"In fact, I suggest you don't speak at all for the remainder of the journey, Mr. de Mordaunt. Whenever you open your mouth, someone wants to silence you."

He didn't acknowledge me, which wasn't surprising. The man held no respect for me, or for women in general. He did, however, stay silent for the remainder of the journey, so perhaps my reasoning sank through his thick skull after all.

We arrived in Harborough, where the Frakingham driver, Fray, greeted us in the large clarence, pulled by the two strongest horses in the stables.

"What do you know of the situation at the house?" Tommy asked him.

"Not overmuch, Mr. Dawson," Fray said, his whiskers drooping with his frown. "But it's not good. Not good at all."

Tommy sat at the front with the driver and our small amount of luggage was strapped to the roof for the short journey. We sped along and I wondered if our swiftness was Tommy's influence, urging Fray to get there faster.

Tommy jumped down from the seat before the clarence rolled to a full stop in the Frakingham drive. Quin, de Mordaunt and I followed. Myer hung back in the cabin, only exiting once he saw that his wife didn't run out of the house like a madwoman to attack him.

"We will assess the situation," Quin said to me. "Go find Hannah and stay with Mr. Langley. Bollard will keep watch, if he's not already. I suspect Dawson will want to come with us."

"And do what? If Edith wants the book…what can be done?" I didn't like hearing the hopeless whine in my voice, but it was difficult not to feel a sense of overwhelming hopelessness at the situation.

"Myer, go into the portal and retrieve the book."

Myer halted and we all stopped too, waiting. "Are you mad?" he spluttered. "We can't give her the book! She'll use it to destroy the portal and then we'll never send her back."

"He has a point," I said. Quin arched a brow at me and waited. "Ah. I see," I said, following. "Perhaps we don't have to give it to her," I told Myer. "We can simply use it as bait. Let her see it, but not hand it over."

"I…I'm not sure," he muttered. "What if she gets her hands on it anyway?"

"Tommy! St. Clair!" Jack trotted down the front steps, exchanging glares with de Mordaunt as they passed one another. He gripped Tommy's shoulder. At Tommy's questioning gaze, he said, "She is unharmed, as far as we know. But they've been down there more than twenty-four hours."

"Down where?" Tommy croaked.

"The basement."

Edith would be getting desperate by now, and Sylvia would be fretting. Poor thing. She wouldn't make a terribly brave hostage. Perhaps that was a little unfair; she did seem to have developed a stronger backbone recently.

"Come inside and I'll apprise you of the situation," Jack said. He paused, once more eyeing de Mordaunt. "Can we trust him?"

"No," I said. "But we have to. He's been tasked with sending the demon back—"

"Demon?" His wide stare swung from me to Quin, to de Mordaunt then finally Myer.

174

"There's much we need to tell you too," Quin said. "Come. Let's discuss it over tea and cake. I'm starved."

"Are you sure it's quite safe inside?" Myer asked, shortening his usually long strides so that he fell behind the other men.

"As safe as can be with your mad wife holed up in our basement, threatening to kill my cousin." Jack strode ahead of us into the house, Tommy at his side.

"She is not really my wife," Myer muttered so quietly that I hardly heard him despite being a mere two paces ahead of him.

"I have to hear her voice," Tommy said once we were inside. "I need to know she's all right, in her own words."

Jack nodded. "We'll go to the basement now. All of us."

"Not the ladies," Quin said.

I wanted to hear Sylvia's voice too, but I wasn't sure I would win an argument regarding my safety. There'd been too many dangers of late, and his anxiety was, perhaps, justified.

"You're here!" Hannah peered over the balustrade from the landing above. She rushed down the stairs and embraced Tommy first, then me. "Thank goodness you've arrived! What a relief to have you back again." Like her husband, she eyed de Mordaunt warily, and Myer too.

"We have to work with him," I told her quietly, nodding at the loutish de Mordaunt. "If he spouts rude sentiments about our gender, just ignore him. He stops eventually, or, if not, someone shuts him up." I looped my arm through hers and gave it a reassuring squeeze.

"With any luck this will all be over by the end of today," Jack said. "And we can resume our normal lives."

Hannah sighed. "I'm not even sure what normal is anymore."

I lifted the veil that I'd kept over my face the entire day, forgetting about the bruise there. She gasped and leaned in closer to inspect it. My skin might be darker than everybody else's, but the bruise on my cheek was still evident and rather hideous. I needed to remember to cover it in public.

"Good lord, Cara!" She touched my jaw, beneath the bruise. "What happened?"

"Lord Alwyn." I waved her and Jack's concern away. "It's all over now. He's been arrested." I took her hand. "Let's go and speak to Sylvia in the basement. I'm anxious to hear her voice, and Tommy *needs* to hear it."

We both blinked sympathetically at poor Tommy. Then I shifted my gaze to Quin. His lips flattened, and I could almost hear him accusing me of being devious. I strode ahead of him to be certain he didn't block my way.

We headed down the back stairs to the service area. The kitchen, scullery and servants' dining room were all empty. Quiet. It was eerie. On the few occasions I'd ventured down there before, footmen and maids were always rushing about, pausing only to bow or curtsy to me. Even in the evenings, their chatter cheered up the simple, functional rooms, and their footsteps echoed on the flagstones.

"We gave what few servants were left some time off," Jack said, anticipating my question. "Only Mrs. Moore remains, and she's been instructed to keep well away from the basement and cellar. Edith Myer caught us unawares. We did not see an attack coming from that quarter."

"No," I said, glaring at Myer. "None of us were warned."

He didn't acknowledge my accusation. Not that an apology would have been enough, particularly now that Sylvia was captured.

Hannah picked up the story. "When Edith arrived, we let her in and offered her tea. That's when she grabbed Sylvia and dragged her to the cellar, a knife at her throat."

"Now we know why she was so strong," Jack told his wife. "She's a demon."

Hannah's lips formed an "O."

Tommy tried to forge ahead of Jack, but Jack caught his arm and held him back. "I have to speak to her," Tommy growled, jerking away.

Jack let him go. He knew Tommy wouldn't do anything foolish to jeopardize Sylvia's life. It was de Mordaunt who worried me more; he wouldn't care about sparing any of us.

"Does Edith have her ghosts with her?" I asked. At Jack and Hannah's blank looks, I added, "She's the third medium. She convinced some disgruntled spirits to possess the living and take up arms against us." Well, arms in the form of boiling hot water and heavy objects. Only Edith had possessed a revolver.

"She was alone," Jack said.

"Good. That will make her easier to kill. Or send back through the portal."

"Send back?" Hannah repeated. "To the demon realm?"

I waved away her questions as we neared the basement steps. "Later."

"Your story will be interesting, I wager," Jack said.

"You have no idea."

Tommy descended the half dozen steps and raised his hand to knock on the door at their base. He paused and glanced at us over his shoulder. Jack nodded for him to go on then joined him on the stairs, Quin at his heels.

Tommy knocked and called through the door, "I wish to speak to Miss Langley."

"Tommy? Tommy is that you?" Her voice sounded distant, like she was much further away than simply on the other side of the door, but that was to be expected; the door was made from very thick oak.

"Sylvia?" Tommy pressed his ear to the wood. "Are you all right?"

"She's unharmed," came the voice of Mrs. Myer. "But I'm growing tired of waiting. Do you have the book?"

"We're seeking a way to get it back," Jack called out. He pressed a finger to his lips, not wanting her to hear either Quin or de Mordaunt's voices, and certainly not Myer's.

"Then you need to hurry, Mr. Langley. I'm not sure how much longer I can bear your cousin's company."

I thought I heard a noise that sounded like a scoff coming from the other side, but it was fleeting and not repeated.

"We need reassurance that Sylvia is unharmed," Jack called out.

There was a pause, then, "I'm unharmed," Sylvia said. "Tommy, are you still there?"

"Yes!" he shouted, pressing his entire body to the door.

"I love you."

His fingers curled against the wood. "I love you too." His voice was softer than hers and might not have traveled through the door. "I'll get you out safe," he said, louder. "Do you hear me?"

"Yes." Her voice quavered. "I know you will. Be careful."

"That's enough!" Edith snapped. "Get the book, and do it now, before I grow impatient with this vacuous twit!"

There were no scoffing sounds this time, only silence. Jack tapped Tommy on the shoulder and signaled for him to come away. Tommy looked as if he wouldn't obey, but then he stepped back from the door and climbed the steps with Jack and Quin. He cast a longing gaze at the basement door then followed us through the service area and into the entrance hall again.

We passed by the main staircase but stopped when Langley hailed us. Bollard carried him, as he always did between levels. De Mordaunt's broad forehead crumpled into a frown as he watched the slow, steady progress of the men. The frown twisted into a sneer of disgust.

Mr. Langley took my hand when they reached the bottom and patted it before letting go. He inclined his head at Quin. Even Myer had a tight smile sent his way. He did not acknowledge Tommy. I didn't necessarily think that a bad thing. No acknowledgement was better than a shouted "get out of my house!"

Bollard set his master down in the ground floor wheelchair. "We need to talk." Langley waved us through to the larger of the sitting rooms. Bollard pushed the chair forward, leading the way.

De Mordaunt followed behind, a swagger in his step. He sniffed. "In my day, if a man's legs didn't work, he would be dead."

"Your legs work and you're still dead," Jack pointed out.

"I would be happy to render them useless for you in this realm," Quin said. "To prove your theory true."

I didn't see de Mordaunt's expression but he mercifully kept quiet. His habit of saying horrid things whenever he opened his mouth was dangerous for all concerned.

Mrs. Moore was already pouring the tea and serving up slices of cake when we entered. She must have guessed the time of our arrival and prepared refreshments early. She greeted me warmly then left, leaving the door open. Nobody went to close it. Mrs. Moore had seen and heard many strange things over the last few months and never told a soul. I suspected she would be loyal to Frakingham and Langley until the day she died, and it didn't matter if she heard something curious now.

"I think you need to tell us what you learned in London," Jack began. "What's this about sending Edith Myer back to her own realm?"

"Her own realm?" Langley was in the middle of accepting a cup of tea from Bollard when he almost spilled the contents over his lap. "What *is* she?"

"Demon," I said. I eyed Quin. He and Bollard were the only ones standing. Jack, Tommy and even Myer sat on the edges of their seats, looking as if they would leap up at the slightest sound coming from the direction of the basement. Only de Mordaunt appeared comfortable. He sprawled in an armchair, his legs apart, and ate his slice of cake in two bites. He swept the crumbs littering his chest onto the rug. Hannah picked up the plate containing the remaining half of the unsliced cake and moved it to a table near her, out of his reach.

I told them what we'd learned about Edith Myer, from Myer himself, and his failed attempts to send her back, with the amulet as well as hypnosis, years ago.

"Hence my need to bring another here to do it," Myer cut in with a nod in de Mordaunt's direction. "The known methods weren't working."

"We were there when De Mordaunt confronted her in London only two nights ago," I said, "but unfortunately he couldn't capture her. She had a few spirits helping her."

"Can't Quin do something?" Hannah asked.

"I can if he fails," Quin said. "Or if he asks for my assistance."

De Mordaunt snorted. "I don't need you, St. Clair."

"Let's not be hasty." Myer nibbled his cake. "We need to do whatever is necessary to force her to leave."

"Why is she even here?" Jack asked. "How and when did she arrive?"

Myer took to eating his cake more vigorously, avoiding Jack's gaze. Quin and I exchanged brief glances. "She came here in sixty-six," I said. "She worked for the royal guard in her realm but, for reasons we don't yet know, she committed a crime and came here to avoid punishment."

Bollard and Langley's gazes settled on Jack. Hannah moved closer to her husband, but he remained perfectly still, his face unmoving. I almost thought he hadn't understood the link, but his eyes gave him away. They were only too aware, too knowing. Jack was far too clever to miss the implication of that date.

"Your mother was sent here to capture her and take her home," I told him.

Jack drew in a long, deep breath, his first in quite some time.

"She got side-tracked," Myer said with a huff and shake of his head. "Had a liaison with Wade, found herself with child, and died."

Hannah's knuckles went white as she squeezed her husband's hand. "Did Edith—the demon inside Edith—kill her?"

Myer nodded. "Her pursuer, as she called Hannah Smith—the original Hannah Smith, your namesake—was weak after giving birth. Edith took advantage of her vulnerability."

Jack leaned his elbows on his knees, taking Hannah's hand with him. He pressed her fingers to his lips, his gaze unfocused, distant. She sidled closer, until their shoulders pressed together, and blinked teary eyes back at me in silent appeal.

"It wasn't the first murder the Edith demon committed here," I said gently. "She killed the real Edith, of course, and Edith's parents and maids when they became suspicious about her odd change of character."

"My God," Langley murmured. "Myer...you knew?"

Myer cleared his throat. "I, er..."

"He knew," I said darkly.

"There was nothing I could do! She was more powerful than me. When I realized that..." He fiddled with his tie and collar again. "It was too late. I was trapped."

"Coward," Jack growled low, ominously. "You should have said something. *Done* something."

"What could I have done?" Myer spat. "Tell the authorities that I married a demon murderess? Ha! They would have blamed me for the crimes."

The muscles in Jack's jaw bunched. He looked as if he would leap across the rug and throttle Myer if it weren't for Hannah's hand anchoring him.

"It's done now." Langley's voice cut through the tension. "She's here. We must get rid of her or..." He broke off, but the words "lose Sylvia" were on *my* lips, and probably everyone else's.

Tommy lowered his head and dragged his hand through his hair. Jack's shoulders were slumped and Hannah's big eyes were full of tears. Bollard's hand rested on his master's shoulder, but it didn't seem to be enough to banish the bleakness in either man's face. I'd never seen the scientist look so distressed before. He and Sylvia may have argued of late, and he wasn't always kind to her, but any doubts I'd held about her importance to him were banished.

I glanced at Quin, feeling in need of comfort myself. But he wasn't looking at me. He'd moved to the window and was staring across the lawn to the abbey ruins and the portal. A terrible feeling tightened my chest. Someone had to go through the portal to get the book back or we would risk losing Sylvia altogether.

CHAPTER 13

"Have you tried tricking her with an old book from Langley's library?" Myer asked Jack. "She's never seen the real one before. She won't know if we wave a fake in front of her."

"Your wife is too clever to fall for that," Jack said. "She won't release Sylvia until she can confirm the book is the right one. I don't want to risk angering her by attempting to trick her."

"I wish everyone would stop calling her my wife." Myer's top lip curled almost to his nose, as if he'd tasted something disgusting. "I'm sure marriages between species is illegal in English law anyway."

"Enough talk." De Mordaunt launched himself to his feet, startling me, and headed for the door. "We're wasting our time."

Jack and Tommy cut him off by blocking the exit, and Quin came at him from behind. He grabbed de Mordaunt's collar. "You are not going anywhere. A woman's life is in danger. You will do what we say, when we say it, or I will hurl you back to the dungeons."

De Mordaunt turned and shoved Quin's hand off. "And risk the administrators' wrath for interfering? No, I don't think you will. You've always done as they say. Always been the good dog, obeying orders without thought."

Quin smirked, the mocking words rolling off him.

"Then what can we do?" Myer whined. "How will we break this impasse?"

We all looked at him, even de Mordaunt.

His lips parted with the release of a wheezy breath. He sat back and clutched the chair arms, as if the object could keep anyone from hurling *him* through the portal to the other realms.

"You have to do it," I told him. "There is no other way. Edith needs to see the real book, and you're the only one who knows where it is."

"It's through the portal again for you." Hannah seemed almost gleeful about the idea.

"No. No, no, no. I can't! The portal…it'll take me to the demon realm, and that place…" He shuddered.

"It is not a bad realm," Quin said. "They won't harm you if you ignore your urges."

"Urges?" Jack asked.

"A person from this realm will arrive there starved, much as the demons that arrive here are. Since you are not summoned, but go of your own accord, you can control yourself."

We all knew how unpredictable and dangerous a demon wrenched here through summoning could be. Those demons needed their summoner to control them, or they would savage everything in their path. Others who'd come here of their own volition, like Edith and the first Hannah Smith, were not so frenzied and were more human. It made sense that the same thing happened in reverse. A human choosing to go through to the demon realm was at least in control of their actions, thank God.

"You coped well enough last time," I told Myer. "Didn't the demon realm authorities send you to the Purgatory administrators almost immediately?"

"It was an anxious wait until they did. I was captured by those hideous beasts and taken prisoner." Another shudder wracked him. "I didn't understand a word of their language, and they didn't understand mine. I was fortunate that those who found me took me to the authorities and didn't decide to make a meal of me."

"They're more accepting of the supernatural than here," Quin told us. "They're aware of the other realms and certain figures can communicate with the administrators of the afterlife." To Myer, he said, "You weren't a prisoner, and I doubt you would have been eaten. They were trying to help you."

Myer sniffed. "They treated me without thought for my dignity, touching my skin, my hair and clothing. It was terribly distressing."

I could imagine it would have been, not knowing their language and customs, or what they planned on doing with him. "Since you've already had some experience, you won't be so anxious this time," I said cheerfully.

"Miss Moreau, I most strenuously object! Why not send St. Clair? Or Langley?" He nodded at Jack, earning him a glare from Hannah that he ignored. "They're his people on the demon realm, after all."

I was a little surprised when Jack made no comment. So, I noticed, was Hannah. "Quin is needed here, to monitor de Mordaunt," I said.

"I do not need monitoring," de Mordaunt snapped.

"And Jack may also be needed if things go wrong. Tommy and Bollard too."

"I wasn't thinking of the dumb one going," Myer muttered.

Bollard didn't flicker an eyelid, but August Langley rolled himself forward and pointed at Myer's chest. "You're going.

You're the one who gave the book to the administrators for safekeeping, you must retrieve it."

"He's right." Quin gave a firm nod of his head. "They might not release it to anyone else."

"It's decided," Hannah said before Myer could think of further excuses.

"Wait!" Myer's fingers dug into the leather arms of his chair. "Once I have the book, then what? You're simply going to give it to her?"

"In exchange for Sylvia, yes. Then de Mordaunt can take it off her again and send her back."

Myer's eyes narrowed. "How will he do that?"

"The exact plan will be drawn up while you're retrieving the book."

Myer groaned and sank even further into the armchair.

Bollard touched his master's shoulder and signed something. Langley nodded and Bollard left the room. "He's going to fetch the parchment." The parchment, torn from the book many years ago, had three spells written on it: one to open the portal, one to summon Quin, and another to close the portal. The book itself had further incantations to perform the same tasks but without it, the parchment was our only resource.

"I won't go." Myer pouted. "You can't force me."

"Yes we can," Tommy growled. "*I* can and I will."

"You? With your useless arm?"

Tommy grabbed Myer by his tie and hauled him out of the chair. He made it look easy, as if Myer weighed nothing. Myer was a little taller, and Tommy dragged him down so that they were face to face. For a moment I thought he would smash his forehead into Myer's nose, as Quin had done to de Mordaunt on the train, but he didn't. "I don't need two arms to hold a knife or a gun. One will kill you as good as two." He shoved Myer toward the door.

Myer stumbled, and Jack caught him. "He's right," Jack said, helping the hapless Myer to regain his balance. "It would be wrong of us to force him."

De Mordaunt muttered something under his breath and rolled his eyes to the ceiling.

Tommy turned on his friend with such ferocity and determination on his face that Jack took a step back. "He has to go! We need that book!"

Jack put up his hands and shook his head. "It would be a low act to push him through when he so vehemently doesn't want to go. I'd feel rotten about it."

"I wouldn't."

Hannah scrambled to her feet. Like me, perhaps she thought they would come to blows over it. Myer slunk away from both men, trying to make himself invisible between the display cabinet and door. Quin edged toward Tommy and Jack—preparing to intervene? Whose side was he on? It wasn't clear from his expression what he thought about forcing Myer to retrieve the book.

I saw my opportunity and seized it. "I agree with Jack. I wouldn't feel right sending Myer through. I'll go."

"No!" came an explosion of voices. I think the only one who didn't speak was de Mordaunt. He seemed to find our squabbling amusing and watched with a smirk on his thin lips.

"Why not? Jack, Bollard and Tommy must remain here to help if necessary, Mr. Langley is immobile, and Hannah…might be with child."

At least that got everyone looking at Hannah and not me. She flattened her palm to her stomach. "How did you know? We haven't told anyone yet."

An awkward round of congratulations followed. It didn't save me from receiving one of Quin's most quelling looks. I tilted my chin at him. I wouldn't be intimidated into backing down.

"I am the logical choice to go through," I told them. "Besides, I'm rather curious about other realms." Purgatory in particular, but I didn't tell them that. I didn't want Quin suspecting anything.

"You're not going," he said coldly. "Do not make me lock you in your room for safety."

"You said yourself that it's not dangerous. Myer wasn't captured, he was helped."

"Something could go wrong. If the demons who see you land are not the understanding sort, you could come to harm. There are all kinds there, as there are here."

"I am going, Quin. I want to."

"You are not. That's final." He gripped my shoulders and dipped his head to peer into my eyes. "I forbid it, Cara."

I clicked my tongue, but before I could respond, Jack cut in. "He's right. Besides, *I* want to go."

"You most certainly will not!" Hannah stamped her fist on her hip. "You are a husband now, and almost a father. You cannot put yourself in danger."

Quin let my shoulders go. "He'll not be in danger."

It was my turn to stamp my fist on my hip. "You just said that *I* would be! How is it different for him?"

"He's half demon. He can use his fire to protect himself and show them his ancestry." He slapped Jack on the back. "It's decided."

"It is not!" Hannah grabbed Jack's hand and dragged him into the corner. Their discussion was heated but not audible. I knew Hannah had won when Jack sighed and lowered his head.

They returned to us, hand in hand. "Myer, you have to go," Jack said. "There's no way around it."

"What? No!" he cried.

Another round of arguing ensued, after which nothing was decided. I gave up and sat down again, frustrated to the back teeth. It seemed I would have to go through while no one was looking. I wondered how easily I could get the parchment off Bollard. And how easy it would be to slip away from Quin. He was already watching me like a caged hawk eyeing its prey. I doubted I could just walk out without him noticing.

I squirmed. Ordinarily I would enjoy being the object of his attention, but this time I wished only to be invisible. Perhaps later, when darkness came, I could pretend to need the privy and go down to the ruins instead.

The rest of the day was a trying experience. Everyone took it in turns to attempt to convince Myer to go, but he wouldn't budge. Indeed, he stormed off at one point and locked himself in the library. Langley shouted at him frequently, his booming voice echoing around the big empty house. Hannah and Jack alternately bickered and made up, doing so quietly, away from the rest of us. Tommy paced around the sitting room while Quin did the opposite; he simply remained standing by the fireplace, watching me. He did not sit, unlike de Mordaunt who sprawled in the armchair, either brooding or snoozing.

The room felt confining, the tension as taut as a bowstring. It wouldn't be long before something—someone—snapped. Thank goodness Mrs. Moore announced that dinner would be served early. Either she had decided we needed a distraction, or Hannah had spoken to the housekeeper earlier and arranged it.

"Jack, fetch Myer," Langley said as Bollard wheeled him out.

I caught up to Hannah. "Poor Mrs. Moore having to cook for all of us without any help."

"Cook prepared pies and some salads before leaving," she said. "Mrs. Moore simply had to place the pies in the oven. But you're right, we've asked a lot of her. She's a good woman."

I looped my arm through hers. "I'm sorry I broke your wonderful news. It was wicked of me. Can you forgive me?"

She hugged my arm and despite everything, smiled. "Of course I can, since you were merely guessing."

I laughed. "Was it that obvious?"

"Perhaps not to everyone." She glanced at Quin, walking behind us. "I agree with him. You can't go. But nor can Jack."

I sighed. "We'll simply have to keep working on Myer then."

We sat at the dining table and waited for the others. Myer arrived within minutes, but Jack wasn't with him and he didn't know where he'd gone. Hannah's anxiety grew until she could stand it no longer.

"I'm going to find him," she declared.

"I'm here," he said, finally walking in. He gave his wife a kiss on the top of her head then sat next to her. The housekeeper bustled in after him. "Mrs. Moore and I took food to the basement door."

Myer pointed a serving spoon at Jack. "They will have to open the door to retrieve it. Why not use the opportunity to snatch Edith then?"

"She gets Sylvia to open the door and retrieve the food."

De Mordaunt bit into a leg of chicken but that didn't stop him from talking. "Even better." He hadn't bothered to use his knife and fork. At least Quin had quickly learned to copy our habits when he'd arrived, and tried cutlery. De Mordaunt didn't seem to care to learn modern manners. "We use the opportunity to remove the hostage and strike the demon."

"No! We do nothing to endanger Sylvia. Unless we can be sure Edith is not near her at the time, we leave them alone."

"This is intolerable," Tommy muttered, dragging his hand through his hair. It was already terribly messy from a long day of worrying.

"Agreed," Jack said. "Myer. Do not force us to throw you through the portal."

Myer gulped. "Y-you wouldn't."

Hannah held up her hands for silence. "Please, let's eat dinner and discuss it again afterwards."

Her request did nothing to vanquish the tension. We all ate quickly to get the infernal meal over with. Instead of returning immediately to the sitting room, Hannah pleaded a headache and retired to her room. Jack went with her, promising to return soon, and Myer requested to be assigned to a bedroom. Langley refused. He wasn't letting Myer retreat anywhere yet. I wasn't sure how effective a tired and irritated man would be in another realm, but I kept quiet.

"Excuse me too," I said to those remaining. "I'm going to freshen up."

"Have Mrs. Moore show you to your usual room," Langley said. "I must apologize for our lack of manners today, Cara. We're out of sorts."

"*She* gets an apology *and* a room." Myer crossed his arms and settled into the armchair. "Bollard, bring me brandy and a cigar."

"There'll be no smoking in here," Langley said as I left the sitting room. "Sylvia says it makes the furnishings smell."

"Then why can't I go to the smoking room?"

"We need to stay together."

"The women aren't here any longer, man! Let's all go."

I hurried down the corridor toward the stairs. Quin caught up to me before I reached them. He took my hand and led me into the music room. The sun had slipped behind the horizon and daylight succumbed to the shadows in the small room. It wasn't so dark that I couldn't clearly see that he was angry with me, and worried.

He shut the door and gently pushed me back against it. His hands rested lightly on my hips, his mouth hovered near mine. I thought he was going to kiss me. I was wrong.

"I know why you want to be the one to go through the portal, Cara. But I will not allow it. Not when you're doing it for me."

"It's not just for you," I muttered.

"I meant what I said; it's too dangerous." He kissed me lightly on the lips then drew me away from the door. "I need to return and watch de Mordaunt. I don't trust him."

"Quin…we cannot go on like this."

"I know. We will force Myer, one way or another." He kissed my forehead. "Go and get some rest. I suspect the night will be a long one."

He let me go and I watched him leave, letting him think that I'd been referring to the hostage situation. In reality, I'd meant *our* situation, as a couple. *I* couldn't continue like this anymore. I would do anything to have Quin with me, and risk much. What did I have to lose?

***

My plan relied on getting the parchment off Bollard. He'd tucked into his inside jacket pocket, where I hoped it still remained. After changing into a more somber gray dress with white trim, I returned to the sitting room. Tempers were as frayed as I expected them to be.

All the men were there and they were arguing. Well, all of them except Quin, who stood like a statue near the door, and de Mordaunt, who seemed to find the whole thing amusing. Even Bollard loomed over Myer, as if trying to intimidate him.

"It would be criminal of you to force me!" Myer shouted.

"Being a criminal is something you know all too well," Jack growled.

Langley wheeled himself over. "It would be criminal of *you* to let Sylvia perish—" He cut himself off with a heavy swallow. Bollard rested a hand on his shoulder.

I approached them, preparing to angle myself close to Bollard, but Quin intercepted me. His bleak gaze told me he knew what I was trying to do. I turned away, no longer able look at him.

"Enough!" Tommy shouted. "This is a farce!" He stormed off, bumping into Bollard so hard that the giant mute lost his balance and fell backward. Tommy caught him with his one arm, but couldn't hold him. They tumbled to the floor together. With a grunt, Tommy picked himself up and walked out.

Jack helped Bollard up and frowned at his friend's retreating back. He went to follow but Langley put up his hand. "Let him go," he said. "He needs some fresh air to calm down."

Quin and I moved to the window and watched Tommy make his way across the lawn. When he was some feet away from the house, he glanced over his shoulder, then broke into a run.

I gasped. "He's going down to the abbey! But he doesn't have the parchment."

Bollard patted down his jacket while Quin and Jack ran from the room. They didn't get to see the servant's dismay when he realized the parchment was gone.

I groaned. "He picked your pocket, didn't he?"

Bollard's lips flattened and he nodded.

"It's not your fault," Langley said. "He was raised a thief. Yet another reason why I never wanted him in this family to begin with."

I picked up my skirts and strode past them. "Perhaps if you hadn't been so intent on excluding him, none of this would have happened. Sylvia would have been kept safe by Tommy if he were here watching over her." Perhaps it was unfair, as nobody could have foreseen this, but I was tired and angry and worried. I was in no mood for Langley's pomposity, especially when Tommy had been the only one willing to take action.

I ran from the house, my skirts bunched in my fists. Both Myer and de Mordaunt followed. With their longer legs both outstripped me, and I was the last to arrive at the abbey ruins. I stopped at the edge of the fallen stones as a strong wind smacked into me. My skirts flapped and my hair was torn from its pins. I pushed it out of my eyes to get a better view.

The portal was already open and I arrived just in time to see Jack leap through the swirling, gaping hole in the air. Nobody stopped him. Tommy was missing. The other men stood in a semi-circle, watching the intense, local storm. The eye began to close as someone—Myer, I think—chanted the spell to close it.

But no, Quin's lips moved too, and I could hear his voice whereas I couldn't hear Myer's. Strange that he would whisper the chant when he must know that Quin was already closing the portal.

"What's going on?" Hannah ran up to me, dressed only in her nightshirt and house slippers, her wrap in her hand. Her curly red hair streamed behind her. "Cara?" She stopped at my side, searching the group of men. Her breaths came short and hard, and I worried that she'd over-exerted herself. I put my arm around her waist and, as if my action confirmed her fears, she burst into tears. "Jack!" she shouted. "Jack!"

I held her tighter as she strained to move forward. "He's already gone through, and you are *not* going after him." I didn't think she would endanger the baby's life like that, but I said it anyway. "He'll be all right. I think Tommy already went through and Jack followed. They're together, and you heard Quin say that the demons aren't as hostile to strangers as we are to them. They'll be all right."

My babbling didn't seem to help. She buried her face in my shoulder and sobbed. I held her and glanced at Quin, but he wasn't watching us. He advanced on Myer, his sword in his hand, his face a picture of fury.

De Mordaunt drew his sword too, but he wasn't watching the other two. He kept his eye on the portal, now almost closed. Just then a creature was spat out, blocking Quin's path to Myer. Its lips peeled back and saliva dripped from its fangs, globules landing on its body fur. It leapt at Quin, but he dodged the creature and raised his sword to strike. It was then that I saw Myer, his lips still moving, edging away from the scene. He clutched something in his hand...

Oh my God. He held an amulet and was chanting an incantation. *He* had summoned the demon and was now controlling it.

I clutched Hannah harder, too afraid to watch but too afraid *not* to. My heart beat madly in my chest and a cold sweat broke out on my brow.

Hannah lifted her head and wiped her cheeks. "There's only one and both Quin and de Mordaunt are excellent swordsmen. They'll get it."

Even as she spoke, Quin and de Mordaunt prepared to strike. But another demon—then two more—jumped through the portal before it closed completely. The men, caught by surprise, had to put up their blades in defense as the three demons descended on them at once. The fourth turned yellow eyes on Hannah and me. We stumbled backward, still holding hands, then turned and fled toward the house.

It was hopeless. A demon could easily outrun us, yet there was nothing more we could do. Quin and de Mordaunt were outnumbered. Jack and Tommy were gone. Bollard and Langley were in the house.

And Hannah and I were exposed and unarmed.

CHAPTER 14

We made it to the edge of the manicured lawn, further than we should have. Bollard approached from the house, jogging rather than sprinting, the revolver in his hand not raised to shoot. Hannah and I turned to look back at the abbey.

It was difficult to see details in the moonlight, but the scene down by the abbey was definitely one of calmness. There were no shouts or screams of agony. The hunched, wolf-like figures of the demons stood placidly, not attempting to claw anyone's skin off. Although Quin and de Mordaunt did not attack them, their weapons were still drawn, their swords raised, ready to strike.

Bollard signed for us to stay where we were, and he continued past. Hannah and I took a moment to catch our breaths before either of us could speak.

"What happened?" she asked. "Not that I'm complaining about the lack of bloodshed."

"I think the demons are being controlled. By Myer, I assume. He summoned them so only he can control them."

"That man is a fool and a danger to others. Does he honestly think he can use those demons to capture Edith? With Sylvia as hostage?"

"That's probably what they're discussing now. Come on, let's see."

I walked off, but stopped when I noticed she wasn't following. Oh, of course. The baby. "You go back to the house, Hannah. I'll tell you what I learn."

She bit her bottom lip, her gaze flicking between me and the abbey. "Come with me."

I shook my head. "I want to know what they're planning. I'll be safe."

She pressed a hand to her belly and sighed. If it weren't for her condition, she would have come with me. She *wanted* to come with me but the situation could still flare up at any moment, and she had another priority now.

"Do you think Jack will be all right?" she asked, her voice small.

I walked back to her and took her hands in mine. "Yes. He's strong and capable. If Myer survived it unscathed, Jack will too."

She squeezed my hands. "You're right. Take care down there. Get away if it begins to get volatile. I don't know that I trust Myer to keep four demons under control."

Nor did I, but I didn't express my concern. It wouldn't help her nerves. She headed back up to the house and I made my way to the ruins again. The men kept a healthy distance between themselves and the four demons.

The creatures weren't so frightening when they were passive. They were somewhat similar to big dogs, all covered in fur, saliva dripping from panting tongues.

Quin intercepted me as I approached. "Would asking you to return to the house make it happen?"

"Not at this juncture."

"I thought not."

I curled my fingers around his arm. The hard muscles beneath his shirtsleeve twitched. "If it begins to look like Myer is losing control, I'll flee. I promise."

Myer did seem to be holding them with his chants, but how long could he do it? What would happen if he stopped?

And then he did stop. It was more of a pause, during which the demons remained where they were, passive and unthreatening. He looked satisfied as he tried it again, this time pausing for longer.

"I have them controlled." The childlike wonder in his voice was odd on the whiskered middle-aged man. "Look!"

"Good," Quin said. "Now send them back."

"I can't do that. They have a job to perform." He began chanting again and the demons turned as one toward the house.

"Stop this!" I shouted at him. "Sylvia is in there!"

He broke off the chant to say, "I will instruct them not to harm her."

"But what if Edith harms her?"

"You can't blame me for her actions. Legally and morally, she isn't my wife."

I threw up my hands. I couldn't believe it! He was going to march his creatures into the basement, willingly putting Sylvia in harm's way. Not to mention that Hannah had gone back into the house. I had to warn her.

The demons lumbered toward the lawn like wound up automatons. I thought about lunging at Myer and snatching the amulet from him, but I wasn't sure if that would cause the creatures to turn on me to defend him.

"Get back, Cara." Quin pushed me behind him and raised his sword. So did de Mordaunt. Thank God we had them both to stop this madness. I'd seen Quin defeat more than four demons, and I imagined de Mordaunt was capable with his weapon too.

"Is your sword demon forged?" I asked him. "Can it kill them?"

His lips curled. "It can kill demons." The grin widened. He switched his focus from the retreating demons to Quin's back, only a few paces ahead of him. "And more." He lunged.

"Quin! Look out!"

Quin spun round, slashing his sword in an arc as he did so. But de Mordaunt leapt out of the way, landing on the ground on his side. He rolled and leapt up onto a stone in a swift, practiced move. He laughed at Quin. Dread sickened me. Bile burned my throat.

Quin thrust and sliced at de Mordaunt's feet. De Mordaunt jumped over the blade then jumped again as Quin repeated the move.

Bollard raised his revolver but didn't shoot. He looked torn between going to the house and helping Quin.

"Go!" Quin shouted, dodging a kick from de Mordaunt's boot. "Both of you! Your weapon will not destroy him."

His words shocked me into immobility. He wanted to *destroy* de Mordaunt, not merely kill his body and send his soul back to Purgatory. It was so final and so cold, particularly since he'd known the man when alive. I found it difficult to believe such a dark sentiment came from *my* Quin. But perhaps it was understandable. De Mordaunt was, after all, ultimately responsible for the betrayal and deaths of Quin's wife and brother, and his own banishment to Purgatory.

Bollard grabbed my arm hard, as if he expected me to resist. I did not. My presence would be a distraction for Quin, and he needed to concentrate on defeating that monster. We ran toward the house, but not before I heard de Mordaunt's accusation.

"I would have been a better brother to him than you. You paraded your whore of a wife in front of him, tormenting him."

The clash of metal against metal was followed by the whine of the blades rubbing. Quin didn't respond verbally to de Mordaunt, and I hoped further taunts wouldn't cause him to lose his temper and act wildly. I dared not look back to check.

I needed to hurry. Bollard was shortening his strides so that I could keep up, but I was painfully aware of how unsuitable my clothing was for physical exercise. The demons and Myer were running now too, and we would not catch them.

A gunshot boomed from the house. Bollard and I dropped to the ground, keeping our heads low. Although we weren't the targets, I wasn't sure how accurate Langley or Hannah would be.

I glanced back at Quin. The gunfire must have broken his rhythm more than de Mordaunt's. He was on his back and de Mordaunt stood over him, both hands on his sword hilt, the point of his blade aimed at Quin's chest. I swallowed my scream and considered snatching Bollard's revolver.

But in the moment I thought it, Quin rolled out of the way and de Mordaunt's blade skewered soft earth instead of flesh. I gasped in relief, and if I hadn't already been on my knees, I would have fallen to them.

Bollard helped me to stand. My body shook, my skin felt cold and tight. He tugged me toward the house, but it was hopeless. The demons would beat us. The bullet hadn't stopped them. Perhaps if the shooter aimed at Myer…

No, he was the only one controlling them. Without him, all of us, not just Sylvia, became vulnerable.

I glanced back over my shoulder at Quin and de Mordaunt. They looked ghostly in the darkness, the moonlight picking out the white of their shirts and glinting off their blades. Blades that would not just kill but destroy. If Quin lost, he would cease to exist in any realm. Not even summoning him would bring him back.

My chest constricted and my breathing became labored. I would have turned back to help him if I knew Bollard wouldn't drag me to safety, risking his own life. Hannah needed him now—needed us. So did her unborn child, as did Sylvia. It would be selfish of me to abandon them and assist Quin.

And yet I felt like I was abandoning *him*.

As if he sensed my conflict, and worried I would make the wrong choice, Bollard pulled me even harder alongside him. We broke into a run, but the demons were already at the front steps. The large doors were closed, probably locked, keeping the demons out. And us.

Bollard stopped and raised the revolver.

The demons suddenly changed direction, darting to the right. He aimed and fired, but the bullet merely glanced off the arm of one. It paused and swatted at its fur, as if nothing more harmful than a fly buzzed there, then turned those yellow eyes on us. One of the other demons slammed itself against the sitting room's French doors, cracking the glass panel. Two more followed suit, shattering the glass.

"Mr. Myer! Please, stop!"

But he didn't respond. He might not have heard me. His hair and forehead were damp with sweat; his breathing came in ragged bursts. His focus was on his creatures, and his words were strange to my ears as he continued the chant.

Inside, another booming gunshot echoed. But the demons didn't care. They spilled through the broken door and into the house. If Hannah was the one firing from in there...

Oh God.

Only three demons entered the house. The fourth kept its focus on Bollard. It came at us, and despite Myer's increasingly panicked voice, it didn't stop.

"Mr. Myer! Control it!"

"I...I can't." He was shouting at the beast now, his words running together. He stumbled backward, away from Bollard.

Bollard raised his weapon, his face a mask of intense focus. He shoved me to one side, keeping me out of harm's way. I screamed and wanted to cover my face with my hands, but forced myself to watch.

Bollard fired, just as another gunshot came from the house. The demon squealed and skidded to a halt, but not before its big paw swiped at Bollard's chest, knocking him over. The demon didn't continue the attack, but clutched at its back and chest, and I realized both bullets had hit it at the same time.

With a whimper, it scampered after its mates, through the door and into the house. Myer followed, still chanting.

I crouched near Bollard. He was bleeding, his clothes shredded, but he was alive. He glanced past me toward the house and nodded once. I followed his gaze and saw Hannah watching us through a window on the ground floor, a shotgun in her arms.

"Are you safe?" I called out to her.

She nodded. "We locked ourselves in here. Cara—" She shook her head and pressed the back of her hand to her mouth, suppressing a sob. "Sylvia."

"I know."

We needed Quin. We couldn't do this on our own. I had to help him, not just for his sake, but for all of ours. With Tommy and Jack gone, and Bollard injured, there was no one else.

I put my hand out for the revolver. Bollard hesitated then gave it to me. *Kill him*, he mouthed.

I hurried to the abbey ruins again. Neither Quin nor de Mordaunt noticed me. I kept the revolver at my back out of view, and slowed my pace as I drew close. They must have seen me, but neither acknowledged me. I suspected Quin was too worried to draw attention to me, and de Mordaunt didn't consider me a threat.

I crouched behind one of the low, broken abbey walls and peeked around it. The scent of the damp earth and grass was strong, the cool stone rough against my cheek. It wasn't a good position to shoot from, so I knelt and rested my wrists on the wall, clutching the gun in both hands. I didn't shoot. I didn't trust myself to be accurate with their positions constantly changing. If I hit Quin...

It worried me even more that I heard nothing from the house. No gunshots, no screams of agony from the demons. They must be at the basement door by now. Perhaps they had already broken it down.

I needed to hurry, but hurrying was the last thing I wanted to do.

I dragged in a steadying breath and willed my hands to stop shaking. I closed my mind off to the sounds of their swords clashing, the grunts of exertion. I focused on de Mordaunt. His moves were fast and perfectly executed, matching Quin's. Too fast. I needed them to be still, just for a moment.

I fired the revolver over their heads. Both paused and spun toward me. I sighted, cocked and fired again.

The bullet hit de Mordaunt's chest. He clutched his heart and stared at the blood seeping through his hands. Shock rippled across his face. Tears clouded his wide eyes.

Quin thrust his blade through de Mordaunt's stomach. Blood poured from the wound and spilled from de Mordaunt's mouth. He coughed up even more, spraying an arch into the air. His damp eyes settled on Quin and his top lip curled in a sneer. "You…needed…a woman. Soft." Then that gaze flicked to me and hardened. "Bitch."

Quin reached into the dying man's chest and pulled out his soul. It wasn't black like the souls of the spirits escaped from Hell had been, but gray and sick looking. I supposed de Mordaunt was a spirit like them, his body not really belonging to him, but granted by the Purgatory administrators, and so his soul had to be removed in the same way. For demons, Quin would have simply left the creature to disintegrate.

De Mordaunt's body and soul crumbled to dust, and his sword vanished. Quin wiped his hand on his trousers and came to me. His body slammed into mine and his arms circled my waist, holding me tight. His breathing was ragged and his chest heaved.

He'd been more worried about losing to de Mordaunt than I'd realized. Or maybe ending the afterlife of a man he once knew well played on his mind. De Mordaunt's soul no longer existed anywhere, in any realm.

I pulled away first, although it was hard to do so. "We work better as a team than apart," I told him. "No more trying to push me away to safety."

His answer was a grunt, and I suspected he would never stop trying to guarantee my safety. I supposed I ought to expect nothing less from him.

I took his hand. "They need your help at the house. The demons are inside and Myer is struggling to keep them under control."

"He's a fool."

"Go ahead of me. You'll be faster."

He took my chin in his hand and kissed me hard on the mouth. Then he ran up to the house. I glanced back at the spot where the portal lay, hidden and calm now. I prayed that Jack and Tommy were all right, and brought the book back with them soon. I abandoned my plan to go through and find it for myself. Tommy and Jack were there now. They would succeed. They had to. For Sylvia's sake.

I ran after Quin, but reached the house well behind him. He climbed through the broken sitting room door and disappeared into the room beyond. When I reached the door, I peered through, checking that the room was empty of demons, then followed. Squealing and snarling greeted my ears from a distance. I crept out of the sitting room and edged along the dark corridor toward the service stairs. My hands shook and my palms grew damp with sweat. I clutched the revolver tighter and cocked it.

"Cara." I jumped, despite recognizing Hannah's whispered voice. She emerged from the shadows of a doorway and hugged me.

"Are you all right?" I asked.

She nodded. "We stayed in here when we saw Quin coming." She moved aside, revealing Mrs. Moore and

Langley gathered around the sofa. Bollard lay on it, his jacket and shirt open, a cloth pressed to his chest wounds. "He'll be all right," she said. "He wants to go and help Quin, but we won't let him."

"I'll check and report back."

"Cara, you mustn't go. It's too dangerous. Let Quin deal with the situation now."

Even as she said it, another demonic squeal ripped through the house. It set my nerves on edge, even though I knew it meant Quin was battling them. Still, what about Sylvia? Had any of the demons breached the door?

"I won't get close enough for them to see me," I told her.

"Those things will *smell* you."

"Myer is directing them to the basement and his wife, not us."

"And we can all see how that is working out." She waved at Bollard.

"I'm not just checking on Quin, Hannah. I want to see if Sylvia is all right too."

As if I'd summoned it, Sylvia screamed. A shiver clawed down my spine. Everyone turned toward the door. Langley's head drooped into his hands. Bollard reached out and touched his master's knee. He cast a pleading glance at me.

I clutched Hannah's arm briefly. "I'll be careful."

She let me go. I continued to creep along the corridor. It grew darker, the further into the house I got. I found the entrance to the service stairs and removed my shoes. They would be too loud. I felt my way down the narrow stairwell, one hand on the wall, the other holding the revolver. How many bullets were left? I couldn't think how many had been fired, but I didn't think there'd been enough for it to be empty.

I reached the bottom without breaking my neck in the darkness. Scuffles and grunts came from my left, where the basement stairs were located. I swallowed heavily, but it did nothing to dislodge the fear clogging my throat and pressing down on my chest. Quin was capable of killing four unarmed demons, but what if he was exhausted from fighting de Mordaunt? And why had Sylvia screamed?

I peeked around the corner and saw the pale glow of lamplight from the basement stairwell, but could not see the stairs themselves from that angle.

"Hurry, Quin!" Sylvia's voice! She was alive, thank God. And she also knew Quin was there, trying to get to her. "She's coming! Please, hurry."

"Myer!" Quin growled. "Stay."

"You fool!" Myer shouted back. "You bloody fool. They were our only chance!"

Did that mean the demons were all dead? I tiptoed to the basement stairs and peered round the corner. Myer stood on the second step from the top, his back to me, lamp in hand. Quin stared at the closed door, hands on hips, his shirt torn and a bloody claw mark across his broad back. Four piles of dust littered the steps.

Quin took a step backward and turned his shoulder to the door. He was going to attempt to break it down.

"Wait," I hissed.

He glanced up as Myer spun round. Both opened their mouths to speak, but I put my finger to my lips. Myer eyed my weapon and swallowed hard.

"I won't shoot you if you do as we say," I told him. "You won't get through that door, Quin. It's too thick and the bolt is enormous."

Quin climbed the stairs to me. "What are you doing here? Go back upstairs."

There was no time for arguing. Sylvia's voice had sounded terrified. Edith could already have killed her, although I doubted it. Sylvia was her bargaining chip. "Do you know what's happening in there?"

"When Edith heard us and the demons, she became distracted," Quin said. "Sylvia managed to free herself from her bonds and arm herself, I think with a bottle of wine."

"She won't be able to hold her off much longer. But perhaps we can still trick Edith." I waved at the piles of demon dust. "Their presence might have actually helped us."

"How?" Myer asked.

"Because if the demons are here, it means the portal was opened, and the portal could have been opened for someone to retrieve the book. Does she know it's in the otherworld?"

He nodded. "I told her. But I also said she'd never get her hands on it. She won't believe I'm now going to hand it over to her. You said yourself she won't fall for tricks. She'll want to see the book first."

"We have to try. It's our only choice. You're still going to refuse to hand it over to her. Loudly."

"I don't understand."

A smile touched Quin's eyes if not his lips. He turned to Myer. "You have to give it to her," he said, voice raised. "Or the Langley girl will die."

Myer, catching on, nodded. "No! You'll have to kill me first."

"That can be arranged," came Edith's voice.

Sylvia cried out in pain. "Stop it! You're hurting me!"

I exchanged a glance with Quin. Sylvia hadn't managed to hold her captor at bay.

Sylvia protested again, but it was abruptly cut off. The basement fell into silence. I stepped down, but Quin blocked my progress. I stood alongside Myer and watched the door. Quin stepped down until he was facing it.

"Is it true?" Edith called out. She sounded like she was up against the door too, on the other side. "You have it?"

"Aye," Quin said, heavily, as if resigned to handing it over. "You have won. The demons came through accidentally when Dawson brought the book back. They destroyed almost everyone here. Myer, Cara and I are the only ones left. Just promise me that you won't use it to harm the people on this realm and I will give it to you."

Loud sobs from Sylvia almost drowned out Myer's voice. "No, you can't believe a promise from her! She's a liar." He seemed to be enjoying himself a little too much. Sick man.

"We need to know that Miss Langley is safe," Quin said.

"Can't you hear the whelp?" Edith shouted.

"I need to see her. Then I will give you the book."

"Who has it? Him or you?"

"He does."

Edith seemed to consider this. "I will crack open the door. He must hold it up."

"I'm not holding anything up!"

I signaled for Myer to put his hands behind his back to pretend he held the book. He set the lamp down on the step and did so.

"When you open the door, I'll force him to show it to you," Quin said.

There was a long pause and I thought our plan had come to nothing. It was a stupid plan anyway. I didn't know why I thought we could bluff her into opening the door.

The bolt slid back on the other side. Myer glanced at me and grinned. Quin kept his focus on the door. The large brass handle twisted and the door opened a fraction.

It was all Quin needed. He wedged his sword blade through the narrow gap. Edith went to slam the door, but it wouldn't close. He pushed all his weight against the blade, using it as a lever to pry the door open wider. An ordinary sword would have snapped at the hilt, but it seemed demon forged ones were strong.

Quin was stronger than her too. He managed to get the door open enough to reach through. My stomach dove, imagining Edith slicing his hand off. Instead, the door flew open wide.

Quin hadn't expected it, and, with his entire weight against the sword, he stumbled forward into the basement. Edith slipped past him in the moment it took him to regain his balance.

"Cara!" he shouted.

But she was already upon me by the time it left his lips. She possessed demonic speed, as well as strength, and pushed me aside before I even registered her presence. She snatched my revolver and aimed it at Myer.

He held his hands up in surrender. "I don't have it!" It was, perhaps, a foolish thing to admit to a desperate and frustrated woman who already harbored deep hatred toward him.

She shot him. The bullet went through his left eye and shattered his skull, sending blood and bits of his head over the stairwell wall behind him.

The sight, coupled with my anxiety, was too much for my stomach. I threw up on the steps.

Quin raced past me and I realized Edith had already left the stairwell. I didn't like the odds of having a gun versus a sword, but I trusted that he would be careful. Or as careful as a dead man could be.

"Stay back!" I heard him shout. "She has a gun. Stay back!"

At least that would keep the others out of the way for now. Sylvia stumbled out of the basement. A bruise bloomed on her cheek, matching mine, and her lip was cut. Her hair fell about her shoulders in tangles and her clothing was askew. I caught her in my arms and she sobbed into my shoulder.

Other arms took her from me. Hannah, I realized. I left her to explain and ran through the house, bumping into tables and walls in my haste. Hannah called after me but I ignored her. I would be careful, and I wasn't going anywhere near Edith Myer. But I had to watch, had to see what happened to Quin.

I ran out through the front door and took the steps two at a time. The gravel dug into my stockinged feet. I'd forgotten I'd removed my shoes for the noise. The night was eerily silent. There were no sounds of night birds in the trees, no sounds of life from the house behind me. I paused on the lawn, deciding that was close enough. Quin and Edith were already at the ruins. She stopped running and rounded on him, revolver raised. He wasn't close enough to use his sword.

"Duck," I murmured. "Get out of the way."

He did not. To my horror, he stood his ground. She cocked the gun and pulled the trigger.

CHAPTER 15

Edith's aim was thrown off at the same moment the gun fired, but from a distance, and in the dark, I couldn't see why. Had Quin hurled his sword at her?

No, he still held it. He used it to knock the revolver out of her hand as a strong wind slapped her hair against her face and lashed at her skirts. It must have been the wind that unbalanced her and saved Quin.

But why was the portal opening *now*? Oh God.

Edith bobbed down behind a crumbling wall, protecting herself from both Quin and whatever was about to come through the portal.

I wanted to scream at Quin to get away and find some protection too, but I doubted he would hear me over the gale. It was too late anyway. A figure burst from the portal's mouth, followed closely by another.

Quin lifted his sword then lowered it again. What was he doing? Why didn't he attack the demons before they attacked him?

The figures picked themselves up off the ground. Not demons. Humans. Jack and Tommy!

I surged forward but paused again before I reached the ruins. In the moment of distraction, Edith had scrambled to the revolver and picked it up. She aimed it at Tommy.

"You tricked me!" she shouted at Quin. "Fetch the book now, or I shoot him."

Tommy, hand raised in surrender, said, "Is Sylvia…?"

"She's alive," Quin told him. "They all are."

Tommy sank to one knee and raised his face to the inky black sky. Jack went to help him up, but Edith cocked the gun. "Get back into that portal and fetch the book." The portal had closed, now that it had delivered its travelers. Someone would need to open it again with the chant.

I pressed a hand to my rapidly beating chest, hardly daring to breathe.

"We can't," Tommy said, getting to his feet. "The administrators won't relinquish it. We already asked."

Edith delivered the filthiest string of words I'd ever heard, and I'd heard terrible ones on the streets in my childhood. She gritted her teeth and tensed her arm, the revolver aimed at Tommy's head.

I shut my eyes. Oh God, please don't shoot him.

"No!" Sylvia screamed from the house behind me.

I opened my eyes, expecting to see Edith shoot. Instead, I saw Quin pulling his sword out of Edith's chest. She dropped the gun and her body began to disintegrate. Her mouth contorted with rage and pain, until it was blown away along with the rest of her on the wind.

I ran down to the men, but held back from embracing Quin. He was still here, but for how long? I steeled my nerves, waiting for his exit. It did not come.

"Why didn't she shoot?" I asked, not taking my gaze off him.

"You didn't see?" Jack said.

"I had my eyes closed."

He smiled as he spotted Hannah behind me. "She fired, but the barrel was empty. Quin must have known, because he was unperturbed when she pulled the trigger."

Either he knew or he didn't care about his body expiring.

"I counted," Quin said.

I'd been wrong. He *was* beginning to disappear, I just hadn't noticed it in the dark. It began at the edges, as if someone were erasing him from the outside in. In moments, there would be nothing left. "Bollard described these weapons to me the last time I was here," he went on. "I knew this one could hold six pellets."

"Bullets," I said, gathering my frayed nerves, trying to hold myself together. "*Bollard* described it to you?"

"With his hands." He poked the gun with the toe of his boot. It went right through. "I prefer a weapon that can be used more than six times."

With each word, his body grew fainter. I watched, helpless, wanting to take him in my arms and anchor him to this realm. But nothing would keep him.

Jack gave him a nod. "Thank you again." He moved away, giving us space.

I didn't need space. I needed time. Time with Quin. Tears burned my eyes but did not spill. He blinked at me, as if he could think of nothing to say. We'd already said it all, and everything I needed to know was in his eyes. Bleakness and love mixed together. So much love.

"Goodbye, Cara."

"Will you...will you request to move on?"

He held my gaze for so long that I thought he would disappear completely before he answered. "I have not decided."

"Please...not yet."

He frowned. "Why?" He took a step toward me. "Cara, what are you planning?"

I paused long enough that he'd faded away to nothing before I answered. I touched the air where he'd stood. It was still a little warm. Or perhaps that was merely my imagination.

I trudged toward the two contented couples, standing at the edge of the ruins. Tommy and Sylvia were embracing and caressing one another's faces as if they couldn't believe they were finally touching in public. Jack had tucked Hannah into his side, and was whispering something in her ear that made her gaze up at him with complete trust and love.

I was so relieved and happy for them, yet my heart felt like it was broken and bleeding. I wanted what they had, but it wasn't possible.

Unless I made it possible.

***

"I don't care!" Sylvia's shout wasn't the first thing I expected to hear upon my entry to the house. I'd thought they'd all be joyous now that they were safe and peace had settled over the estate. But Sylvia's clenched fists and fierce scowl indicated otherwise.

"My dear, I understand that you've had an ordeal," Langley said. He was relatively calm, considering his niece was defying him in the entrance hall with everyone listening in, including me, a guest. Only Mrs. Moore was absent. Bollard looked a little pale, his clothing in disarray, but he was standing straight, as usual, at his master's back.

"Yes, I have had an ordeal," she snapped. There wasn't a tear in her eye or a wobble in her voice. Everyone kept their distance from her. Except Tommy. He rested his hand on her lower back and faced down Langley too. They were a team, a united couple, and I was pleased to see their open defiance. "Being held captive in a basement all day and night made a lot of things very clear to me. I love Tommy, and he loves me. We're going to be together, whether you like it or not. It would be much easier if you accepted that fact. If you don't…we're leaving Frakingham."

Langley's breath hitched. He attempted to cover it with a cough. "We'll talk about this in the morning after you've rested."

"We'll discuss it now." She leaned into Tommy's side and he kissed her temple. "When I thought he was dead…" She choked on the last word, proving that her tears weren't completely banished after all. "When I thought Tommy was dead, I didn't want to live either. Not without him. He went through the portal for me! If that's not love and loyalty, what is?"

"Sylvia—"

"What do you know of love anyway? You treat poor Bollard like a servant."

Langley's face darkened. His lips pressed into a ruthless line. "He *is* a servant."

Hannah and I exchanged glances. I thought Jack might say something to diffuse the situation, but he didn't.

"He loves you!" Sylvia cried. "And you love him, so why try to hide it from us? Your family and friends don't care about…"

Bollard's face had gone paler and his eyes wider. He probably wasn't used to this sort of discussion, perhaps not even with Langley. Some things are just too taboo to talk about, even in private. He signed something to Sylvia.

"It does matter," she told him hotly. "I'm tired of subterfuge and awkwardness. I'm tired of everyone being afraid of you, Uncle."

"Afraid of me? Who is afraid of me?"

She threw up her hands. "Everyone! But not me, not anymore." She tossed her head. I am going upstairs to have a bath. Hannah, please send Mrs. Moore in with some supper and hot chocolate. Then I'm going to bed. We'll discuss this again in the morning, Uncle, after you've had time to give it some serious consideration."

"Good," Langley said tightly. "That is what I was trying to get you to do all along."

She sniffed and with another toss of her head, marched off, only to return to Tommy, kiss his cheek, then leave again. She stomped up the stairs, her shoulders square, her head high. I was rather proud of her. From the small smile on Hannah's and Jack's lips, I suspected they were too.

Jack rested a hand on Tommy's shoulder. "You go too. There'll be time for discussion when we've all recovered."

Langley huffed out a long breath and wheeled himself away. When Bollard followed and grabbed the handles to take over the pushing, Langley growled, "I can do it."

Bollard moved to where Langley could see him, and signed something. He pointed at the stairs.

"You're injured," Langley snapped. "Jack!"

Jack rolled his eyes, earning him a smile from Hannah. He picked Langley up and carried him up the stairs. Bollard stood with his hands at his sides, watching his master—lover—go without him.

Hannah touched his elbow. "He'll be in a better temper in the morning."

Bollard looked at her as if he thought she was being overly optimistic. Then he followed Jack and Langley. I wondered what their conversation would be like when they were finally alone.

Tommy hovered nearby, in the shadows, but emerged once the others were out of sight. "Hannah, may I have my old room?"

"Of course not! You're no longer a servant. The rose guest chamber is yours for now. And don't worry about Sylvia."

"I'm not." His gaze lifted to the top of the staircase. "For the first time in, well, ever, I'm *not* worried about her."

"She has come a long way."

His gaze softened. "She's become the woman I always knew she would be."

I thought his faith in her admirable, considering *I* had no inkling Sylvia could ever be so strong, or so willing to give up her pampered life for the man she loved.

Tommy headed up the stairs and Hannah finally turned to me. "Are you all right, Cara?"

"I'm fine. I'm growing used to Quin leaving. But I think I'll go upstairs and rest too. It has been an eventful day."

"Very true." She eyed me warily, so I quickly took my leave and followed Tommy.

I caught up to him on the second floor landing. "Tommy," I whispered, trotting after him. "May we speak?"

He looked a little surprised that I wanted to talk to him privately. We had never been alone before, and I'd never had reason to have a private word with him. "Is something the matter?"

I sucked in a deep breath. "I'd like the parchment. Do you still have it?"

His lips parted in a quiet gasp. "Why?"

"I want to go through the portal. I think I can help Quin stay on this realm."

"What? How?"

"The book contains all the information. It's been done before. Gilbert de Mordaunt was sent to Purgatory and managed to return here and live a normal life."

"But he was a demon. Quin is—was—human."

"Then it should be even more natural for him to come back."

"Won't there be consequences?"

I shrugged. "There weren't any for Gilbert."

"Are you sure? What happened after his death? His second death, I mean."

"I…I don't know for certain." It was the only fly in the ointment. The book had warned that something terrible would happen to the soul that tried to follow those instructions. Yet Gilbert had lived a full life here. If something happened to him in the afterlife…well, it was something to find out beforehand. Somehow.

I held out my hand. "Please, Tommy. May I have it?"

His mouth twisted to the side, unconvinced.

"I saw what you did for the one you love," I said. "And I know you would have done anything to save her. I want the opportunity to do the same for Quin."

"Your situation is different."

"No, it's not. It all boils down to being with the person you love."

He dragged his hand through his ragged crop of hair. "I don't know, Cara. Jack and I landed in the demon realm together after leaving here. It was...a strange place."

"Were you in danger?" Quin had said the demons weren't as threatening to us as we were to them, unless we appeared dangerous. Much as we treated those from their realm who came here and killed, of which there were all too many lately.

"We were only there briefly. I think the same people who found Myer found us. They didn't seem surprised by our presence, or worried, and we were immediately sent through another portal to Purgatory. The administrators there sent us back here after an all-too-brief discussion."

"Without the book."

He nodded. "They claim it's too dangerous to release back into this realm. I have to agree with them. Humans can't be trusted with such knowledge. I'm just glad we didn't need it in the end."

"I have to at least try and convince them. All I want is an opportunity. Please, Tommy. You did the same thing for Sylvia."

"Yes, but you're a woman. Like it or not, you can't punch a demon in the face and expect him to be knocked unconscious." He didn't look quite so opposed to the idea of me going, however. It gave me hope.

"By all accounts, yours included, I won't have to punch anything in the face." I crooked my fingers at him. "Please, Tommy. I will support you against Mr. Langley."

He smirked. "I'm not sure you'll need to. Sylvia's doing a fine job on her own."

"I'll name our first born child after you."

He laughed. "What if it's a girl?"

"Thomasina."

He pulled a face. "Perhaps as a middle name." He reached into his jacket pocket and pulled out the flattened and crumpled roll of parchment. "Be careful, Cara. Please."

I took the parchment and kissed his cheek. "Thank you."

"When you get to the demon realm, try to resist the hunger and…fear. Everything will go better for you if you remain calm."

"I will. With any luck, I'll be back by the morning."

"You had better be. I don't want to be the one to tell the others that I assisted you to go through the portal."

I tucked the parchment up my sleeve and headed back along the corridor and down the stairs. The household was quiet; everyone had gone to their rooms to rest and recover. It was easy to slip out and reach the ruins undetected. There was enough moonlight that I didn't fall over any stones, but not enough that I could be easily seen from the house if someone looked out a window.

I unrolled the parchment, drew in a deep breath, and spoke the words from the ancient spell. A breeze caressed my skin then grew in strength until my hair was rippling behind me. The air in front of me swirled then the center yawned wide. I could not see an end to the black tunnel beyond.

I drew in a deep breath and then, before I lost my nerve, jumped through.

Darkness surrounded me. It sucked at me, pulling me through the portal. I'm not ashamed to say that fear gripped my insides, and I almost regretted choosing this path.

But then the darkness ended and I was spat out…somewhere. I lay on the ground, unharmed. The earth smelled of damp soil and grass, just like home. I was in some sort of meadow, with yellow flowers sprouting in clumps and trees surrounding it on two sides. On the other sides, more fields stretched as far as the eye could see, over a series of gently rolling hills. A cloudless blue sky was exactly where I expected it to be. The place looked so *English*. Surely there'd been a mistake and I'd simply traveled from one portal to another within the same country.

My curiosity gave way to a more pressing need. I was starving. My stomach felt like a giant cavity in my body. I tried to ignore it, but it growled in protest. The need to eat was overwhelming, and drove me to get up and explore.

I checked for signs of life, hoping to beg a pie or slice of bread from a kind farmer. A slender stream of smoke rose from behind the trees, so I headed in that direction. The air was clear, the walk easy, and the trees not overly dense. They were similar to trees that grew in our realm, although not quite like any species that I'd seen. Their trunks had a blue-gray tinge to them, and their leaves were larger, greener, and the forest canopy denser.

The smoke came from a small settlement nestled in a clearing. I pressed myself into a tree trunk and watched people—demons—coming and going. The buildings reminded me of something from history books, with mud and daub houses, thatched roofs, and unpaved streets. There were no vehicles of any kind that I could see, and no horses, although I did spot pigs in a pen. It was all so quaint and domestic. So normal.

Except for the demons wandering about. They wore no clothing, but walked upright, not hunched like they were when they came to our realm. Nor were they the snarling, saliva-dripping creatures I was used to seeing come through the portal. These were civilized by comparison. The creatures that were wrenched from here to our world resembled wild, vicious wolves. These ones, while still having the same features, were more like pet dogs, albeit on two legs. There was nothing threatening about them.

It made me feel horrid for the ones forced through the portal against their will. Being summoned turned them into creatures of death and destruction, but I could see what Quin meant when he said they were a peaceful species on the whole. I supposed Jack's mother was a testament to how they could be gentle-natured if they came through the portal of their own volition.

A paw clamped down on my shoulder, shoving me into a tree. Bark scratched my face and the wind was knocked out of me. I gasped and spun round, my hands up to defend myself.

The large, furry demon face peered back at me, so close that I could smell its putrid breath. Its small, yellow eyes peered back at me from beneath a thick brow. It sniffed my hair and throat, then licked me with a slippery tongue.

I screamed. Despite Tommy's warning, I felt anything but calm. If this creature was peaceful, why had it shoved me into the tree? Why was it baring its fangs and snarling at me? Its paws waved in the air, so close to my head that I feared it would knock me out. It continued to snarl and growl and gesticulate. Then it clamped its paw over my mouth.

No peaceful creature would treat a stranger like that. It was just my luck to be found by a demon of Edith Myer's ilk, with a nasty streak.

I tried to suck in air, but that only drew the stench of demon breath and fur into my nostrils, my lungs. I coughed, but with the paw still over my mouth, it was more of a choke. The creature moved closer, smothering me with all that fur. The long teeth were frighteningly close. One bite could rip off half my face.

With a surge of fear-fueled energy, I shoved it in the chest. I didn't think I was strong enough to push it away, but the demon let me go. It stared at me through those yellow eyes with what I thought was curiosity. Perhaps it hadn't meant to hurt me or scare me. Perhaps our meeting had simply got off on the wrong foot and I'd overreacted.

But then it grabbed both my wrists in its paw and jerked me alongside it.

"Stop!" I shouted. "No, please! I don't wish you any harm! I want to get to Purgatory."

It didn't acknowledge my words, just marched me forward. I tried to pull away, but it tightened its grip. I winced as pain spiked up my arms, but didn't try to escape again.

The demon hailed someone in the village as we walked in. Several of them stopped what they were doing and stared at me. Jaws dropped. Eyes widened. Perhaps they'd never seen a female human. Or perhaps this village had never seen humans before at all. I couldn't be certain if the portal had spat me out in the same place Myer or Tommy and Jack had found themselves.

"Please, I mean you no harm. Let me go." I struggled again, but that only resulted in a more bruising grip. The blood slowed in my veins; my arms grew numb.

I whimpered with the hopelessness of it all. How could I communicate with them without words or gestures? Two demons came up to us and exchanged words with my captor. They seemed heated to me, but it was difficult to tell. Their natural speech could be snarling, grunting and growling for all I knew.

One of the demons nodded then walked off, while the other lingered, its eyes skimming my length. Was I being sized up for the dinner table?

I shuddered, but tried to keep Quin's assurance at the forefront of my mind—demons weren't a dangerous species. At that moment, I wondered how well he knew them.

The one holding me jerked me forward. It let go of my hands, finally, and I rubbed them until my circulation returned. The demon prodded me in the back then pushed me through the door of a crude building. I landed on my hands and knees, my sore cheek smacking against the hard packed earth.

The door behind me slammed shut and a bolt slid home on the other side.

I scrambled up and shook the handle, but nothing happened. I banged on the wooden door, but nobody came to rescue me. If anyone was on the other side, I couldn't tell. There were no voices, no sounds of footsteps walking past.

I looked around the room, but there were no windows or other doors. Light filtered through the small gaps between the walls and roof, but it only showed me that the room was entirely empty. It didn't even contain a chair.

I pressed against sections of the wall, but it was solid. Perhaps the roof would be weaker, made only of thatch, but how to get up there? The walls were too smooth and too high to climb. I could dig under them, but with what tools? Perhaps later, if they fed me and gave me a spoon, I could hide it and use it at night. Then I could flee to one of the more peaceful settlements the others had spoken of.

But what if they didn't feed me? What if I was the meal instead?

I sat down on the floor, pulled my knees up, and sobbed into them.

At some point I must have stopped crying. I lost track of time completely. I was no longer ravenously hungry. Anxiety had replaced hunger. The minutes—hours?—became an endless stream of nothingness. It was still daylight, but perhaps the days and nights in the demon realm were different to ours.

The sliding of the bolt jerked me fully to attention. I scrambled backward into the far corner and cursed my foolishness for not bringing a weapon with me. Why had I come so poorly prepared? Because Quin had said the demon realm was unthreatening.

Quin. The figure standing in the doorway, outlined by the light behind, had his shape. I rubbed my eyes and got to my feet. When I pulled my hands away, the figure had moved. He stood in front of me, scowling.

"You look a mess," Quin said.

I bit my wobbly lip, but that didn't stop my tears. He opened his arms and I stepped into them. I buried my face in his bare chest and breathed in the familiar scent of him. My relief at seeing him was overwhelming and utterly consuming. I couldn't stop crying, and I hated my weakness as much as the fear that his arrival had now banished.

He swept my hair off my shoulders and massaged my neck, shushing me like a baby. "It's all right, Cara. No one will hurt you." He stroked my back, my head, my neck, and waited patiently until I finally composed myself.

He grasped my shoulders, but I didn't want him to move away. I circled my arms around his waist and clung to him. I wasn't the brave, defiant woman I wanted to be. Not always, anyway.

"Cara, you should not—"

"Don't. Don't tell me I shouldn't have come. It won't change anything."

He sighed. "Very well." He took my hand and went to walk off.

I snatched my hand back. "Where are you taking me?"

"Home." He spoke with tired resignation, so unlike him. Had the events at Frakingham exhausted him? But he was no longer on our realm. Surely he didn't need sustenance and sleep in Purgatory.

"Did the administrators send you here to rescue me?"

He shook his head.

"Then why are you here? Some other warrior business?"

He looked away. "Come. I'll take you home."

"No, Quin. Tell me why you came? And how?"

He crossed his arms but still did not look me in the eye.

"If it's not warrior business, then...are you here unofficially? Because you knew I needed you?"

When he didn't answer, I grabbed his arm and shook it. He sighed again. "Aye."

"Oh, Quin." I stood on my toes and brushed my lips against his.

He responded with a brisk, dry kiss, then drew away.

I regarded him levelly. "Is your unofficial visit here going to be a problem?"

"No."

I couldn't tell if that was a lie to appease me or not. His face was a closed mask. "Go on."

"I knew you were here and that you were scared when the demon found you. You shouldn't have resisted, Cara. The demon mistook your resistance for hostility."

"But he was so rough with me."

"They are a naturally strong species. Those paws do not know how to be gentle."

"But its words were harsh, like it was angry at me for intruding."

"And he said your screaming hurt his ears. He had to make you stop, so perhaps that made him rougher with you. They have very sensitive hearing."

"Oh. So they weren't going to roast me and eat me for dinner?"

The corner of his mouth twitched. "No, even though you look like a tasty morsel to me."

His teasing eased my mind somewhat. Yet he hadn't fully answered my questions about his timely arrival. "You say you heard about me being here. Did you ask for permission to come?"

"Aye."

"And?"

"And the administrators refused. They said it wasn't warrior business."

"Really?"

"I came of my own volition."

"You defied the Purgatory administrators? Is that allowed?"

"It's...not ideal."

"Not ideal! Quin! What will happen to you? What punishment...?" I broke off. After his first visit to our realm undertaken without permission, he'd suffered a flogging upon his return to Purgatory. The spirit of Father Ignatius from St. Etheldreda's church had said Purgatory kept a tight leash on its warriors. A leash that Quin had broken twice now. They'd punished him and given him a second chance after the last time. Would they be so forgiving now?

"Don't fret, Cara." He gripped my arms and dipped his head to meet my gaze. "I'll be all right. Now, you must go home."

I sucked in my wobbling lip and waited until I had control over my tears. "No, Quin. I've come this far. I must speak to them. Take me to Purgatory, please."

His fingers squeezed then sprang apart, letting me go. "Are you mad? Aye, you must be. Go home, Cara. Accept that this is the way it has to be."

"I can't accept!" I was shouting now, but I didn't care. It wasn't like the demons could understand me. If the administrators were listening in...good. "You have rescued me countless times, Quin. Now I want the chance to rescue you."

His mouth twisted as he tried to hold in his emotions. His mask rarely cracked like this, and I welcomed the rare glimpse into his deepest thoughts, even though they were troubled ones. "You can't."

"I only want the chance to try. I have to try. I'm compelled to do so."

"Why?"

"Why did you defy the administrators and come here against their wishes?"

His heavy swallow was loud in the silence. "Because I love you," he whispered. "I love you like I've never loved anyone before. I ache to see you, and I hated knowing you were afraid and alone." He lifted his gaze to mine. Raw emotion pooled in the depths of his eyes and threatened to spill out.

I touched his face, stroking his cheek, wishing there was something I could say to ease his pain. But how could I when I felt so much pain myself?

"Cara, I'm afraid to exist without you, yet I don't want to move on until I know you will be waiting for me at my destination."

My cheeks dampened, and I realized I was crying. "Then let me fight for you to come and live with me."

"It has never happened before."

"Everything has a first time."

"They won't want to set a precedent."

226

"They don't have to tell anyone."

He sighed heavily, and his shoulders drooped with the effort.

"I know the chance of success is slim," I said. "But if I don't try...I'll have to live with the guilt of giving up for the rest of my life."

He pressed his forehead to mine. "And I cannot live with the guilt if they condemn you for the attempt."

"How can they condemn me for doing everything I can to save my love?"

His lips touched mine in a tender kiss that was more powerful than any he'd ever bestowed on me. I placed my arms around his neck and pressed my length against his. We held each other as close as possible, not willing to let the other go. Not *able* to.

Suddenly he was pulling me and swirling me around and around, like an out of control waltz. No. Wait. Something else was dragging at us, whisking us out of that mud hut, out of the demon realm. I felt like I was being sucked through a hole and into a void by a strong cyclone.

"Quin!"

"It's all right." He held me against his chest. "It will end soon."

"Where are we going?"

"Purgatory."

CHAPTER 16

I clung to him and lifted my face from his chest. We were surrounding by a darkness that felt even emptier than the room we'd just left. "Are you doing this?" I asked.

"No."

"Oh."

"Cara, whatever they say...do not be afraid. You've done nothing wrong and they cannot hurt you or keep you here."

I took his hand as the swirling slowed. "I'm not afraid when you're with me."

He squeezed my hand. "Remember what I said. You are free to go whenever you wish."

I was about to toss back a quip about leaving only with him, but he was suddenly ripped from my side. I reached out into the darkness, but there was nothing there. "Quin? Where are you?"

"Gone." It was his voice, but it was muffled and came from a distance.

"Gone where?"

"Back where he belongs." The second voice sent my heart leaping into my throat. It sounded so close, but

228

another tentative search with my hands revealed no one nearby.

"Who are you?" I asked.

"An administrator." It was a woman's voice, soothing and gentle.

"Can I see you?"

"I have no form."

"Can I have a light anyway, to see what this place looks like?"

"It looks like nothing, and therefore no light is necessary. A void cannot be illuminated."

"I thought this was a realm, not a void."

"It is a place in between realms."

"I remember Quin saying that too. Where is he?"

"Back in his cell."

I swallowed. He told me not to be scared, but it was so hard without his solid, reassuring presence. I curled my fingers and dug my nails into my palm. The pricks helped remind me that I was still real, that I had a body, and I was alive. As Quin said, they couldn't keep me there.

It was time to see how reasonable these administrators could be. "Do you know why I'm here?" I asked.

"Of course." It was the same voice. I wondered how many others there were and what they sounded like. Were they all women, or did the voice change depending on whom they spoke to? "You wish us to free your lover."

"When you call him my lover, it sounds sordid. What we share is not sordid. It's rare."

"We know that."

"And it's beautiful."

There was no response. I took it as a good sign.

"Anyway, you're not quite right. I do want him freed, yes, but I wish for him to be allowed a life."

"Cara," Quin's voice held a warning, but he still sounded so far away. How could he hear me from his cell? This place—realm—was strange indeed.

"I told you, Quin. I will do everything in my power to have you with me. My voice, my words, are the only power I possess."

I thought I heard him chuckle, but it could have been an echo from some other distant noise. "Not the only power," he said softly.

"We have discussed his case," the woman's voice cut in, "and have decided that he has completed enough tasks and performed a valuable service. Since we promised him his freedom, if he wished it and proved himself worthy, we will allow him to move on, despite his two transgressions."

"No, you're not listening!" Hands on hips, I spun round, trying to pinpoint where that voice was coming from. "I don't want him to move on to his afterlife yet. I want him to come back and live with me on the human realm. As a living, breathing human," I clarified.

"Who would want that?"

"I do."

"As do I," came Quin's voice.

I smiled. My heart lifted. Did his agreement mean he thought we had a chance of success? I hoped so. "Well?" I prompted.

"We do not allow such a thing," the administrator said.

"You do not allow such a thing *yet*. Just because it has never been done before doesn't mean it cannot be done."

"That is no reason to make something so."

My heart did a flip in my chest. She hadn't said no that time. "I know it's possible. The details are in the book, and Gilbert de Mordaunt did it. He lived heartily on our realm after freeing himself from here."

"He *escaped*. And he may have lived well and long on your realm, but he did not die well. We had to wait to punish him, but we did it eventually. Upon his death, his soul went to the dark place known to you as Hell."

"Oh." We had come so close to condemning Quin to the same fate without realizing it.

"I told you that you saved me by not giving me the book that first time," Quin said.

I almost smiled at that. "Yes, but I almost sent you to Hell this time. I came for the book," I told the administrators. I hoped my honesty would go some way to swaying them to my thinking. "So...will you grant him a new life anyway? Without condemnation at the end of it? As you said, he has performed a valuable service for you over a long time. He deserves to come back."

"He deserves rest, in the afterlife."

Very well. It was time to tell them what I really thought, without holding back. I crossed my fingers and prayed it didn't backfire. "He deserves to have a chance at living. The chance *you* robbed him of."

A sharp intake of breath echoed through the darkness. Quin's? The administrator's?

"Quin only lost his life as a result of the your mistake."

"Explain," the voice snapped.

I swallowed and forged on. I'd come too far to back down now. "What he did to his brother wasn't his fault. It wasn't murder. Guy gave up. He wanted Quin to end his life and put *him* out of *his* misery. Guy felt guilt for his affair with Quin's wife, and felt he deserved to die. Quin, filled with rage, fought with him on the battlefield but did not wish to kill him. Sadly, Guy had other ideas. He essentially laid down his sword at the worst possible moment."

There was more silence, and this time it seemed to stretch on forever. I was about to call out to Quin to see if he was still there and had heard me, when the administrator spoke.

"If that was so, and Quintin was not to blame, why didn't he ask us to reconsider our judgment? We are not unreasonable. If he did not murder his brother, we could have sent him to his afterlife immediately."

"He blamed himself. He didn't want to move on. He felt he deserved this place, this endless punishment. Until relatively recently, anyway."

"We saw the gray stain on his soul upon his death."

"Gray stain?"

"A black, rotten soul is sent to the dark place by the waiting area administrators. A gray, uncertain one comes here. If Quintin *felt* he had murdered his kinsman, it would explain the color, even if he were indeed innocent."

"He did feel guilt. He hated himself for killing his own brother. He welcomed your punishments because he felt he deserved them."

"Perhaps."

I bit my tongue. She was being unreasonable, but I wouldn't say it out loud.

"You claim it was our mistake that resulted in his death," she went on. "But you have not explained."

"Gilbert de Mordaunt escaped from here and lived a normal life on the human realm. He had children, and his children had children, and so on, until Edward de Mordaunt was born. Being part demon, he shifted shape into Quin's wife's form. He then used that form to seduce Guy St. Clair, and begin the chain of events that led to both Guy's and Quin's demise. If Gilbert had not escaped from here in the first place..."

"You blame us for his treachery?" The voice sounded utterly surprised. By my accusation or my audacity?

"He learned how to get out somehow, somewhere. Or perhaps a door was left open..." I winced at my own pathetic attempt at a joke.

The administrator snorted. "There are no doors in Purgatory."

"I wasn't being literal."

"Enough! You dare to come in here and make light of your request? Of us?"

"No!" Hell. Think, Cara, think. "Please. Whatever mistake led to Gilbert de Mordaunt's escape cannot be undone. Guy St. Clair has long ago moved on to his afterlife, but you can atone by giving Quin his life back."

"*We* do not need to atone."

I cleared my throat. "My apologies. But what I say is not wrong. Gilbert escaped from here and is ultimately responsible for Quin's death, his guilt, and his long presence here. Please, look into your hearts and be compassionate. Release him to me."

"We do not possess hearts."

I drew in a deep breath. Was I imagining it, or did she sound less angry, and almost…resigned? "Quin has learned much over the centuries. He's learned not to blame himself anymore, or to blame his wife either. If he hadn't, he would never have allowed himself to fall in love with me. He would never have let anyone into his heart again."

"This is a truth. You are a willful, clever woman with the power to rip out his heart if you chose. Yet he trusts you, where for so long he could not trust any woman. Or human."

"That proves it! He's a better person. A better *human* now."

Another long silence which did nothing to mend my shredded nerves.

"Are you still there? Quin?"

"I'm here," he said gently. "I love you, Cara. With all my heart and soul."

I smiled as tears slipped down my cheeks. "I love you too. No matter what, and no matter where you are. There will never be anyone else for me but you."

I heard his raggedly drawn-in breath, then even that stopped. The silence thickened around me, cloying and hot. I clasped my hands over my stomach. I needed to hold onto something, but there was nothing within reach.

"We have made our decision," came the silky voice.

I gripped my own hands harder and shut my eyes to stem the tears. If they said no, would they let me say goodbye to Quin? Or would I be sent back without even a moment in which to think?

"Quintin will return to the human realm with you. He will become mortal again."

I'm not ashamed to admit that I squealed like a little girl. And then I cried like one too. I couldn't stop myself. I was full of relief and happiness, far too much to be contained, and it spilled out of me in the form of tears and spluttered laughter.

"Thank you," I choked out. "Thank you, your...highnesses."

A pair of arms circled me, pinning me against a hard, warm chest. I recognized Quin's scent and shape, and the lips that crashed into mine were wonderfully familiar. I clasped the back of his head, not wanting him to break the searing, delicious kiss. It stole my breath, sent a jolt through my heart, and swamped me with so many emotions that I felt like I was drowning in them.

I relished every moment, not wanting to part. *Never* wanting to part again. We didn't have to now. There would be no more goodbyes, only a lifetime of good mornings and these kisses.

The kiss consumed so much of me that I was only distantly aware of the breeze and motion. Suddenly the darkness lifted, and we tumbled to the grass together, still clutching one another.

We broke the kiss to investigate our surroundings. I laughed. We lay on the dewy grass in the Frakingham Abbey ruins. The pink sky in the east heralded dawn and what promised to be a sunny day.

I tried to sit up, but Quin gently rolled me onto my side instead and pinned my legs with one of his. He kissed me again, gentler this time. I stroked his back and shoulders, relishing the magnificent man claiming me for all to see.

Finally he sat up and helped me to sit too. He tucked my hair behind my ear and stroked my face, skirting the bruise, down to my chin.

"I shouldn't have doubted you, Cara."

"Why not? I doubted myself."

"Nevertheless, without your persistence—"

I pressed my lips to his, silencing him. "Let's not think about it. We are here, together, and our lives will be long and full."

He kissed my nose, my eyelids. "You are quite the brave little warrior."

"I am, aren't I?" I grinned and he laughed.

"I cannot call you that in public, however."

"True. What about partner?"

He forked an eyebrow. "Partner?"

"For the business endeavor we'll start together. You'll be the public face of our private inquiry business, specializing in paranormal problems. It'll be a roaring success with our combined knowledge and abilities. I can't wait to get started."

He glanced shyly down at our fingers twined together. "Partner has a nice ring to it. But I prefer wife."

"Oh. Oh! Yes, of course."

He watched me through his lashes. "Is that yes, as in yes you will marry me?"

"Yes!"

He threw his arms around me and we fell back onto the ground all over again.

The sun was fully over the horizon when we came up for air. He helped me to my feet and we walked with our arms around one another toward the house.

"I ought to warn you," I said. "We have to name our first born after Tommy."

"What if she's a girl?"

"Even then."

He pulled a face. I smiled and tilted my face up to see him better. He bent to kiss me, and we stopped walking.

It took a long time to reach the house. Only Mrs. Moore was awake when we did. She cooked us breakfast and we ate in the kitchen while we waited for the others to come downstairs. She found Quin a shirt and he buttoned it up but did not tuck it in. He didn't have his sword.

"You do look a mess, Miss Moreau," the housekeeper said as she cracked eggs into a bowl.

"It's been a long and eventful night, Mrs. Moore. Did anyone notice me gone?"

"I don't think so. No alarms were raised, no searches conducted." She eyed each of us in turn. "Were you in the village?"

"We were somewhat further afield."

Quin smiled. "But we're here to stay now."

"You're not going back to that colony on the other side of the world, Mr. St. Clair?"

It took me a moment to realize she was referring to Melbourne. We'd told everyone Quin was from that distant shore, and it seemed we'd been believed.

"I have good reason to remain here now," he said.

I placed my hand over his, and was about to tell her that we were going to be married, but Hannah entered the kitchen. She broke off her yawn when she saw us.

"Quin! What are you doing back?" Her gaze darted to the high kitchen window, and worry shadowed her eyes. "What's happened?"

"I have returned," he said. "Forever."

Her jaw dropped. "How?"

"Cara can be very persuasive when she sets her mind to it."

"I think I need to hear more."

"And you will," I told her. "After we tidy up."

She eyed my hair and filthy dress. It was covered in dirt from the floor of the demon hut, and I hated to think what state my hair was in. "You do look like you've had an interesting evening."

I was reluctant to part from Quin, but Hannah wasn't liberal minded enough to allow us to undress in front of each other, even though I told her Quin and I would marry as soon as possible. We met up again in the formal drawing room. I was the last to come down, even though Hannah helped me with my hair. She'd already woken the rest of the household, and everyone was present.

Quin rose upon seeing me and held out his hand. I took it and we shared a warm gaze that made my heart do little flips in my chest.

"Now, will you please explain what is happening?" Mr. Langley said. "St. Clair wanted us to hear it from you, Cara."

I raised my eyebrows at Quin. "It is your doing," he told me. "You should have the honor of telling the tale."

We sat together on the sofa, one of the rare times in which Quin sat down when he was at Frakingham, and I told them what I'd done. Unfortunately I had to mention Tommy's role, but nobody gave him an admonishing glare. Not even Mr. Langley. I finished by telling them that Quin and I were getting married. A round of congratulations followed.

Then Sylvia burst into tears. "See, Uncle!" Her face was red, her eyes swollen from what I suspected was a night of crying. "Even they're going to marry and you cannot get two more unsuitable people. Quin was dead! He's not even from this time! Yet they're allowed to be together. Why can't we?"

She looked as if she was about to run from the room, but Tommy took her hand before she had a chance to flee. Despite the presence of Langley, and all of us, he folded her against his chest.

"We'll be together, my love," he murmured into her hair. "I'll take care of you, no matter where we are."

She smiled through her tears and put her arms around him. "And I'll take care of you."

Langley cleared his throat, and they separated, but held hands. "It seems Cara isn't the only one who can present a persuasive argument." He glanced first at Bollard then Jack. "I have been convinced that giving my blessing to your marriage will be best for this family. The alternative was...not favorable."

Sylvia stared unblinking at him. Tommy let her go and stepped forward. He extended his hand to Langley, and Langley took it without hesitation.

"Thank you, sir. I will take good care of her, despite..." Tommy indicated his weak arm.

"You've also been reinstated as my assistant," Jack said, beaming at his friend. "I can't manage alone."

Sylvia continued to stare, but her lower lip began to wobble. Langley stared back at her. He looked uncomfortable, as if he didn't know what to say or do. Bollard wasn't quite so apprehensive. He pushed Langley's wheelchair forward and stopped it in front of Sylvia. Then he stepped around it and drew her into a hug. It was the most emotion I'd ever seen him express, and I suspected even Sylvia hadn't received such a reaction from him before. She hugged him back and thanked him through her tears.

He drew away and signed something to her that made her cry harder. I looked to Hannah for a translation and she whispered, "He said their niece will make a beautiful bride."

Their niece. It seemed Sylvia was gaining a fiancé *and* another uncle in one morning. And I thought I was blessed.

Langley cleared his throat then he too opened his arms to receive her hug.

"Oh, Uncle. Thank you!"

"It doesn't come without a condition attached." His voice sounded strained, thick.

She drew back and narrowed her gaze at him.

"Anything," Tommy assured him.

"You must promise to stay here at Frakingham. The house needs you, and Jack and Hannah. And your friends. It needs laughter and conversation. Balls and dinner parties too, if you insist."

Bollard signed something again, and I didn't need Hannah to interpret the simple signals. '*We* need you.'

Sylvia beamed at Tommy, and Jack laid his hand on his wife's belly.

Quin tilted his head closer to mine. "How long before we can wed?" he whispered.

I met his heated gaze with my own. "In a hurry, are you?"

He nibbled my ear. "Aye."

I giggled at the tickling from his lips. "We'll leave tomorrow to visit Jacob and Emily, then begin organizing things for a small wedding as soon as possible. I'm not waiting for Celia and Louis to arrive in the country." I stroked his cheek, his jaw, his hair. "We've waited long enough."

EPILOGUE

Samuel and Charity's wedding was a quiet affair, but as elegant as their small circle of friends expected it to be. After all, Charity did have exquisite taste and the groom's mother had been excluded from as many of the arrangements as possible. They married in the church the Gladstone family frequented in the village, then meandered back to the house afterward for the traditional wedding breakfast. Nobody hurried. The late summer sunshine was warm but not hot, and many of the villagers came out to watch the procession and marvel at the beautiful bride in her white silk gown trimmed with lace and organdy. She smiled at them all and accepted flowers from the little girls with enthusiasm, even though some of the blossoms had wilted in the sun.

Her four bridesmaids also wore white, with coronets of pink roses in their hair. Two of them strolled arm in arm with their husbands along the path to the house. The third was accompanied by her fiancé, whose arm hung limply at his side, and the fourth, the most interesting looking girl of them all, beamed up at a broad-shouldered man at her side, who also happened to be her fiancé. He, poor fellow, looked uncomfortable in his formal frock coat and cravat, but no less happy than the other groomsmen.

The little ring bearer and flower girl, children of the Beauforts, skipped along hand in hand, then raced ahead, trying to beat one another to the next tree, and then the next. The boy, being the eldest, and with long legs like his father, always won, except for the last time when he let his sister have some glory.

The four couples stayed overnight then departed the next day in two carriages. The newlyweds occupied one of the Gladstone coaches, making up the third in the convoy that reached Frakingham House late in the day. The housekeeper greeted them with a fine supper, put on by the cook and her assistants who'd all returned, along with the other servants, after a brief absence.

Despite their long day on the road, the couples wanted to enjoy a few more hours together before the newlyweds continued on with their honeymoon to the continent in the morning. They sat on the terrace, arranged in couples, and gazed across the sloping lawn to the ethereal abbey ruins and the glossy lake beyond.

"It's so peaceful here," Emily murmured, sinking back into Jacob's arms.

Jack kissed his wife's temple. "Hard to believe what has transpired over these last several months here."

Charity shuddered, and Samuel hugged her tighter. "It's all over now," he said quietly. "The Myers are gone. All the souls we've encountered along the way are back where they belong."

Cara and Quin exchanged a glance and her heart filled. Yes, Quin was exactly where he belonged: in her arms.

"Is it wrong that I feel no sympathy for the Myers?" Sylvia asked, her pretty brow wrinkled.

"No," Tommy told her. "They deserve no such kindness."

"What will happen now, with the portal?"

241

Everyone looked to Quin, as if he possessed the answer. Once, he could have asked the Purgatory administrators what they wanted him to do about the portal, but not anymore. Any link to them, to the otherworld, was severed. He couldn't be happier about that. The only supernatural phenomenon he wanted to be near was his wife, in her capacity as a spirit medium. If a paranormal problem came their way via their inquiry agency, then so be it. He would do his best to help others, but not if it required putting himself or his family in danger.

He smiled down at Cara. *She* was his family, and any children they may one day be granted. He still wasn't sure how—or why—he'd been so lucky to win such a remarkable woman, and be given the opportunity to live again, but he wasn't going to question it. Nor was he going to leave her side if he could help it. Why, indeed, would he want to?

"We'll be the custodians of the portal," Jack told his cousin. "You and Tommy, Hannah and me."

"And our uncles." Sylvia giggled. "I still can't get used to thinking of Bollard as an uncle. I mean *Livingston*."

"I think August is having trouble coming to terms with it too. It'll take time for him to stop treating Bollard—Livingstone—as a servant. At least he has decided to do so. It's a big step for him, but a good one at that."

"I can't get used to calling him Livingston." Hannah smirked. "It doesn't suit him at all."

Cara snorted. "I always thought Bollard was his first name." She settled back in Quin's arms and breathed in the scent of late summer roses hanging on the dusk air.

"This is Heaven," Charity said, also settling into her new husband's arms. He kissed her and tightened his arms around her.

"Aye," Quin murmured, his gaze on Cara and not the pretty, peaceful landscape. His fiancée was far more beautiful to look at anyway, her features never failing to intrigue him, or amuse him, depending on her expression. She was, quite simply, a marvel. And she was all his.

The group fell into silence, although the distant sounds of the children's laughter came from somewhere in the house. They were probably tormenting August Langley, who'd promised to supervise while their parents enjoyed some peace and quiet on the terrace. Actually, he hadn't volunteered for the job, Bollard—*Livingston*—had volunteered them both, suggesting they needed experience with children now that Hannah was expecting. Emily did wonder if Mrs. Moore was helping them, since she couldn't imagine those two men knew how to get children to laugh like that.

The five couples watched as the sun whispered its final goodbye then sank below the horizon. No, not goodbye; merely farewell for now. Goodbyes were painful, as the ten people lounging on the terrace knew all too well, though not necessarily permanent, thank goodness. Sometimes the unexpected happened. Lovers and friends reunited, and life went on, better and richer than it had been before.

THE END

Get a FREE Freak House Story

This is not the end of the Freak House series. You can read a short story featuring Hannah and Jack Langley, set during their honeymoon. It wasn't quite the carefree and uneventful holiday they let everyone believe. While the story can be read as a standalone, it contains spoilers of the 1st Freak House Trilogy. The best part is, it's FREE, but only to my newsletter subscribers. So subscribe now if you haven't already. The short story, titled STRANGE HORIZONS, will be made available in July 2015. Full instructions in my next newsletter - but you must be subscribed to receive it! Subscribe via my website: http://cjarcher.com/contact-cj/newsletter/

LOOK OUT FOR

The Last Necromancer
The first MINISTRY OF CURIOSITIES novel.

To be notified when C.J. has a new release, sign up to her
newsletter. Send an email to cjarcher.writes@gmail.com

ABOUT THE AUTHOR

C.J. Archer has loved history and books for as long as she can remember. She worked as a librarian and technical writer until she was able to channel her twin loves by writing historical fiction. She has won and placed in numerous romance writing contests, including taking home RWAustralia's Emerald Award in 2008 for the manuscript that would become her novel *Honor Bound*. Under the name Carolyn Scott, she has published contemporary romantic mysteries, including *Finders Keepers Losers Die*, and *The Diamond Affair*. After spending her childhood surrounded by the dramatic beauty of outback Queensland, she lives today in suburban Melbourne, Australia, with her husband and their two children.

She loves to hear from readers. You can contact her in one of these ways:
Website: www.cjarcher.com
Email: cjarcher.writes@gmail.com
Facebook: www.facebook.com/CJArcherAuthorPage